Moses Migrating

Moses Migrating

a novel

Sam Selvon

with an introduction
by Susheila Nasta

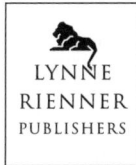

LYNNE
RIENNER
PUBLISHERS

BOULDER
LONDON

Published in the United States of America in 2009 by
Lynne Rienner Publishers, Inc.
1800 30th Street, Boulder, Colorado 80301
www.rienner.com

and in the United Kingdom by
Lynne Rienner Publishers, Inc.
3 Henrietta Street, Covent Garden, London WC2E 8LU

Library of Congress Cataloging-in-Publication Data
Selvon, Samuel.
Moses migrating : a novel / Sam Selvon ; with an introduction by
   Susheila Nasta.
    p. cm.
  ISBN 978-0-89410-872-3 (pbk. : alk. paper)
  1. Trinidad and Tobago—Fiction. I. Nasta, Susheila. II. Title.
PR9272.9.S4M6 2009
813—dc22

                                                              2008050311

British Cataloguing in Publication Data
A Cataloguing in Publication record for this book
is available from the British Library.

Printed and bound in the United States of America

       The paper used in this publication meets the requirements
  ∞   of the American National Standard for Permanence of
       Paper for Printed Library Materials Z39.48-1992.

    5 4 3 2 1

To Debra Jane

Contents

Introduction

Susheila Nasta

Sam Selvon is one of the Caribbean's most popular and internationally distinguished writers. Commonly seen as a major pioneer of the Caribbean literary tradition and the father of black writing in Britain, he was to publish several highly influential works during the course of a literary career that stretched across fifty years.

Selvon was born in Trinidad in 1923, the son of an East Indian dry goods merchant and a half-Scottish mother, and he grew up in a culturally and racially mixed world. He began writing during World War II while working as a wireless operator for the Royal Naval Reserve. After the war, he became a journalist with *The Trinidad Guardian* and literary editor of *The Guardian Weekly*. During this period many of his early short stories and poems were published locally under a number of pseudonyms.

In 1950, like many other Caribbean writers of his generation, Selvon left his native island for the metropolitan atmosphere of London. His first novel, *A Brighter Sun*, set among the East Indian rural peasantry in Trinidad, was partially composed as he sailed across the Atlantic. Published in 1952 to much metropolitan acclaim, it established Selvon as a major voice in international contemporary literature. It was swiftly followed in 1955 by *An Island Is a World* (one of his favorite works), a novel that explores the existential and metaphysical crises of the educated urban middle classes still resident on the island after Indian independence in 1947.

The Lonely Londoners, set among the rootless community of black immigrants in a bleak and unwelcoming "mother country," marked the introduction of another major dimension of Selvon's art. Published in 1956, it was the first in a series of three London novels concerning the trials and tribulations of the now iconic immigrant character Moses Aloetta, who reappears in *Moses Ascending* (1975) and *Moses Migrating* (1983). Keen to develop a medium that would capture the experiences of these early immigrants, Selvon developed a distinctive creolized voice for the language of both the narration and the dialogue, an idiom that modified the oral rhythms of Caribbean speech into a frame that transported the trickster, calypsonian culture of his island "boys" to the "diamond" pavements of West London. Bridging the difficult gap between the teller of the tale and the tale itself, he thus created a means not only to revision the "grey world city," but also to reshape its geography, giving his previously unlettered and voiceless characters a place to live in it. Often now heralded as an ingenious alchemist of style and the master of a new calypso aesthetic, Selvon's work has influenced several generations of writers who have followed on. Interestingly, Caryl Phillips, now a major writer himself, has located this aspect of Selvon's art not only in terms of its forging a tradition of black writing in Britain—a body of now well established work by contemporary writers such as David Dabydeen, Zadie Smith, and Andrea Levy—but, more significantly, as a key force in the literary reimagining of Britain during the postwar years. Not surprisingly, perhaps, the two settings of Trinidad and London formed the major focus of Selvon's work. Yet, while the Indian sugarcane community is carefully observed in his best-known Trinidad novels—*A Brighter Sun* and *Turn Again Tiger* (1957)—Selvon did not himself come from a rural background, nor was he "Indianized" in any sense. As a descendant of an indentured East Indian family, Selvon, like his contemporary V. S. Naipaul, grew up as a middle-class colonial in the multiracial world of Trinidad, a world that reflected the layers of a mixed colonial history and was situated at the crossroads of a number of cultures—Indian, African, North American, English, French, Chinese, and Spanish. Unlike Naipaul, however, who was often unsettled by the cultural admixtures of his Brahmin East Indian/Trinidadian background, Selvon was keen from the outset to find a creative means of drawing and building on the rich potential and diversity of all of these worlds. Speaking of the Hindi language he once said: "I just ignored it. . . . I grew up so Creolized among the Trinidadians. . . . Not as an Indian, but as a Creolized West Indian as we say."[1]

The tensions implicit in the idea of creolization are a frequent preoccupation in Selvon's fiction, whether his subject is the East Indian peasantry, the urban middle classes, the rootless street characters of *Ways of Sunlight* (1958)—a collection of stories set in both London and Port-of-Spain—or amid the enclaves of black immigrants in his London novels. Clearly the "ideal" notion of a creolized identity does not provide an easy resolution for any of Selvon's fictional characters, who, despite their well-worn, shape-shifting strategies for survival, still struggle for self-definition and remain caught between the interstices of several different and often competing cultural worlds. In interviews, Selvon frequently articulated his own sense of the difficulties of straddling several worlds. Once commenting on the colonial history of Trinidad and his own sense of the complexities of living in diaspora, he said: "It's all well and good to appreciate what the world is like and what people are like, but, who the hell am I? And where do I fit into it, have I got roots, am I an Indian? Am I a Negro? What is a Trinidadian?"[2]

Selvon lived in London until 1978, returning to Trinidad only infrequently and for relatively brief visits. His longest period back "home" was in 1969, when he visited the small rural village of Tacarigua to compose *The Plains of Caroni* (1970). In 1978, he left the UK for Canada, eventually taking up permanent resident status as a Canadian citizen. He died in 1994 on a brief trip to Trinidad.

The "Moses" Novels

Selvon's sojourn in London acted as a crucial catalyst in the development of his work: it became possible for him to move, on the one hand, toward a more fully realized picture of the world back home and, on the other, to define and establish a specifically Caribbean consciousness within a British context. Through the demythologization of the "mother country," the energy to confront the self could be released. "Only in London," said Selvon, "did my life find its purpose."[3] It was "the first time that people from all the different parts of the Caribbean were meeting."[4] This sense of the birth of a Caribbean identity is portrayed in *The Lonely Londoners* (1956), where we see a black community (made up of a variety of islanders and also a Nigerian) established for the first time within the heart of the city as England begins, as Jamaican poet Louise Bennett once put it, to be colonized in reverse.

Moses Aloetta, the veteran black Londoner, is first introduced in *The Lonely Londoners* and reinvented well over two decades later in *Moses Ascending* and *Moses Migrating*. Although Selvon's Moses has today gained mythical status in the history of Caribbean and Black British fiction (much like V. S. Naipaul's Mr. Biswas), many critics have observed that the Moses figure as reconstructed in the later novels is not necessarily consistent with the figure whom we meet in *The Lonely Londoners*.[5] This is not just because of the different periods in which the works were written, but also due to identifiable shifts in mood and tone reflecting a significant difference in the author's perspective and the nature of the comic vision (which I will return to later). At the end of *The Lonely Londoners* we find a Moses who is becoming frustrated with the repetitious lifestyle and circularity of existence that characterize the activities and experience of Selvon's picaresque "boys" in the city. The term "what happening," which echoes with comi/tragic resonance throughout the novel, comes to suggest less a calypsonian mode of survival than a dislocating sense of incoherence and emptiness. Beneath the "kiff-kiff laughter, behind the ballad and the episode, the what-happening, the summer-is-hearts," Moses perceives a "great aimlessness, a great restless swaying movement that leaving you standing in the same spot" (*LL*, p. 125).* The deliberately disjointed nature of the novel's form and the ironic undercutting of the characters' melodramatic but two-dimensional identities—the self-caricatures that "the boys" have created for security within the closed immigrant group—bears close parallels to the tradition of calypso and looks forward in some respects to Selvon's drama of impersonation, when Moses returns to Trinidad for Carnival in *Moses Migrating* (1983).

It was once said of the early period for the West Indian abroad that one is either a performer or has no personality. And the need for drama as a shield from suffering recurs as a theme in several novels of migration and exile written during this period. V. S. Naipaul, for instance, treats a similar theme in *The Mimic Men* (1968), where, as Naipaul's protagonist and narrator, Ralph Singh, frequently tells us: "from play-acting to disorder: it is the pattern."[6] Interestingly, Selvon made several similar observations concerning the nature of drama and the use of the comic in his work. Laughter, he once said, often acts as a "sort of protection, a defense mechanism against tribulation and hardship. . . . But every joke is made out of the facts of a tragic situation."[7] The conclusion to *The Lonely Londoners* captures this bitter-sweet quality with Moses's bleak, almost desperate vision of purposelessness and stasis, despite the surface comedy of "the boys" escapades. In addition, the question posed by Moses at the close of this first novel, regarding his need to separate himself from the community and develop an individual consciousness, looks forward to Selvon's more self-conscious attempt to explore Moses's predicament as a Black British settler twenty years later in *Moses Ascending*. In that novel, Moses, now having "arrived," attempts to make a mark on Britain by writing his memoirs.

In this second novel, we meet Moses actively attempting to "draw apart" from all the hustling of the early days. At an

---

*All references to *The Lonely Londoners* (hereafter *LL*) are to the edition published by Longman in 1985.

important level—given the changed social and political climate of the 1970s, a world where repressive immigration laws had begun to have a substantial impact on entry and departure— Moses's endeavors to construct a fully realized persona are explored metaphorically. He buys his own, admittedly dilapidated, house (due for demolition in three years); he is no longer a tenant, but a landlord; and furthermore, he wants to be a writer. Moses ascends for a brief spell to live in the attic, or "penthouse" (his castle), of his own house and can leave the basement days of *The Lonely Londoners* behind him. But the parodic treatment of Moses's aspirations and pretensions— reflected throughout in Selvon's use of language (which is a conglomeration of Moses's "mongrel" consciousness, a hodge-podge of Trinidadian English, Shakespearian allusions, the new Black Power usage, advertising jingles, etc.)—only highlights the gravity of his predicament. Moses is plainly striving to build a home on shaky foundations. Even though he feels that he has reversed the colonial relationship with "old Brit'n," to the point of having an illiterate, white Man Friday, Bob, from the "Black Country" (playing of course on one of the novel's major inter-texts, Daniel Defoe's *Robinson Crusoe*), Moses's dream of having finally made it is slowly shattered. A series of absurd reversals leads to his steady descent back down to his own basement where, dispossessed of his newly acquired rights as a black land-lord, he is forced to allow Bob and Jeannie (his tenants) the full use of his penthouse.

Moses Ascending marks an important stage in the Moses story. Though that story spans Selvon's own period of residence in Britain, Moses is not simply an autobiographical figure, but a representative voice of the old generation of immigrants who came to Britain in the 1950s. As Selvon tells us, Moses, in spite of all of his "presumptions to be English . . . remains basically a man from the Caribbean."[8] Based on a "true-life" character, Moses also typified "all that happened" during that phase; importantly "he . . . spoke in the voice, in the idiom of the people which was the only way that he could . . . express himself."[9] Yet, by the close of *Moses Ascending,* with the growth of a new generation of Black Britons, the Black Power movement, the growing hostility between Asian immigrants and blacks, we become aware of the impossibility for Moses of forming an organic relationship either with his own community or with the white world outside. He is outdated, a misfit, a black colonial adrift in the city, straddling or attempting to straddle both worlds. As is the case in *Moses Migrating,* where Moses is introduced by Galahad as a kind of Rip Van Winkle who has lost touch with the world, the often archaic and inappropriate language Moses speaks reflects the confused and increasingly serious nature of his situation.

As noted earlier, there would appear to be a substantial shift in the nature and purpose of Selvon's comic vision in *Moses Ascending* and *Moses Migrating,* as we seem to have moved from a genuinely felt sense of pathos combined with a vision of hope in *The Lonely Londoners* to what becomes a biting and increasingly disillusioned portrait of Moses's "progressive deterioration," a decline accompanied by a growing cynicism that is described but not accounted for.[10] Significantly too, as Kenneth Ramchand has noted, the cumulative impact of the satirical reversals has moved to a more "agnostic" vision, one in which "all sides of every question" are deftly mocked through farce and burlesque, but which lacks any clear sense of direction.[11] In fact, Selvon's resourcefulness, his subversion of the "Queen's English," and his iconoclastic techniques, which playfully unite the traditions of calypso with Western literature, only serve to heighten our awareness that Moses cannot yet fully inhabit any "home"; he is not yet master of his own house nor of the language with which he wants to compose his memoirs. After twenty-five years in "old Brit'n," then, Moses remains trapped and entrapped, as if he were still caught in the hold of a slave ship.*

There has been much debate in recent years as to whether Selvon's three Moses novels should in fact be termed a trilogy.[12] Selvon himself once referred to *Moses Migrating* as a "sort of

---

*Unless otherwise noted, all subsequent page references are to this new Lynne Rienner Publishers edition of *Moses Migrating.*

sequel" to *Moses Ascending*, and there are certainly several direct
intertextual links made among the novels as details, stories, and
characters (Galahad, Tolroy, Big City, Bob, Jeannie, Brenda) are
carried forward or interweave.[13] In addition, the Moses story
when read as a sequence can be seen as the construction of a
recognizable immigrant life cycle, as we first encounter Moses
as community liaison officer and voice of the embryonic black
community in *The Lonely Londoners*; then meet him again as
budding writer/landlord/Black Briton attempting to build his
own "castle" in *Moses Ascending*; and, finally, find him as a
deluded and unreconstructed black Anglophile settler returning
home in *Moses Migrating*. The books are also directly connected
by Selvon's continuing experimentations with form and his sustained attempts to create a counter-discourse that can explore
the clichés and racist stereotypes of the canon. Yet, it would still
seem that the notion of a "sequel"—a term that by its nature
suggests development and growth—might in some ways be
inappropriate to describe the cumulative impact of Selvon's
subversive methods in this cycle of works. For Selvon's constant
undermining of a structural sense of progression, as well as the
seeming impossibility of any real growth for Moses in Britain,
suggests a different kind of destination as Selvon continually
launches his anti-hero into yet another mock pilgrimage, a
quest by way of which it becomes impossible to ever reach a
"promised land."

Moses Migrating

Moses Migrating, Selvon's tenth published novel, is illustrative of
Selvon's continuing preoccupation with the theme of migrant
displacement. As in the earlier novels in the Moses cycle, the
frothy humor and pace is barbed with a disturbing ambiguity
and irony. The comic-grotesque reversals of the colonial
encounter already exploited in the iconoclasm of *Moses
Ascending* are thus further explored, as Moses finally decides to
leave London and return to Trinidad for Carnival. After traveling third class on an ocean liner (Selvon mock-seriously invokes

the trials of the Middle Passage), Moses stays in the "upside-down" world of the Trinidad Hilton (p. 83)—becoming a tourist, in other words, in his own country. The metaphorical possibilities of rooms and houses as a correlative or frame for the lack of a firm cultural identity are thus extended; but now it is neither basement, nor attic, but hotel room that bears the weight of significance. The quintessential transitoriness, artificiality, and unreality of the hotel room (which is underground) give image to the special hollowness and disorientations of Moses's split and confused postcolonial identity. Moses seems fated to find no true home in either Britain or Trinidad. Selvon's use of the hotel room as symbolic motif for Moses's plight invites comparison again with V. S. Naipaul's representation in *The Mimic Men* of Ralph Singh's final refuge in a suburban English hotel.[14] Significantly too, like Naipaul's Ralph Singh, Moses becomes increasingly reliant for survival on various forms of play-acting, adopting a series of masks in a masquerade, which points to the continuing power of racial and cultural stereotypes while at the same time offering the author and reader strategies to decode and destabilize them.[15]

In *Moses Migrating*, Selvon provides his first fictional portrait of the black Londoner and Anglophile returning home. The dream of return, the nostalgia for a childhood lost, friends and relations never seen, and the yearning for a landscape possessed rather than adopted had played an important role in Moses's nostalgic conversations with Sir Galahad (his alter ego) in the early days of *The Lonely Londoners*. He yearned to end his days in "Paradise," a small village somewhere between St. Joseph and Tacarigua where "I would get a old house and have some cattle and goat" (*LL*, p. 114); yet, at this stage the sentimental nostalgia for a life lost is not accompanied by a desire, or the opportunity, to return. *Moses Migrating*, in contrast, opens with the accretion of several years of disillusionment as well as the possibility offered by the British government to repatriate. After twenty-five years as a stalwart black servant of the "mother-country," Moses, now self-deluded Black British subject, writes a concerned letter to Enoch Powell thanking him for his generosity in helping loyal black Londoners to return to their native lands: "Dear Mr. Powell, though Black I am writing you to express my support for your campaigns to keep Brit'n White.... I have always tried to integrate successfully in spite of discriminations and prejudices according to race" (p. 29).

Galahad (one of the only remaining characters from the early days and a member of the Black Power group) ridicules Moses's misplaced patriotism and focuses our attention on the extent to which Moses, still caught in a colonial mindset, has lost his grip on political developments. "You remind me of that fellar who went to sleep for years and get up, Rip Van Winkle" (p. 30). Nevertheless, Moses's resolve, based from the outset on a serious misreading of the government's objectives, remains firm, and he plans to depart "merry England" as an "ambassador not only of goodwill but good manners" (p. 55). His ambitions are further fired by the desire to proclaim at home that "the British bulldog still had teeth, that Brittania still ruled the waves" (p. 56). In an absurd portrait of Moses as blinkered Black British "native informant," the firmness of Moses's declarations are undercut sardonically by Selvon's biting irony. Moses does not sell his "mansion" in Shepherds Bush, but leaves it reluctantly in the hands of Galahad, thereby maintaining at least a foothold in the "land of milk and honey" (p. 35). Moreover, the more serious psychological impact of Moses's time in Britain is palpable when he expresses his significant fear of departure, a departure that, despite his confident declarations, seems far from "heroic":

> As I shuffled up the queue I thought of several things to tell the Officer . . . like I was chief instigator of a race riot in Notting Hill, or that I was responsible for that bomb what explode in Oxford Street. . . . I even thought of fainting: it occur to me I should of learnt some of them Paki tricks. (pp. 49–50)

From the outset, Moses is presented as a jester, an actor and a chameleon who inhabits a series of roles to survive not just on board ship, but in Trinidad itself. And Moses takes several elements of his London life with him. Bob (the white Man Friday of *Moses Ascending*) and his wife, Jeannie, are also on the voyage as tourists, but traveling First Class. Having rehearsed their roles in front of Moses before departure, and complete with safari hats and colonial shorts, they too have the intention of holidaying at Carnival time in "the-land-of-the-humming-bird" (p. 33). On board ship, the Upstairs-Downstairs relationship already established with Bob and Jeannie in *Moses Ascending* is further extended. Only now Moses is trapped in the "bowels of the ship" instead of the basement of his own house. He had left Britain "with a flourish" (p. 50); but now, Selvon's sardonic depiction of Moses's new accommodation as being like the hold of a slave ship heightens our awareness of his real predicament (see pp. 50–51).

Moses insists, of course, on presenting the journey as a kind of heroic mission—not a voyage to rediscover his roots, but a courageous, patriotic pilgrimage on behalf of old Brittania. Yet, his cabin, 13B, is the nearest one to the engine room: "they couldn't get any lower unless they bore a hole in the bottom of the ship" (p. 50). In a mock-heroic vein, mimicking the style of Bunyan's *Pilgrim's Progress,* Selvon presents Moses's reactions to his cabin and his quest:

> Was I never to rise to heights again? Was I wrong . . . ? My times would come: there would be moments when suppliants bend their knees to me for alms. . . .
>
> So I pass that hillock of despair, but not the Ben Nevis of my desertion of Brit'n in her hour of need. How would the country survive with all these blacks returning to the islands? (pp. 50–51)

Moses, absurd black Anglophile and fantasist, is further ridiculed in his encounter with his black cabin mates. Dominica mocks him with a laugh that is both derisive and penetrating. While Dominica sounds to Moses like an "insecure jester" (p. 59), his laughter has bite and "puts you in your place." More important, Dominica's typical Caribbean "big-talk" clearly opens up and mirrors Moses's own insecurities. Moses, too, is the clown as he inappropriately dresses formally for dinner Third Class—and it is only the clientele in the First Class bar, "mostly whites . . . that helped me to unwind a little" (p. 53). In addition, the derisive comment from one of the other inmates of 13B that "Brit'n must of blow [Moses's] brains" (p. 57) echoes Galahad's earlier observations that Moses has not only lost the plot, but has lost his bearings altogether, leaving us with a sense of the vulnerability of the skin of Moses's camouflage and regular protestations.

Once at sea, "seeing nothing but grey sea and grey sky," Moses's real sense of terror and displacement is expressed: "I feel like one of the crew on Columbus ship as it sail across the Atlantic who shitting his pants wondering if the ship would topple over into oblivion" (p. 58). Clearly, Moses is on no voyage of discovery; nor, it would seem, is he about to enter any New World. In addition, as in the voyages—literal or metaphorical—plotted in the other novels in the Moses cycle, his return to Trinidad, his native land, for Carnival only signifies yet another false start, a journey to another illusion.

Yet, when Bob becomes seasick, the resourceful possibilities of Moses's chameleon-like persona are brought to the fore. Encouraged by Jeannie, Moses returns to the sexual antics already established in Shepherds Bush, thereby settling an old score with Bob and continuing as cynical sexual opportunist. At this point, as enthusiastic player of the game and universal playboy, he lives out a philosophy of "what's writ is writ":

> Circumstances that are predestined are not to be baulked by a change of dirty underwear nor shifting from a black ghetto in London to a ship in mid-Atlantic. None shall escape: indeed in fleeing one situation for another it is often a case of out of the frying pan into the fire. . . . I am easily reconciled to the thrusts and parries of Fate. If all the men in the world was a pack of cards, . . . I would come out the joker. (pp. 73–74)

The voice here is one of a confident Moses, a trickster who enjoys his freedom and is devious enough to use situations to his own ends. Moreover, on his arrival in Trinidad, we are told that Moses was apparently so unconcerned about his destination that he was "sound asleep, having drunk myself into a stupor the night before" (p. 81). This Moses does not allow himself to eulogize the first sight of the tips of the Northern Range or to fall at his knees to kiss his dear native soil. However, his intense anxiety about the "alien culture" (p. 81) that he will encounter once he leaves the sanctuary of the ship is also made blatantly apparent.

Moses's sense of real estrangement and dislocation once he disembarks is portrayed cumulatively by Selvon. On arrival, he unnerves himself by directing a taxi driver the wrong way to the Hilton; once within the security of the rootless community of expatriates in the hotel, he reflects nervously on Queens Park Savannah outside (p. 85). Significantly too, he begins at this point to recount some specific details of his past, information about his ancestry that he never dared expose in London (pp. 84–85) and that adds to his fear of arrival. "Other fellars," we are told, "have it jammy, at least with brother or sister if their Pa and Ma dead, . . . who would . . . celebrate the return of the prodigal son," but Moses, it would appear, is an orphan brought up by the childless Tanty Flora, a forceful matriarch, "heavy on religion and saving souls" (p. 85). And he has not been in touch with Tanty Flora during all his time in England. So weak, in fact, is Moses's link with his childhood in St. John that he is unsure of Tanty's identity when he first sees her. Perhaps most significantly, Moses, as an orphan of the world, has developed agoraphobia and is increasingly fearful of venturing out of the safety of the Hilton walls to confront his past (see pp. 84–85).

Selvon's focus here on Moses's previously undeclared orphaned status clearly has far broader symbolic implications in terms of his exploration of diasporic identities and the complex question of colonial and postcolonial lineages. For, like many other immigrants and returnees, Moses is both child of Empire and foreigner within it. In addition, the precise details of Moses's cultural and biological parentage are deliberately obscured by Selvon. We have not heard such stories about his past before (in *The Lonely Londoners*, for example, or *Moses Ascending*), and we wonder indeed whether they are true. These inconsistencies not only complicate our view of Moses's accounts of his past, but also draw our attention to the difficulties, after so many years living abroad, in making such linkages.

When Moses first sees Tanty—an old woman selling oranges across from the hotel—the almost willful lack of recognition is mutual: "You don't sound Trinidadian to me no more," says Tanty. "You sounding strange. . . . You learn to talk like white people" (p. 88). In his reactions to the sight of Tanty, Moses voices similar observations about his lost sense of self: "I began to rue my impulsive dash from the hotel. Not that I wasn't please to see Tanty, but it was as if out here . . . I lose my identity and become prey to incidents and accidents"(p. 88). In this brief encounter, the construction of Moses's mythological Trinidadian face is shattered. Not only does Tanty not recognize him, but he offends her by his initially superior attitude, the extent of his difference, and his obvious Anglophilia. She cannot take him seriously (unless, as we learn later, he inhabits the role of Britannia subsumed by his Carnival mask). Tanty would in fact prefer to leave Moses as a figment of a Carnival imagination, part of a fantastic vision of madness and illusion. Thus, by the end of the novel, when the festivities are over, she even refuses to bid him goodbye. "She say," says the perceptive Doris, also one of her adopted children, that "she would pretend, it was somebody who masquerade for the Carnival as you" (p. 193).

Carnival provides the central symbol for the novel's action and is the major motivating force for Moses, its prime masquerader. From the outset, Moses's main motivation is to be an "Ambassador of Her Majesty's Service" (p. 109). It is the prime reason that he is in Trinidad, and his plan to "play mas" by donning the costume of a "black Britannia" (using Jeannie and Bob, as white handmaiden and slave) continues the series of absurd comic reversals that proliferate throughout the novel. Ironically too, although Moses attempts through his portrayal of Britannia to further pursue his "civilising mission" by drawing attention to the iconic coin of Empire, the Carnival judges and audience read his performance "subversively—as a counter-colonial inversion of the historical hierarchy."[16] As Helen Tiffin suggests, Moses's apparently "obedient gesture is thus interpreted by his Trinidadian audience as deeply disobedient." It is a performance that not only destabilizes the imperial stereotype, but literally "sets it spinning."[17] Not surprisingly then, it is

Carnival that in the end signifies Moses's real arrival in *Moses Migrating*, providing him with the perfect platform, as archetype of the "whitewashed black man," to act himself. This is an irony, as Roydon Sallick has pointed out, that he sadly misses.[18] It is Carnival, too, and the carnivalesque that offer Selvon the satiric potential as author to continue his sustained deflation of Moses's pretensions and further develop his broader critique of the authority of colonial and canonical discourse.

In contrast to the fantasy world offered by preparations for Carnival, any contacts with the actual realities of postcolonial Trinidad are disturbing for Moses. The episode, for instance, when Moses ventures out to Frederick Street in search of a much longed for "glass of mauby" illustrates his loss of touch with island culture and also pinpoints the way others regularly perceive him, as a "madman." The climax of this scene, with the echo of voices in the drinks parlor (pp. 103–104)—"he must be drunk"; "or else a drug addick"; "go in Woodford Square if you want to make speeches mister"—doesn't deter Moses from his misguided sense of commitment and pilgrimage: "I could see that I would have a hard time as Jesus with the Pharisees spreading my gospel in Trinidad" (p. 104). Yet, as the afternoon goes on amid hundreds of excited shoppers for Carnival, Moses, the worldly black Londoner, begins to lose his grip. Feeling like a "piece of flotsam and jetsam," with perspiration trickling all over his body, he fortuitously bumps into Dominica (his ex–cabin mate) and grabs him "like a drowning man clutch a straw" (p. 105).

Similarly, when we listen to Moses's versions of his conversations about Carnival with Lennard, a local reporter for *The Guardian,* we realize that there is constantly a biting irony in the comedy at Moses's expense (pp. 120–121). Whether within the walls of the Hilton or outside, Moses remains the jester and buffoon. Attempting to explain the seriousness of his idea of representing Britannia for Carnival, he still fails to understand that Lennard's real motive is to make a fool of him: "It was to be expected that a philistine like Lennard would snort and guffaw at my efforts" (p. 125). Even Doris, when Moses makes his first trip up the hill to John-John—an episode that reflects a movement in Moses's consciousness toward real sentimentality for his lost past (see pp. 110–111)—sees through his thin disguise. When Moses introduces himself self-importantly as ambassador of Britain, Doris retorts with stinging mockery: "Is that what you playing for Carnival?" (p. 109).

The formation of Moses's relationship with Doris is important, as it signifies one of the only possibilities that Moses has for real integration and return. However, the meetings between the two are framed from beginning to end by preparations for Carnival and the creation of his costume. Initially, Moses as sexual predator is captivated by Doris's "pot-pourri" beauty, though she also represents, as one of Tanty's other adopted children, a symbol of home and the possibility of growth. Moses even believes at one point that he has fallen seriously in love with Doris and contemplates settling down, blaming the "bastard" cupid for waiting until he arrives in Trinidad "up on John-John hill, to fire at me" (p. 115). He writes poetry to Doris, contemplates selling his house in Shepherds Bush, and goes so far as to ring Galahad in London (who later uses this as an excuse to turn up in Trinidad with Brenda and to stay at the Hilton at Moses's expense!). But Moses's budding love is not taken seriously by anybody; and eventually, true to form, he calculatedly lifts his Muse off her pedestal by deflowering her on Jouvert morning (p. 182).

It is during the episode when Moses proposes to Doris on Jouvert morning that he comes closest to release and a possible embrace of his past. Dancing all through the night in a frenzy of potential birth and destruction, he glimpses for a moment an organic vision of community and the central forces at work in the subversive energy of Carnival:

> I don't know what come over me that morning, if memories of bygone Jouvert return after all my years in stuffy old Brit'n, or if it was that I was in the midst of my countrymen now, the pulse and the sweat and the smell and the hysterical excitement, but my head was giddy with a kind of irresistible exultation like I just get emancipated from slavery. (p. 180)

The depth and potential seriousness of Moses's brief epiphany here is highlighted by the rhythmic tonality of Selvon's prose, which modulates at points into a stream of consciousness chant celebrating the regeneration of a deep ancestral awareness of a shared Caribbean identity. "All of we chanting and slaving to out the fire in Massa sugarcane plantations; foreday morning come; Jouvert, Canboulay, Massa come to play was too, mas in your arse" (p. 180). Moses almost convinces us that he is truly "home." But he is unable to sustain his sense of communal identity or the blurring of illusion and reality that enables the insight. After the climax of the celebrations and his sexual experience with Doris, the self-protecting mask of the uncommitted survivor resurfaces:

> Of course, in real life one goes from climax to climax—one thing leads to another, as it were, and you have to apply yourself to the continuation of your existence. The onlyest thing I know that have one definite climax is fairy tales. . . . Even Doris had to go with the tide. (p. 182)

Significantly, Moses cannot escape his role as masquerader even when Carnival itself is over. Moreover, the nature of the forces generating Carnival become a paradigm or metaphor for Moses's condition, a crucible in which he ends up playing himself so consummately as "whitewashed black man" that he wins first prize. But, even before the final parade, Moses is repeatedly described as representing a kind of "sanity in madness" (p. 175). Bob and Jeannie perpetually tease him about his mongrel background. "You are just a fluke," says Bob at one point, "a random bastard who adopted England as his home. No wonder you don't know if you're coming or going" (p. 148); similarly, Brenda calls him a "composite man among mimic men" (p. 176). The language of mimicry is further extended when Moses accuses the others of making a "pappyshow" of his intended marriage to Doris (p. 192). Moses responds to such taunting with characteristic flippancy, but his jester-like reactions are also illustrative of an ultimately self-denigrating philosophy: "orphans like me are content to let the dead bury the dead and be thankful for little happinesses and small mercies that God mete out" (p. 147). And there are several other more disturbing implications in his response. As buoyant figure and successful Carnival masker, Moses may be briefly uplifted by the noise of the masquerade, but he is also left dancing on the precipice of a dangerous self-deception. In true Carnival spirit, Moses may not divulge his impersonations to anyone, but those very disguises might result only in further entrapment. Like the calypsonians of the Carnival bands, it would seem that Moses's private identity can remain intact only within the extrinsic bounds of the game.

Selvon's use of Carnival as the central symbol and unifying force of *Moses Migrating*'s action is essential to understanding the novel's themes, purpose, and episodic structure. As an annual fete that involves the whole community, Carnival (particularly in Trinidad) represents one of the most vigorous and spectacular expressions of community and folk art in the Caribbean. Many critics have commented on the significance of Carnival as central to the evolution and history of the Caribbean novel and its innovations with literary form. The preparation of sensational costumes and music as everyone, rich and poor, "play mas" expresses a frenzied cunning for fantasy and release, drawing on the history of slavery, on a time when slaves were allowed a brief respite during Carnival to play the roles of fairy-tale kings, queens, and princesses. In the same vein, the pulsating vibrancy of the festivities—the maskers and the glittering bands—come to an abrupt end as day breaks on Ash Wednesday. Like Tanty and Doris, the poor return to their previous powerlessness and anonymity, while the social-political tensions of the society remain unaltered. When the costumes are removed on Ash Wednesday, the fete is over.

Moses's Jouvert morning with Doris and the Carnival procession itself, with the ironic reversal of Moses as Black Britannia led by his white slaves (Bob and Jeannie), are carefully interwoven into the structure of the narrative, Moses's betrayal of Doris culminating with explicit echoes of Peter's betrayal of Christ (see pp. 192–193). Once the spell of Carnival is broken, Moses finds it necessary to turn away, not only from his newly discovered Trinidadian ancestry, but also from all the possibilities that love might entail. He can be no more an organic part of

Tanty and Doris's world than he can of his own house in Shepherds Bush. As the novel builds to a climax, paralleling the preparations and expression of the Carnival spirit, there is a corresponding sense of withdrawal and deflation that signifies the inevitable return to reality after the rituals of the procession are over: "Even the evening itself was sombre . . . no gay calypso steel band music on the hill, and the sun . . . painted the sky in mournful shades of grey and deep purple, like funeral drapes" (p. 193). Moses's predicament once the masquerade is over is double-edged. Beneath the drama of impersonation, there is a disturbing sense of spiritual desolation; beneath the mocking irony of the opportunist's wit, a sense of despair. It would seem by the close of the novel that Moses is even further caught between worlds than he was at the start. While he might have succeeded, almost despite himself, in engaging with the subversions of Carnival and with the various masquerades that he has taken on as playboy of the born-again New World and colonial orphan, the dual worlds of London and Trinidad seem to be increasingly unreal. "Playing mas" may be fun, but it is ultimately an evasion and can only last so long. The lack of resolution, and perhaps the lack of a possible resolution, is demonstrated in the open-ended quality of the novel's final episode—with Moses literally caught at the close in a kind of suspended state, just outside the doors of Britain, "like I was still playing charades" (p. 194).

Structure and Language

The narrative of *Moses Migrating* (as is the case with several of Selvon's other novels concerning exile and migration) does not conform to an explicitly linear form. The three major episodic sequences of the novel—it is not divided into obvious sections or chapters—relate primarily to Moses's time on board ship and his arrival in Trinidad; to his portrait of island life, past and present; and to his various sexual exploits, including his passion for Doris and the preparations to "play mas" as Britannia at Carnival. While Moses is not always the instigator of the action, he is usually a willing participant and frequently turns events to his own advantage. Moses and his narration of events is the only clear thread of continuity, and that narrative, as we have already seen, is frequently unreliable.

Similarly, Selvon's depiction of the other characters does not follow an easily identifiable pattern of development, as all the significant figures—Bob and Jeannie, Brenda and Galahad, Doris and Tanty, Lennard—are largely set up as mirrors of Moses's shape-shifting Carnival identity. Although these characters do serve the purpose of bringing together the two worlds of Trinidad and London, enabling different perspectives that cover Moses's past, present, and future, they never have a significant impact (apart from Doris) on the psychological or emotional substance of Moses's life.

Selvon devotes only a very short description to the third and final sequence of the book, where Moses is caught clutching his chalice outside the gates of Heathrow airport in Britain (p. 194). But it is of course a crucial moment in the novel. Moses has resisted the possibility of staying on and bonding with Doris in Trinidad. Instead, clinging desperately to his recent success as Carnival Queen and pathetically clutching his romantic trophy of the "Holy Grail," he is caught in limbo as the passport officer goes off to check whether he can indeed re-enter Britain and return to his house in Shepherds Bush.

As with the different faces that Moses adopts, Selvon's language adjusts accordingly. Written with an artful elasticity, versatile enough to make the most of the comic incongruities that are inherently linked to Moses's unstable persona, the first-person narrative juggles a vast reservoir of jostling cultural images and intertexts, Moses perhaps coming closest to inhabiting a convincing voice in the resonantly sentimental descriptions of his encounters with Tanty and Doris in St. John. It is in these scenes in particular that a creolised Trindidadian register becomes most marked, the climax being the expression of a communal consciousness and the potential for emotional consummation with Doris on Jouvert morning (p. 182).

Clearly, Selvon wants to demonstrate shifts in tonality and rhythm to express Moses's changing image of himself, however suspect. And, interestingly, whereas in *The Lonely Londoners* Selvon used comparisons from a Caribbean landscape to define a West Indian presence in the gray metropolis, he now reverses this technique to create a picture of Trinidad from the viewpoint of a returning black Anglophile. But just as Moses's identity cannot be pinned down, neither can his language. The slippery tones of the narrator's unreliable voice in fact only serve to further confirm the novel's main purpose, as we are left wondering whether Moses is victim of his mongrel language or master of it. Like the dominant motif of Carnival, which provides the metaphoric and symbolic structure for the action, Selvon's linguistic confection in *Moses Migrating* acts both as "power and . . . prison . . . liberating force and . . . agent of alienation."[20] Through Selvon's construction of Moses's divided and mosaic-like identity, the creative as well as the potentially destructive elements of Moses's "return" are stressed. While his delusions and cultural contradictions are sustained on the whole by an apparently fast-moving optimism, buoyed up by the overarching structure of Carnival, Moses appears by the close to have made little progress. He may mistakenly believe that he has realized the heroic fulfillment of his quest, but where do we expect him to go from here? Sadly for us, Selvon did not ever complete his next novel, which sought to return, as in *An Island Is a World*, to larger existential questions of Caribbean identity and consciousness, raised but not resolved in this, his final London work.

Notes

1. "The English Novel Abroad," Samuel Selvon interviewed by Gerald Moore, BBC Radio broadcast, January 4, 1974.
2. Peter Nazareth, "Interview with Sam Selvon," *World Literature Written in English* 18, no. 2 (1974), p. 426.
3. Michel Fabre, "Samuel Selvon: Interviews and Conversations," in *Critical Perspectives on Sam Selvon,* edited by Susheila Nasta (Washington, DC: Three Continents Press, 1988), p. 64.
4. "The English Novel Abroad."
5. Helen Tiffin, "Under the Kiff-Kiff Laughter: Stereotype and

Subversion in *Moses Ascending* and *Moses Migrating*," in *Tiger's Triumph: Celebrating Sam Selvon*, edited by S. Nasta and A. Rutherford (Hebden Bridge: Dangaroo Press, 1995), p. 131.

6. V. S. Naipul, *The Mimic Men* (London: Andre Deutsch, 1967), p. 184.

7. Susheila Nasta, "The Moses Trilogy: Sam Selvon Discusses His London Novels," *Wasafiri,* no. 2 (1985), p. 9.

8. Frank Birbalsingh, interview with Sam Selvon, 1986 (unpublished; included here thanks to the author).

9. Ibid.

10. Kenneth Ramchand, "Comedy as Evasion in the Later Novels of Sam Selvon," in *Something Rich and Strange*, edited by M. Zehnder (Leeds: Peepal Tree, 2003), p. 88.

11. Ibid.

12. Roydon Salick, *The Novels of Sam Selvon* (Westport, CT: Greenwood Press, 2001), pp. 132–161.

13. Fabre, "Sam Selvon," p. 75.

14. Salick, *The Novels of Sam Selvon*, pp. 152–153.

15. Tiffin, "Under the Kiff-Kiff Laughter," pp. 131–132.

16. Ibid., pp. 136–137.

17. Ibid., p. 138.

18. Salick, *The Novels of Sam Selvon*, p. 154.

19. Ibid.

20. Edward Baugh, "Friday in Crusoe's City: The Question of Language in Two West Indian Novels of Exile," *ACLALS Bulletin* 3 (1980), p. 9.

Moses Migrating

The idea of depicting Britannia on the face of a coin origi-
nated with the late Mr. Wilfred Strasser, who played the
part in the 1948 Carnival celebrations in Trinidad. I have used
the idea for my own purposes in this work of fiction.

—s.s.

A Special Preface by
Moses Aloetta Esq.

It have a lot of myths and legends and nancy stories that circulate since I, Moses Aloetta Esq., presented my credentials to the literary world. Some people think I am an arsehole, some people say I am an enigma that never arrived, the chosen few consider me a genius, and one evening at a big literary conference at the Commonwealth Institute in London whilst I was reading a bawdy passage from one of my tomes in front of a big audience that included *Whites,* a black Guyanese bitch walked up to the microphone and slap me bam bam in my face. I wouldn't of minded if *Blacks* alone was present, but to slap me in front of White people really hurt.

The author has often been asked how much of the books is himself, or the fictional character, or the actual person who inspired him. In the process of creativity, unknowingness is the quintessence that propels me—I want to know as much as the reader what happens next, or what shit "Moses" is going to come up with, and when I emerge, your guess is as good as mines as to who is the culprit. So that when literary critics—seeing some significance in the name as the biblical Moses who led his people out of bondage—ask me, "were you thinking of that when you were writing about your Moses and the black immigrants settling in England," I can only say, "no, the name is common in Trinidad, and I just pull it out of a hat." But they dig and delve. Look for plot and subplot. Climax and anti-climax, purpose and motive. The machinations that went on in my mind whilst I was writing, if I had them all the time I would be writing books like peas.

Of the factual human being that Moses was based upon, I know that under the welter of adversity, and the wonderment of living in the heart of the Mother Country after coming from a small island known only to map-readers, was the yearning to be a writer. "Boy," he told me, "is as if I only start to live since I come to Brit'n. I wish I was a writer like you." Instead, he was a master raconteur. Not that he held forth recounting the ballads and episodes: he would drop a hint or a clue and leave it up to his listeners to embellish or elaborate. His word-to-the-wise economy sometimes exasperated me, and I would ask, "but what actually happen?" and he would shrug and say, "imagine if you was me . . . what you would of done?"

I did nothing about writing down his adventures until I got the "distant perspective" from a writers' colony in the United States. I started to make notes, and when I returned to England I sat down to write *The Lonely Londoners*. I couldn't make any headway; was totally frustrated until I realised I was using the wrong kind of right English. I tried the "nation language" of the English-speaking Caribbean, and everything fell smoothly into place. I made some slight modifications, mainly by not spelling phonetically or shifting a phrase to make it more understand-able. Some diehard Caribbean critics claimed that it lost authenticity.

Be that as it may, the book was highly praised in England and the United States, special reference made to "the injection of new blood into the English language."

Some twenty-five years went by before Moses appeared again *(Moses Ascending)* to depict the changes during that time—a new generation of Black Britons, and an influx of Indians and Pakistanis to add *more* colour to the scene. Moses has ascended to being a landlord, and his language has escalated from the basement to the penthouse, a kind of hybrid mixture of ye-olde and what-happening. Once again the language swept the book along like a cork on a tidal wave, and the critics were full of praise.

In fact, though I had not anticipated doing another book on the life and adventures of Moses, I was in high gear. As it happened, the true-true Moses felt that Brit'n had taken its toll not only on his philosophy but his physiology, and he decided to peter out his days in the warmth of the tropic sun in his homeland of Trinidad.

I well remember some faithful friends saw him off at Waterloo Station, in good time to catch the boat-train. . . . This was where it had started, and this was where it was going to end as far as his life in London was concerned. There were no tight throats, no gruff voices, no loose-fingered hand raised surreptitiously to wipe away a tear. We covered sentiment with banter and old-talk, recalling the old days, joking about how he would miss scouting the streets of London to pick up a sleeper. Finally we all shook hands and embraced him. And he left London.

Truth is *stronger* than fiction. Who knows what ballads and episodes more graphic and pertinent than any I have tried to describe in the books he might have taken away to reminisce over in his rocking-chair days?

He might well have rested in peace had I not decided to follow him to Trinidad in the present novel *Moses Migrating*. And considering the characteristics that are his trademark—the mimicry, the convolutions of irony and satire, the ambivalences nothing seemed more appropriate than the celebration of Carnival, a national, emotional event that is more important to the people than voting for Prime Minister or taking precaution against a devastating hurricane. Somewhere between the actuality and the dreamworld of fiction, the truth about Moses—the truth about the whitewashed Black man torn apart by the circumstances of living in a white society—exists. If I as author consciously strived at anything when he gave me a chance, it was to keep some thread of authentic commentary of the tribulations of Black people surviving away from their roots, which I tried to weave into the kiff-kiff laughter: there is no question that Britain's image needed a boost at the time of his migration: there is no question that *any* Black immigrant returning to his homeland would have qualms about resettling.

The humour and entertainment that Moses provides some-

times tend to whelm the serious side of his nature. It is a knack
that all Black people acquire to survive. In my own years in
London, any hardcore material I wrote about Blacks had to have
ha-ha before any English publisher would touch it.

So laugh your guts out. But remember there is more in the
mortar than the pestle.

—*M.S./S.S.*
January 1991

I don't rightly recollect when it was the idea of going back home hit me. It could of been one time of any time when I was down in the dumps, my back aching from bending down to pick up the apples that fall when my cart upset. But I could tell you one thing for sure, that down there in that grimy basement in Shepherd's Bush, feeling like a trapped animal while my erstwhile lackey Bob and his bride Jeannie occupied my penthouse on the top floor, it was not hard to wish for a change of scenery and circumstances. And topping that was the daily dread that the pigs would come a-knocking at the basement where Galahad and Brenda conducted their Black Power party affairs, to arrest somebody for something, or merely to give me the shivers.

Just entertaining the idea of leaving Brit'n gave me the creeps. I swear a tear fell on the paper as I sat down to write Enoch of my intentions:

"Dear Mr Powell, though Black I am writing you to express my support for your campaigns to keep Brit'n White, as I have been living here for more than twenty years and I have more black enemies than white and I have always tried to integrate successfully in spite of discriminations and prejudices according to race. Though I am deciding to return to Trinidad it is grieving me no whit and it is only your kind offer to subsidise such black immigrants as desire to return to their homelands that will make

29

it possible for me. I will therefore be grateful to receive my assist-
ed passage money, and the £2000 capital which will start me off
when I go. As a proof that I have no ill-feelings or animosity for
your sentiments re blacks, and in gratitude for your assistance, if
I open a business when I go home I will call it Enoch-aided
Enterprises, or some such title that will show what your true
feelings are, and not like the newspapers and television that try
to defame you, though I would not bother with that so much if I
were you, as they do the same thing to black people."

I did not know my benefactor's home address, and I did not
want to send my application to his office in the House of
Commons, so I waited until I saw Galahad to find out.

He went into an apoplexy of laughter. "Man," he gasped,
"you have really retired from the scene. Do you not know that
like most of Enoch's brainwaves, that one got the thumbs-down
from Parliament? You remind me of that fellar who went to
sleep for years and get up, Rip Van Winkle!"

I lied glibly. "Of course. It's just a personal, private plea
which he might view sympathetically."

But coming to think of it, I should of realised that if Enoch
finance an exodus of all the blacks in Brit'n, he would be in a
worse state than the country itself.

"However," Galahad say, "you are a landlord, a man of
means. If I were in your shoes, I would be out of this country in
a jiffy, the way how things are going. Bad enough being black
and unwanted, but the whole economy collapse. If they don't
hurry up and start pumping oil from Scotland, I won't be able
to drive my car."

I did not say anything. I knew from experience the best
thing to do when Galahad talk was to pretend to listen and then
forget every word, or else you would find yourself compromised
or beholden to him in some way or manner. Indeed, the next
thing I knew was that everybody in the house was talking about
how I was leaving Brit'n after all these years to go and live in
Trinidad, while I myself was merely toying with the idea.

Bob came down from the penthouse to see me. During this
time, from odd bits of gossip I gathered, it appeared that he had
not only taken over the highest flat but had risen in the world in

other respects. Gone were Batman and Spiderman. In their stead were Tolstoy and Thomas Hardy, a copy of Fowler's *Usage of English,* and a tome called *Progress of Man.* Canned beer and sweet stout were out: port and claret were offered guests, though Bob being what he was, more spirituous liquors were available if desired.

All I could offer him was wood cider from a cheap shop in the Harrow Road, which he politely declined.

"We shouldn't live as enemies, Moses," he said. "Why not come up and visit this evening?"

"Okay," I said, a little dubious.

"Right." He nodded. "I'll get Jeannie to prepare a meal. We've got some venison down from Scotland. She could make a curry or stew."

I couldn't help shuddering. "Perhaps she could roast it instead, or make a casserole? It should be marinated with gin and served with a caper-sauce."

Bob smiled. "Your tastes haven't declined. We'll see."

Later I hauled my vicuna suit out of the cupboard, and start to dust off the dust that collect, and the webs. I did not want to turn up like a drop-out. In fact, why not show them that I was still of the gentry, in spite of my circumstances? I donned waist-coat, and spats, and evening jacket, and brushed my bowler to a shine before putting it on.

But it all turn out useless when I arrive. Bob hail me in jeans and Afro-shirt and a pair of sandals what show his dirty toe-nails. And Jeannie flounce up in an open-neck shirt—open-breast, really—and red cotton slacks.

I feel like a prat in my evening jacket and bowler.

"Well come and welcome—" Jeannie began, but Bob interrupt sternly, "I told you to cut out all that relic, Jeannie."

She began again. "Oh hello, Moses."

"Hello Jeannie," I say. "Long time no see."

"It's good to see you," she say, taking my bowler, and casting an anxious eye at Bob, as if wondering if she was acting the right way.

"You've made some changes, I see," I say.

"Well Moses," Jeannie say, "Bobbie is a changed man. Since

he is educating himself he is like a stranger to me. For normal
visits, now, he would be dressed like you. But he wanted you to
feel at home."

I do not think Jeannie meant to be ironic with that last
remark but I was as sensitive as a G-string and winced. Bob told
me the drinks were on the sideboard and I could help myself
and pass him a claret if I wouldn't mind. I got myself a heavy
Scotch, him his claret, and I poured Jeannie a gin and tonic.

"Thank you, Moses," she say. "Where have you been? Have
you been doing anything interesting?"

She sound great, except she flick cigarette ash on the
Axeminster carpet though it had a big ashtray on the coffee
table.

"Did you see that Pinter play on the Beeb last evening?" Bob
ask.

"I haven't got a television where I am," I say.

"I forgot. Perhaps we could let you have our old black and
white set. Pity about the play, I thought we could discuss it."

"Maybe Moses would like to talk about something else,"
Jeannie say hopefully.

"How's the dinner coming?" Bob ask her.

"Yes, I'd better take a look," she say, and went to the sideboard and topped up her glass and went into the kitchen.

Bob watch her going, and shook his head. "She doesn't fit
into my scheme of things. I am leaps and bounds ahead of her,
and she cannot cope. However, I have got her to start a collection of old and rare coins as a hobby."

I had other things on my mind. For one, it was time to stop
this nonsense of him and Jeannie living in my flat. Now that
Bob was an educated man I felt sure we would be able to settle
our differences in an amicable manner.

"I'm thinking of selling up, Bob," I began.

"I say!" he say. "Really?"

"I'm a bit fed-up with things," I say.

"Yeah. The country's affairs are in a deplorable state."

"I'm even thinking of going back home."

"Really!" he cried. "That's a coincidence! Jeannie and I want
to go to Trinidad for the Carnival." He moved to the sideboard

and drowned the rest of his claret with a whisky. "That's great, Moses."

He saw me looking at his glass and explained, "Claret and port are okay, but a good scotch takes a lot of beating."

Jeannie came back from the kitchen at this moment, wringing her hands.

"Oh, the dinner is all burnt! I had it in the oven—"

"You can't do any bloody thing right, can you?" Bob snarl.

"It's all right," I say.

"The same thing happened the other night," Bob say. "We had an American actor and his wife to sup, and she made a mess of the food."

"I'm all right with mash and veg," Jeannie say, "and I make a good Lancashire hot-pot. I never cooked venison before."

"Don't worry, Jeannie," I say, relaxing my gastric juices and stomach muscles, which were anticipating a decent meal. "I will settle for a cup of tea."

"You think you can manage that?" Bob sneer at her.

Jeannie tossed her head and went back in the kitchen.

I said to Bob: "You'll have to look for another place when I sell."

"Go ahead. I'm a sitting tenant." He did not seem concerned. "Let's talk about our trip, Moses. It would be great if we could get a Caribbean cruise, touching at all the islands, Jamaica-where-the-rum-comes-from, Trinidad-the-land-of-the-humming-bird, Barbados-the-little-England. I'd like to see that little island where Princess Margaret hangs out with that pop singer, too."

He drank and filled his glass again. One thing with Bob: once he take a sip it is the start of a marathon. As no food was forthcoming I joined the race and charged my glass too.

By the time Jeannie brought the tea—China pot cups, I noticed—Bob was high and I was mellowing.

Jeannie did the honours. You could see she was trying, but the dainty cups and saucers rattle, and she didn't ask before or after with the milk when she pour the tea, nor one lump or two with the sugar. The poor girl was a bundle of nerves, especially as Bob stop talking while she perform the ceremony, and look at every move she make.

As she lifted her cup and took a sip he broke the silence.

"Now now, Jeannie," he say, his own cup and saucer up to his chest like the genteels, "didn't I tell you?"

"What, Bobbie?" Jeannie ask.

"Look at me."

I look too. He was wiggling the little finger of the hand he was holding the cup with. Then, having caught her attention, he crooked it and took a sip of tea.

"Oh," Jeannie say, and crook her little finger. "Sorry, Bobbie. But Moses isn't doing it!"

"Of course I am," I say, crooking the little finger what holding the saucer by mistake.

Jeannie laugh. "That's the wrong one."

"I am left-handed," I say.

"Don't make a joke of it, Moses," Bob say. "I have enough trouble teaching Jeannie the rudimentaries. Little things like that count in the right society."

"Would you like to see my coin collection?" Jeannie ask me.

"Not now." Bob frowned. "Tell her your news, Moses, about going back to Trinidad."

"Are you really?" Jeannie exclaim.

"I am thinking about it," I say.

"Oh Moses, come with us!" Jeannie cry. "You can guide our tour, tell us what is taboo and what is custom, so we wouldn't be embarrassed making silly mistakes. Say yes, Moses, say yes!"

I laugh, or rather the free whisky inside me laugh.

"Hold on, Jeannie. There are several matters to consider even before I come to a decision."

She gave me a winsome smile. "Oh Moses, I have this dream of bathing in the turquoise-blue waters of the Caribbean sea."

I could hardly hide a smirk. In a claustrophobic bath in a derelict terrace house in Shepherd's Bush, she earnestly desired her back to be scratched. What would she want when she found herself in the wide open spaces of the sparkling surf in my tropical island?

"It would be splendid if were together, old boy," Bob say, "maybe our plans will coincide."

But not a word of sorrow or sadness, from either of them, that in the event I decide to return, they would miss my presence in Londontown. Perhaps I was premature to tell Enoch that I have more black enemies than white.

It occurred to me that I would be a fool to burn my bridges and sell my mansion. I could leave someone in charge while I do some reconnoitering in Trinidad, just in case I wanted to come back to the land of milk and honey. But I almost cancelled the idea when I realise the only one was Galahad.

I broached it to him cautiously. "I've changed my mind about selling," I tell him. "I think it prudent to hold on to the house. Only thing, I got nobody to look after it while I'm away."

"Leave the keys with me," he say promptly.

"You!" I exaggerate doubts and mistrusts in my tone. "I rather leave it vacant at the mercy of squatters."

"I wouldn't do nothing you wouldn't do yourself," he say. "I will put the rents in the bank regularly every week please-God. I wish you had a garage, though. My Mercedes looks incongruous parked in front of your house."

"You talk as if I've given you the assignment," I jeer. "I wouldn't trust you with a straight-pin, Galahad."

"Okay," he say, as if he didn't care, but knowing full well that I had no one else to turn to. I could see a gleam in his eye, like a drop-out foraging in a rubbish tip and coming across a old suitcase stuffed with money.

"If we had a written agreement, I might consider it," I say.

"We've been friends for years, Moses," he say.

"It will all have to be down on paper, legal, duly witnessed and attested by a reliable firm of solicitors."

"I know a firm," he say.

"One of my choice," I say, and sigh. "I will have to go on drugs and tranquillisers when I think of you here as landlord."

"Don't exaggerate," he say.

"You'll have to occupy the basement room, you know. Don't imagine you are going to live it up in my penthouse. I want it let as soon as I leave."

"Sure, sure. Put it all down in written agreement."

Doubts assailed me again: what protection was a scrap of paper against Galahad? "I will tell Brenda to keep an eye on things," I say. "In fact, I will appoint both you and Brenda as trustees."

"Two heads are better than one," he agree.

"But two wrongs don't make a right," I say, already regretting my proposal.

I suppose I could of gone to some house agency, or rent-collectors. But I wanted someone around all the time. Any day the walls might want shoring up, or some beams of wood jammed under the roof to stop it caving in.

I went into the Black Power office a little later to see Brenda, and Galahad was there. The both of them was laughing and slapping one another on the back, and when they see me they quieten down, but I was filled with foreboding. I was mad to negate the idea and keep my arse quiet.

"We won't do nothing we didn't do while you were here, Moses," Brenda say. "I will see that Galahad behaves himself."

"And who will keep an eye on you?" I ask.

"I'm doing you a favour," she say, "but if that's your attitude, you can stuff it."

"I just want to warn you, that British justice will protect me from any misdemeanours. It will all be legal."

"Ah, how lucky you are," she say. "What wouldn't I do to quit this miserable, god-forsaken country and go to live somewhere in the Third World."

"Yeah, boy," Galahad chimed in, "at last you are realising your dreams. And you will be in Trinidad for Carnival!"

"Don't crow too loud," I say. "I have not gone yet. And if I do, I may return. Unexpectedly."

"You will always have a home to return to here, Moses," Brenda say. "I think this calls for a little sherry." She open the drawer in her desk and haul out a bottle of cheap synthetic British sherry, and some paper cups. "I must say you've timed your departure well. Anyone with sense would get out."

"Here's your hat, what's your hurry?" I sneered, remembering a line from a film.

"I have a duty to My People," she say.

In due course the agreement was drawn up, and I kept a copy to stowaway with my luggage, for when I got depressed to look at and remind me that British law, the greatest in the world, was in there pitching for me.

Meanwhile Bob and Jeannie were wildly excited and going apace with their plans. One evening they asked me up. I found them browsing through a great collection of tourist leaflets, and there was a copy of Errol Hill's *The Trinidad Carnival* on the coffee table.

We all had some port. Then Jeannie, who appeared to be restless, say to Bob: "Shall we do it now?"

"Why not?" Bob say, and the both of them got up. "Just help yourself to the drinks, old boy. We'll be back in a jiffy," and they went into the bedroom.

I thought perhaps they had deferred a sexual intercourse until I came—some whites are switched on by blacks—and was trying out a little Tia Maria when they came back.

"Don't turn round yet, Moses," Jeannie call, as my back was turn, "wait until I say now!"

"What's up?" I ask.

"Now!" she say.

I turn. I stare.

Jeannie had on leather boots coming up to her knees, a thick furry-looking midi-skirt belted at the waist, a white cotton shirt, a colourful bandanna round she neck, and one of them cork hats like what you see film stars wear on safari. The hat was trim with mosquito netting material, like what demure brides wear.

Bob, standing at her side, had on heavy, black boots, white stockings up to his hairy calves, a short pair of khaki drill trousers, a safari jacket with a pipe sticking out of the top pocket, a cork hat like Jeannie but without the veil, and he was sloping arms with a great elephant gun.

Oh, and both of them were wearing giant sunglasses, so big almost covering their faces.

I did not laugh. I looked them over appraisingly. I went and do a parade inspection, straightening Bob's hat, patting and turning down the flap of the pocket over Jeannie's left breast, then I stood in front of them, frowning a little.

"Well?" Bob say.

"I assume those are your costumes for playing Carnival?" I ask.

Bob frown now. "It's our tropical gear."

"It might do for Port-of-Spain," I say, "but when you get into the interior the natives will laugh at you. You'll have to discard all that."

"You mean walk around starkers?" Jeannie ask interestingly.

"I won't have that," Bob say. "It's okay for Moses if he wants to revert, but we have to toe the line somewhere."

"Oh dear, now you have me worrying about my bikini," Jeannie say, "it might be too daring."

"Better let me have a look, Jeannie," I say.

She flew into the bedroom to change.

"I don't want to go around looking like a proper Charlie," Bob say. "What do you think? Don't they have safari trips? I always fancied getting a lion or an elephant in my sights"—he brace the elephant gun on his shoulder and squint along the barrel aiming at my chest—"bang! One shot."

"Can you really shoot?" I ask.

"Sure. I did my National Service stint." He put the gun aside and sat down. "Would we need any phrasebooks?"

"Oh God, Bob," I say now. "You've met a lot of Trinidadians in London."

"But I don't know what they're like at home," he say.

I gave up. Why the arse should I worry if he landed there dressed as an Eskimo? Or Jeannie—she came back just then with bits of cloth covering her tits and private parts and walked up and down posing like a model.

"It doesn't look safe to me," Bob mutter.

"You selected it," she remind him.

"Okay, okay, you can stop all that wiggling and waggling and go and put on something decent. And what about a cup of tea?"

He watched her going and sighed. "That woman! Moses, she is so untrained. She will not learn one of the social graces, or interest herself in the arts. She is really a handful."

"That's true, Bob."

"Sometimes I think I was better off without her."

"Oh no, she's an asset," I say.

"Maybe. But things used to be good with us before she came, eh? Sometimes I wish things could be like that again."

He grew thoughtful, raking up the past in his mind. I kept quiet, for I had other matters to think about.

When you making a big move, after a long time, it got problems you don't foresee. My passport, for instance, was a British one which expire aeons ago, as I never left these beloved shores, not even for a day-trip across the English Channel. But when I went to the Passport Office to get a new one I got the shock of my life. Did I have citizenship papers? they ask me. I laugh. (The white English clerk was even younger than I was.) He said if I hadn't, I would have to go to the office of the High Commission for Trinidad and Tobago in Belgrave Square. But, I said. Don't hold up the queue, he said. I will complain to the Citizens' Advice Bureau, I retorted. Do that, he said.

I had half a mind to, too, but being as things was getting imminent I went to Belgrave Square. I had a funny feeling when I get to the place. They say that once your foot is on the territory, so to speak, of the country of your birth—represented by the premises of the Embassies of all nations on whatever foreign soil—you are safe from persecution even if you commit the worst crime. At the least, temporary sanctuary. (I always remember that film *Hunchback of Notre Dame* how Charles Laughton hop into the cathedral and lisp, "Sanctuary, sanctuary!" and the bastards who was chasing him couldn't do nothing whilst he was in there). And I used to think, being British, that if ever I found myself in crucial straits, like if I walk on the grass or loiter on the pavement, that I would run and hide like Quasimodo in the House of Commons or Parliament.

It now look like this place in Belgrave Square is where I would have to come to lay low, so I tread warily, as on hallowed ground, and I look about me to see if they had any moats or battlements erected to protect Trinidadians from the Metropolitan Police Force. But there was nothing like that—in politics, it is all a matter of diplomacy, of which the English are past masters, though I do not think they can pull the wool over the eyes of any Trinidadian.

I won't assume that the others in the passport queue I join was stupid like me and wanted to go back to Trinidad. Some might of been travelling to China, or the Seychelle Islands, or going on a business trip to the North Pole—you could never tell where you will bounce-up with a Trini. I had to fill up so many details, and there was so much protocol about dual nationality and if I was a British or Trinidadian that I just tell the clerk to give me any passport, and give him my Woolworths photo-machine photos. But that wasn't good enough for them, I had to go out and get expensive photos from a studio. And after all that I was still waiting for my passport as they said they would post it.

I was still waiting to hear from my Tanty Flora too. Naturally I had thought of letting all my friends and relatives know I was coming: I bought a dozen air-letter forms, then found that the onlyest one I could remember was my Tanty Flora living up in John-John, who look after me when I was small. All these years in Brit'n I never wrote nobody: I didn't even know if she was alive or dead. I had to give Brenda the eleven air-letter forms that remain, for Party use: she did not offer to reimburse me, and I wasn't silly enough to ask.

Bob broke into my thoughts. "You know, Moses," he say, "there is some personal business I have to see to when I go to Trinidad."

He gave me time to ask what but I didn't, so he went on, "I've been trying to trace my family tree. I went to Somerset House, and from what I could gather, it would appear that there may be some Caribbean connection."

I did not ask him what in the first place because I thought it would be some shit like that. I yawned.

"You're not interested?" he ask.

"I've got my own problems," I say.

"You're troubled about leaving Galahad in charge, eh? I don't blame you."

"I wasn't thinking about him," I say, "but it reminds me that he wants me to take something back for him. He's bringing it tonight—I'd better go."

I got up.

"Aren't you waiting for tea? I wanted to discuss this matter of tracing my ancestry—"

"Yeah," I interrupted, "that's why I'm going. Say good-night to Jeannie for me."

I went down to the basement, and repacked one of my suitcases to make a little space for Galahad.

When he came I asked him for it as I wanted to get my luggage out of the way.

"I left it outside," he say. "It's all crated, I got the packers to do a nice job."

"Crated?" I was puzzled.

"Yeah," he say, "come and see."

I followed him out and saw a massive wooden crate jam-up and towering in the basement door.

"I couldn't quite get it in," Galahad say apologetically. "Can you give a hand?"

I swallowed hard. "That's the little parcel you want me to take?"

"Don't be dismayed," he say. "Look, it's even stenciled 'This side up' and 'Handle with care.'"

I laughed.

"It's a deep-freeze," he say. "The latest model. I got it on the H.P."

I was feeling weak at the knees. I propped myself against the crate to stop from fainting.

"You all right?" Galahad ask.

"Sure."

"Maybe Brenda has some sherry in the office." He went and come back with a glass. "Take this."

I gulped it down.

"Feeling better?"

I couldn't think of anything funny to say.

"Don't be unreasonable," Galahad say. "You know how risky it is to ship things abroad. "The last time I sent a parcel to Trinidad it ended up in Peking. Funny, eh?"

"Yeah," I say, "you're slaying me."

"Don't think I expect you to take it on your back!" he say indignantly. "I have arranged transport to the docks. I couldn't pay to keep it in storage. I just wanted you to see it, that's all, so you could keep an eye on it in transit, and make sure them stevedores don't mash it up when they taking it off in Trinidad."

It was a bright morning in February when me, Bob and Jeannie stood on the pavement waiting to get into Galahad's Mercedes. We did not have much luggage, as we had sent most of the stuff to the docks in the van that came to collect his deep-freeze. Mines was the biggest item, which Galahad had to put in the boot, and it wasn't even mines, but Brenda's, who decide at the last moment to send an old sewing machine to a relative.

Brenda had come out to wish us goodbye, and even Paki was waving from the penthouse window.

"I would have liked to throw a farewell party for you," Brenda say, "but you've been so busy these last days."

"It's the thought that counts," I say drily.

"But I have a memento of London for you," she say, and handed me a cheap ball-point pen what had a picture of Piccadilly Circus on it, that you could pick up in any sweet-shop for a few pee.

"I'll treasure it," I say, clipping it in the breast pocket of my jacket.

"All *abroad*?" Galahad call gaily, from where he was tinkering with the engine.

"Here, hold on a minute," Bob say, "Jeannie's forgotten her sun-lotion."

"Oh God," I said.

"Is that Paki at the penthouse window?" Jeannie ask plaintively, glancing up. "What is he doing there, Bobbie?"

"I'll soon find out," Bob say grimly, turning to go in.

"Watch it," I caution, knowing all them Oriental tricks of hari-kari and kung-fu Paki was capable of. And my nerves was so bad that I snarl to Jeannie, "You and Bob behaving like West Indians!"

"Now now, Moses," Brenda say, "I can understand your feelings, but not your comparisons."

"Fuck all of you," I say, getting into the back seat, hoping Bob would sit with Galahad in front and I would have Jeannie on the way to Plymouth.

But Galahad took care of that. "Come in front with me," he told Jeannie. "Moses is overwrought," and he gave her a heavy wink.

I peeped out of the car-window to see what was keeping Bob: he was waving frantically from the penthouse.

"Galahad!" Brenda drew his attention. "Bob's in some trouble up there with Paki!"

Galahad dashed upstairs—fearful of anything that might threaten our departure—and came back escorting Bob, who had a black eye and was limping. Galahad himself was favouring his right foot.

"Fine thing," Bob mumbled through swollen lips. "Assault and battery in my own flat!"

"What happened, Bobbie?" Jeannie ask. "Was he after the silver?"

"What about me?" Galahad yell. "The bloody Paki stamp me on my big toe. I may not be able to drive properly!"

"Nonsense," Brenda cry. "You've got to get them to Plymouth, Galahad! Pull yourself together."

It was lucky thing we didn't have neighbours—at least the kind who come to offer sympathy. No doubt they knew I was on my way out of Brit'n—I saw a few window curtains shaking and knew they was hiding behind there peeping, indulging the favourite English housewife pastime.

I was anxious to get moving, if only to get away from the scene. The Mercedes was just going gr-r-gr-r-r as Galahad step on the X, but wouldn't start.

"Jesus Christ," I say. I was beginning to sweat.

"What's wrong, Galahad?" Jeannie ask.

"Pull the choke," Bob say.

"You want a push?" Brenda ask, worriedly.

"Cool it," Galahad say. And then, with dwindling confidence, "I sure I full up with gas last night. Maybe the tank overflowing. Give me a push, Brenda."

Brenda was behind in a jiffy, straddling her legs to get a firm grip. She braced her hands on the boot, lowered her head like a bull about to charge, and pushed.

The Mercedes edged a few inches, and the engine stutter as Galahad try to get it going.

"You pushing?" he yell.

"What the arse you think I'm doing?" Brenda shout.

"No good. No good." He turn around. "You and Bob better get out and push. It give me this trouble sometimes."

I got out. Bob get out. We start to push. Galahad was helping, with the driving door open, one foot in and one foot out, and one hand on the steering.

Suddenly she start!

"Hop in, hop in!" Galahad cry.

By this time the Mercedes was about twenty yards from me and Bob.

I turn to wave Brenda goodbye, and she yell, "Moses! The milkman! You remember to tell the milkman not to leave milk for you?"

"Oh God, Brenda, I forgot!" I shout.

"All right, don't worry! How much you owe him?"

"Forty pee!"

"Jesus Christ, Moses, hop in before she stall again!" Galahad shout.

And that's how I left Shepherd's Bush, London West Twelve, when I departed London. No sentimental glance at my house or street, no bemused frame of mind leaving the place where I live. Just dashing exhausted into the car lest they go off without me. By the time I catch my breath we pass the market where I used to get pigfoot, and the Woolworths where I get cheap watchekongs, and the little corner shop where I used to buy my Oxo cubes and Instant Mash.

"Oh God," I cried, "oh God."

"I hope we can make it to Plymouth," Galahad say. "You got some change for gas, Moses?"

Bob absolve himself before I could answer by saying that all his money was in dollars and he only had a few loose pee for those new Gents what you have to pay to get into.

"Never mind, we might just make it," Galahad say, flicking glances all over the dashboard, like an airline pilot facing a battery of dials. "I hope the windscreen wipers working."

I was recovered enough to sit back and laugh at that, and it make everybody laugh, which shows you the nervous state we was all in, though each for different reasons. For myself, I was pretty glum, especially when I had to hand over a fiver to Galahad to buy gas on the way, from which I got back a half-pee change—"you could use it as a small screw-driver," he said. Once or twice I thought we would never make it, when the

Mercedes wouldn't start after a stop at a pub for refreshments, and another time at a traffic lights, where Galahad toot the horn in exasperation and got it going. I don't think anything would of stop him from getting us to the docks, even if he had to change horses at Jamaica Inn. He kept a wary eye on the clock, and in fact got us there with a good two hours to spare.

How different were my thoughts and feelings in the forties, when, from this very same port, I caught my first glimpse of merry England! How my heart bounded as they sent a tug to take our luggages off the ship, for we was anchored a little way offshore, and I could see the greenery of the coast hills, the pretty little houses, and seagulls hovering and fluttering around, waiting to drop a welcome on the heads of we black adventurers! A Grenadian standing at the rails next to me had water in his eyes, and a old woman, come no doubt to join a pioneering son or husband, raised arms to the sky and cried Hallelujah like a old Mama from the Deep South.

I thought now, as I stand in the customs shed with Galahad —Bob and Jeannie having gone off to sort out some problem with Immigration Control—how I did never plant a flag, nor wrote my name on a wall, when I first came. And I had the feeling, that somehow I should leave my mark in Brit'n before I go, some sign or symbol that Kilroy was here, for I was saddened beyond measure. To have spent all those years toiling, to have witnessed the death of His Majesty King George VI and the coronation of Her Majesty Queen Elizabeth, and just vanish without a ripple or a blink!

"What can I do, what can I do?" I ask Galahad, helplessly wringing my hands.

"Eh?" he say.

I knew he was sticking around grudgingly, forced into some show of friendliness and concern, the while he was yearning to get back to Shepherd's Bush and instal himself.

"You've got no feelings, have you?" I said, bitterly. "You can't appreciate my depression and gloom."

"Yeah," he say, "we got here too early. My timing was bad."

"Galahad," I say, "tell me honest. Will you miss me?"

"Sure," he say quickly. But his eyes were flicking around, assessing the possibility of picking up a few passengers to take back to London, for there were many such about, come to bid farewells. Even in my blues I could not help observing that there were quantities of Our People milling about or standing in little groups of goodbye.

"Who and what are all these people, Galahad?" I ask. "Have they just disembarked from a vessel to try their luck in Brit'n?"

"They're going back home," he say briefly.

"Going back?" I was nonplussed.

"Of course," he say easily. "Immigrants don't only come, old man. They go. But you don't hear about the departures."

"They go back voluntarily?" I ask, amazed.

"Sure. They serve their periods of indentureship, or do their stints in the salt mines, then return to the islands."

"I don't believe you," I said firmly. "I can't conceive of anyone stupid like me to leave Brit'n."

"My regret is that they deplete the Black forces in the country. The Party grows weaker with each shipload of departures, and it is getting harder every day for newcomers to get in."

The sight of so many black ones chattering and chuckling, as if they were happy they were going, accentuated my gloom. How could they find the heart? How could they, on this last day, put up a brave, indifferent front, as if it didn't matter? I cast about, truly wretched, to see if I could do some kind act to some Englisher, help a porter shift a heavy load or give directions to the Gents or Ladies, or anything to soothe my troubled mind.

Galahad wanted to go to the bar, and I was about to succumb when I felt a tap on my shoulder. It was a white woman.

"Here, my good man," she say, "will you help me with my baggage?"

"But of course." I beamed.

"Come on, man," Galahad already stepping off, "she take you for a porter because you black."

"Leave this gentlewoman in the lurch?" I arched my eyebrows at him.

"I can't find a porter," Gentlewoman say. "I'll pay, of course."

"Oh, in that case I'll be glad to be of service," Galahad say.

"I will do it for nothing, dear lady," I say.

"It's against Union rules," Galahad say.

"Well," Gentlewoman say, a little bemused.

"Where are your encumbrances, ma'am?" I ask, rolling up my sleeves.

"Follow me," she say, heading for the entrance.

I dash up to a black who was unloading his gear off a trolley. "Let's have that," I say, tumbling his things off.

"What the arse—" he begin, but I was trundling the trolley in the wake of Ma'am.

I was almost light-headed with joy: it was so crowded in the customs hall I couldn't even scrawl my name anywhere, and to think that Fate answered my plea this way!

Galahad was waiting to help unload as I came back staggering behind the trolley packed dangerously high. As we finished unloading Gentlewoman opened her purse.

"No no!" I cried, and presumed to touch her hand briefly. "Spare me that indignity!"

"That was a heavy load," Galahad say. "An ordinary porter would of charge more than a quid to bring that in. Union laws."

"A qu—you mean a pound?" Gentlewoman was horrified.

"It was nothing, ma'am," I wave my hand. "It was a pleasure to be of service."

"I'll have to see someone about this," she say, getting nasty and reverting to basics. "I think thirty pee—pence—is generous," and she moved the filthy lucre towards me.

"I won't touch it!" I say, and turned aside.

"You mean thirty pee as a tip, lady," Galahad say. "I seen these porters charging fifty pee minimum to bring in black people luggage."

"Well, I'm in a hurry." She take out a fifty-pee piece and add it to the thirty. She threw me a dirty look as she stalked off. "Just as I thought. God alone knows what you're like in the islands."

"Come on Moses," Galahad say, "I can buy you a pint of bitter now."

A pint of bitter—you cotton? I was so deflated I just followed him.

Bob and Jeannie join us in the bar shortly after. Bob was fuming.

"Here, Moses," he say, "you have any trouble with any officials?"

"Not yet," I say.

"Well, they kept me and Jeannie in that office for hours, asking all sorts of questions. They even wanted to *examine* her!"

"We have to conform with the laws, Bobbie," Jeannie say.

"They should question people like Moses and his lot," Bob
say, quite disgruntled.

"They don't care about the blacks who are going," Galahad
explained.

"I will miss you, Galahad," Jeannie say, and to Bob, "Did you
go to the Bureau de Change so we can buy some drinks?"

"I've only got dollars, I told you," he say.

"I've been hiding an odd pound or two for just such an
emergency," Galahad say, digging into his pocket. "I thought you
might need it."

He and Bob do a transaction, exchanging dollars for
pounds, and Galahad try to make a joke, saying, "I rather have
Trinidad dollars in my pocket than pounds, the way how things
are."

The three of them begin celebrating the trip, but I had
nothing to be jubilant about. I give them their due—they saw
my mood and plied me with drinks, trying to jerk me out of it.
Bob was toasting every drink with a we-will-be-together theme.
I don't know what he meant—he and Jeannie were booked in
first-class, and I had a third-class cabin next to the engine room
in the bowels of the ship, sharing with three others. I had left all
those arrangements up to Bob, being loath to sharpen the cutlass to cut off my own head, as it were, and he said that was the
only berth he could get me, though I suspected he wanted to
keep up the Upstairs-Downstairs fallacy.

The drinks only made me feel worse. I wished the ship's
engines might need overhauling, or that an Official might
appear and challenge my right to depart. I even pretended to
be sick, holding on to my left side and rubbing it in agony, but
none of them paid attention until I deliberately pushed my
finger down my throat and brought up some bile in Galahad's
lap.

"Jesus Christ!" he say, and get a dirty washing-up rag from the bartender to wipe it off. We moved off to a table in the corner as the bar was getting overcrowded.

"I think I got an appendix," I moan. "Call a ambulance. I can't make it."

"Pull yourself together, Moses," Bob say.

"It couldn't be the drink," Jeannie say.

I think if was only Bob and Jeannie there, I might of pulled it off, but Galahad say, "Cut out all that shit, Moses."

"I might die making the Middle Passage," I say. "You know what happened to blacks in transit, how they were tossed to the sharks?"

"Pack it up," he say. "It's too late now."

"I'll look after you if you get sea-sick" Bob say, "I am a seasoned traveller."

"Why don't you have something to eat, Moses?" Jeannie suggested.

"Good idea," Galahad say. "Have a sausage roll—or something expensive like potato chips."

Galahad was growing restless and getting fidgety. He look at his watch and said it was time we cleared Immigration and got aboard and settled in nice and cosy.

"Aren't you coming on the ship to see us off?" I ask, aghast.

"Oh. Well, you need a pass for that."

"And you didn't think of getting one?"

"See if you can get one now, Galahad," Jeannie urge. "You may never see Moses again."

"That's what he's hoping," I say, "that's the sort of friends I have."

"Just to show you I'll make a try," Galahad say, and left us.

We went over to Immigration, but of course separated at the First-class and Third-class barriers.

"See you on board," Bob say cheerfully, "we'll find the Third class bar."

I grunted. The drinks was wearing off, and I was back in the dumps as I find myself in the line of departing blacks. As I shuffled up the queue I thought of several things to tell the Officer to prevent my departure, like I was chief instigator of a race riot in Notting Hill, or that I was responsible for that bomb what explode in Oxford Street, and not the Irish terrorists. I even thought of fainting: it occur to me I should of learnt some of them Paki tricks like going into a trance so everybody believe you dead. With each inexorable step forward, I counted the inches that was taking me away from Brit'n.

Suddenly I was in front a Officer and he look at me and say, "What's up with you?"

"I don't really want to go," I blurt out.

He guffawed. "Back to all that sunshine?"

"I rather the bitter cold and the nasty smog," I say sincerely.

"You enjoyed your visit, then?"

"Visit?" I choke. "I am a citizen. I am a landlord!"

"Yeah? Well, don't hold up the queue," he said happily, "lots more behind you!"

I hand him my passport automatically, and he stamp me out of Brit'n with a flourish and turned beaming to the next person.

I can't remember how I went up that gang-plank: some people push me out of the way because I was walking too slow and they wanted to hurry. Halfway up I look down over the side and see a piece of the English Channel, and realise that already I was on the ocean just standing up on a piece of wood. I almost collapse. It was more the press of surging crowds behind that got me on board than my own volition.

I descended into the bowels of the ship seeking my cabin, 13B. Or rather, our cabin, as I remember when I open the door and see luggage scatter all about, suitcases and briefcases and boxes and cartons wrap up with twine, and plastic bags stick up with scotch tape. I had no idea who my three cabin mates was, but obviously they had come in early and bags the three best bunks and stake their claims about the cabin.

Cabin 13B was the nearest one to the engine room: they couldn't get one any lower unless they bore a hole in the bottom of the ship. Was I never to rise to heights again? Was I wrong to hoard my money for rainy days and take the cheapest berth I could get? Was I a *masoshit* suffering like this, when I could of afforded to charter Queen Elizabeth II for my own self, and travel in luxury and style? No. I was convinced I was doing the right thing. I remember a dustman in Shepherd's Bush what used to clear all the filth and refuse. In the day he look besmeared and begrimed and lowly: in the evening he was in glad rags and sleek, driving about in a Jaguar with a painted blonde. My times would come: there would be moments when suppliants bend their knees to me for alms: days when I could afford to scatter largesse wantonly.

So I pass that hillock of despair, but not the Ben Nevis of my desertion of Brit'n in her hour of need. How would the country survive with all these blacks returning to the islands? When the streets were paved with gold they came a-running: now that the humble potato was princely they were rushing out to the Third World to eat rice instead, having made their kill in the British Isles. What did they think they were, film stars and lucrative pop singers, who flee to Jersey or Switzerland after reaping a harvest without putting anything back in the kitty? I had no quarrel with these latter, you can't expect better of them, it was the black ingrates who raised my hackles. Indeed, if it were left to the socialites, they would want the blacks to stay and keep the home fires burning while they themselves go to frolic in the sunny climes of the Caribbean! I thought of the poor suffering whites left behind trying to raise a little econo-mince to feed their families, and I worked myself into a towering rage against my countrymen. I was in such choler that I felt like chasing them off the ship: maybe at this last minute I could cause one of them to change their minds and return to the millstone.

I was about to do just that when a black man appeared and exclaimed, "Aye man! What you want here? This is my cabin!"

"Aren't you ashamed of yourself?" I cried.

"Eh?" He peep to see if all his things was intact. "You belong to this cabin?"

"Alas."

"Oh." He mumbled something else I didn't catch.

In the short dialogue I was trying to identify him. Jamaican? Barbadian? Trinidadian? I could tell a Cockney, and a Welsh, or a Devonshire accent and a Scottish brogue, and I would recognise the Queen voice anywhere.

"What the arse you mean by if I ashame of myself?" he ask.

"You've made your packet, now you don't care about the hand that fed you," I told him.

He laugh. It was a kind of Caribbean laughter, derisive and mocking, what put you in your place. I was affronted. I stiffened.

"Man," he say, "you some sort of social worker or Welfare State or something?"

"I'm just a loyal Briton," I say shortly.

"Oh," he say, then "Jesus!" and he laugh again. "I just come down to check. If you belong to this cabin, okay."

"Where you from?" I ask.

"Dominica," he say.

I teased my memory, but at the moment it slipped me which island it was.

"And where you from?" He ask.

"Brit'n," I replied unhesitatingly.

"I mean before," he say impatiently.

"Oh. Trinidad," I mutter.

"Huh. I thought so." He sound disgusted. "You can't take it, eh?"

"Me!" I spluttered. "It's you who's sneaking back after enjoying the benefits of National Security. You've got no conscience."

He laugh again. One thing with a Caribee: when he can't talk, he laugh. "That's how I know you are Trinidadian, you talk big. Who told you I was going back to Dominica? I am going to Trinidad for the Carnival."

"I don't care. Who will take your place here? What work did you do?"

"I was a hospital orderly."

"That's a vital job, isn't it? One could imagine the life of a patient hanging in the balance between orderly and surgeon."

"Yeah," he say doubtfully, "something like that, eh? Yeah."

"If all the black orderlies left they'd have to shut down the hospitals."

"I don't know about that. The staff gave me a sendoff. All of we was pissed in the pub, and the Matron say she wish she was in my place."

I left him rummaging in a suitcase, and trudged up the stairs. I did not have any trouble finding the bar, as that was where everybody was heading. I looked around but didn't see any of my friends. I bought a drink and went and sit down by a window where I could watch the land. I had lost all spirit. All I could wish for was that the ship was in mid-Atlantic, for I knew my fate was sealed.

Bob found me drowning my sorrows, and took me to the first-class bar, where Galahad and Jeannie were involved in a fond farewell. The clientele here was a different sort, mostly whites, and that helped me to unwind a little.

"I wish Galahad was coming with us," Jeannie say.

"The best of friends must part," Galahad say jovially. "We just have time for a last drink."

"I'll get it," Bob say.

"No, my turn," Galahad say.

"Call the waiter, Bobbie," Jeannie say.

Bob raise his hand and try to snap his fingers but couldn't. I did it for him. Catching the eye of a waiter was an accustomed gesture with me and I did it with such flair that when he come he come straight to me and said, "Yes sir?"

"What'll you have?" I ask Jeannie.

"My turn, Moses," Galahad say.

"Gin and tonic, please," Jeannie say.

"Bob?"

"My turn, Moses," Galahad say.

"Double rum punch," Bob say.

"And you?" I look at Galahad.

"My—same as Bob," Galahad say.

When the drinks came I paid the waiter and gave him a tip.

"Really, Moses," Galahad began, and same time, the ship's horn make a loud blast. "Saved by the bell," he ended.

Jeannie was startled. "Are we off?"

"That's for visitors to leave," Bob say.

Galahad gulped his drink and rose. "Well, bon voyage and all that." "I will send you a postcard," Jeannie say.

"Well, boy, Moses," Galahad clear his throat, though it wasn't obstructed, lying in action as well as in words. I waited to hear the platitudes fall, and they fell. "Best of luck. Say hello to everybody for me. Don't do anything I wouldn't do. Take care of yourself."

We drank our drinks and got up to follow him.

"No need to see me off," he say, "I won't stowaway."

I tried to laugh like Dominica.

When we was out on the deck, I was assailed by melancholy again, seeing the visitors go down the gang-plank to rest their feet on Brit'n.

Galahad shake hands with Bob, and Jeannie demurely turn her cheek for him to kiss it.

"Have a wonderful time, Jeannie," he say, "and look after yourself and come back safe and sound to London."

I waited quietly in the background, and the bastard actually began to go without a last word to me.

"I almost forget you, Moses," he laugh. "Don't forget to look out for my deep-freezer." One would of thought he was the voyager and I the visitor.

"I am trusting you with all I possess, Galahad," I say. "I expect you to maintain regular correspondence, and keep an account of outgoings and overheads."

"Yeah, yeah."

"I don't know," I cried in despair. "It seems an occasion for earnest exchange of sentiments, but nobody appreciates what a wrench this trip is to me."

"You mean you feel like you feel when you was leaving Trinidad to come here?" he ask.

"No. This is different. I wouldn't of minded if Brit'n was in better shape. I feel like a traitor."

"Never mind. It is an English ship, with an English crew, so you won't feel so badly. And by the time you hit the rock and drink a fish-tea and a coconut water, such fancies will flee."

"Yeah," I mutter. "You better go, Galahad, before you begin to shed crocodile tears."

"Take it easy," was his last words to me. I watch him disappear in the crowds. He didn't look back once: he just sort of burrow himself quickly into the mass of people, as if the police was after him to deport him.

"Well, we'll soon be on our merry way," Bob say cheerfully. He had donned a yachtsman's cap, and now paced up and down the deck, hands clasped behind his back, like a mariner impatiently waiting on the tide to set sail.

"I think I'll go to the cabin and put away our things," Jeannie say.

"Good idea. I'll come and help you." He asked me if I was staying on deck.

"Yeah," I say. "I got nothing else to do."

So I stayed there like a *masoshit*, in all the hub and hum of excitement, feeling like a wallflower at a gay ball. I could not help noticing the lack of tears. On the contrary, all the black people were laughing and giggling and expressing great joy and happiness, from two points of view: (a) those that was leaving was laughing with relief to get away, and (b) those that was staying was laughing to think that with the exodus, chances would increase of employment and occupation of basement rooms and derelict houses.

For myself, what can I tell you? As the ship's horn make three toots and we cast off and headed down the English Channel, I strained my eyes to catch a last glimpse of the land, my emotions all churned up like the water the ship was leaving in its wake.

Another occupant of 13B turned out to be a youngish Trinidadian name Owen who just finish studying law at Gray's Inn and going back home. As I enter Dominica say to him, "This is the guy I was telling you about."

"I'm sorry, man," Owen tell me.

"Don't mention it," I say from habit.

Out on deck, ere we left the English Channel, I had come to the conclusion as Brit'n faded on the horizon that I would be a credit to the country, an ambassador not only of goodwill but good manners. The idea put a different complexion on my circumstances. I now had a purpose, which was to show the outlanders in the Caribbean that Brit'n was not only still on her feet, but also still the onlyest country in the world where good breeding and culture come before ill-gotten gains or calls of the flesh. I would go forth with a stout heart and proclaim that Johnny Walker was still going strong, that the British bulldog still had teeth, that Britannia still ruled the waves. This self-imposed undertaking not only steeled me but fired my ambitions. I was fortified for whatever lay ahead, resolved to make the best of my sad lot, and actually turn the course of events to the advantage of my beloved country!

Owen's apology was slightly puzzling until he went on to explain, in that pseudo-Oxford accent that a lot of black people feel is distinguished: "I couldn't find my box camera and I thought it had been stolen. Dominica said you were down here and might have borrowed it. But I just discovered it's still in my suitcase."

I glare at Dominica. "I hope we shall have a happy voyage as fellow-travellers," I say. "All of we got to spend time in this little cabin, and it don't make sense to get off on the wrong foot."

Dominica make his laugh and say, "I got two Trinis to cope with!" A white man appeared at the door with his luggage and Dominica say, "Wrong cabin, mate."

"This is 13B, isn't it?" he ask.

"Are you with us?" I ask, scarcely able to believe my luck.

"Yes. I'm Walter."

I grasp his hand and shook it fervently. "I'm Moses," I say, "that's Owen, and he's Dominica."

Walter acknowledged the introductions with two nods.

"It seems they've chosen their berths already," I say. Dominica was lying down in a top bunk, and Owen was sitting in the one below. On the opposite side was the other two. I gestured at them and ask Walter which one he rather have.

He shrug. "Doesn't matter," he say.

For a fleeting moment I thought of giving him the upper one, but maybe subconsciously I had bad memories of being relegated to the bottom of things. "I'll take the upper, if you're sure?"

"That suits me," Walter say.

We all began to ensconce ourselves properly, putting away our things in the lockers, squeezing and jostling about to avoid collision, so reminiscent of the rooms immigrants have in London.

"Is there a loo down here?" Walter ask.

"You've got to go up the stairs," Owen told him.

Walter went out. The moment he left Dominica exclaim: "Jesus Christ, what this white man doing down here?"

"I hope you're not racial," I say. "I for one don't want any trouble down here. He appears a nice bloke to me."

Dominica sneer. "You only seen him for a few minutes, how the arse you know he nice?"

"He's white," I explain.

Dominica laugh. "Who're you, man?" His voice come out in a squeaky high C. "Some dictator or administrator, telling me what I must say and do? You better keep your arse quiet before I bust a cuff in your face!"

"Sticks and stones may break my bones," I say.

"Like we got a right one here," he tell Owen. "Brit'n must of blow his brains."

"Just leave me out of it," Owen say. "I don't want arguments."

"You got to be able to argue if you want to be a lawyer," Dominica say.

I left them to argue and went out to get some fresh air. In fact I decide that I going to live in the open as much as possible and only go down to the cabin when I had to. I walked around a bit, then climb up the ladder to Deck B, and walk around that too, getting my sea legs, and acquainting myself with the ship. When I climb up the ladder to go on Deck A, I meet a notice: STRICTLY FIRST CLASS PASSENGERS ONLY. I looked about, seeing mostly whites, standing by the rails or sitting in deck chairs. The cabins look posh, even with curtains at the windows—they didn't have portholes up here.

I climb back down, again regretting that I did not travel First and avoid the rabble. It was getting towards evening now, and I wonder about Bob and Jeannie. Would I ever see them on the voyage? Would they keep to themselves in style and luxury, ignoring my presence on the ship until we got to the tropics and they needed assistance with their luggage? Up there on Deck A they had everything—their own bar, their own dining-room, and even a swimming-pool. There was no need for them to come down. When we was in Shepherd's Bush planning the trip, we say what a great time we would have together on the ship, promenading the decks and taking the ozone, lolling in the sun, playing deck tennis and quoits, and I, in my ignorance, did even book a set with Jeannie for the Captain's Ball!

They say that once at sea a great peace comes to a man, and clarity of thought, as if he get away from the milling masses of humanity and the din and cacophony of life on land, that out here on the bosom of the ocean, under the canopy of the wide skies, he can come to grips with Eternity even. I look out to the horizons but I couldn't see Eternity, nothing but grey water and grey sky. Instead of feeling philosophical and meditative, I feel like one of the crew on Columbus ship as it sail across the Atlantic who shitting his pants wondering if the ship would topple over into oblivion when it reach the place where sky meet sea.

I decided I needed a aperitif before dinner, and slouched to the bar, where I easily spotted Walter as he contrasted with the black background.

"Hello," he say, "what're you having?"

"Allow me, old boy," I say, glad of his company. He was just finishing off a beer so I got him another and a Campari Bianco for myself.

"Quite a shipload, isn't it?" he say. "Have they all got jobs in the islands to return to?"

"Some of them might," I say. "Others are merely going for a holiday in the sun."

"What about you? Trinidad is your home?"

"I came originally from Trinidad," I admit, "but I have lived in Brit'n for longer than I can remember."

"You're only on holiday?" He sounded disappointed.

I shrug. "I haven't decided. How about yourself?"

"I got a contract to work in the oilfields."

"Point-a-Pierre?"

"Yeah, that's the place. You know it?"

"It's about forty miles south of Port-of-Spain."

"I hear it's hot as hell down there. Trinidad is near the Equator, ain't it?"

"Yeah. I'll feel the heat as much as you, being away so long."

"Soon be time for dinner."

"Yeah. We'd better get changed."

"Changed?" He frown at me.

"Yeah, for dinner."

"This isn't first class. You changing?"

"But of course. One always dresses for dinner aboard ship."

"You think that lot are going to change?" He wave about him.

"I don't care about them," I say, "but I know the decorous procedure. I'm sure all whites will appear suitably attired."

"Not me."

"You ought to, you know." It was ironic that the first man I try to inculcate some culture in was a Englisher. "You ought to set an example for those who don't know."

"Yeah? I'm okay, though."

I finish my drink. I wasn't going to let Walter put me off. White he may be, but handsome is as handsome does.

I went below. I had a shower on Deck B and went down to the cabin. No one else was there so I was able to get dress in comparative comfort. The dinner gong went as I was combing my hair.

I went to the dining-room, full of confidence. This was going to be the first evening, and like everybody was hungry, for all the tables was full up. I strolled casually but elegantly to the table where the other occupants of 13B was seated.

"You going ashore, Moses?" Dominica laugh.

It was a habit he had, that he usually laugh either before or after anything he say, like an insecure jester. He had on a dirty wind-cheater with no shirt underneath, and a pair of worn corduroys. It didn't look as if he even wash his face or brush his hair.

I sat down and spread my serviette on my lap. Owen and Walter were discussing the menu.

"Shall we pool and have a bottle of wine?" I suggested.

"I don't drink wine," Walter say. "Beer's my thing."

"I don't drink at all," Owen say.

"I'll drink if you're buying," Dominica say.

"Let's forget it." I had to remember that I wasn't being paid expenses to spread British culture. Though I admit I was a little disappointed with Walter: *he* should of been the one to make the suggestion.

The waiter came with starters: it did not seem as if they was taking orders, but serving out everything on the menu. I tried to make some light conversation as we ate, but nobody took me on. Dominica wolfed his food down, finishing each course first and waiting impatiently for the next.

After dinner I took a promenade. When I went down to take off my dinner suit, Dominica and Owen was there. I was just waiting around in the hope they would go out and give me a chance to move about.

There came a knock on the door and I open it. It was Jeannie, looking quite distressed.

"Oh Moses," she cry, "I'm so glad I found you!"

"Jeannie!" I exclaim.

"Aye-ay-aye!" Dominica open his eyes wide, and Owen back up against the wash-basin, as if making room for her to come in.

"Is anything wrong?" I ask.

"Oh Moses," she wail, "Bobbie is seasick. Terribly!"

"What!" I couldn't believe it. "The sea is as still as a millpond, and the ship is as steady as a rock!"

"Please come, Moses, and see for yourself. I've been all over the ship looking for your cabin. You're almost in the engine-room."

"What about introducing your friend?" Dominica move forward.

I had no intention of that. Perhaps Walter, if he was here.

"You work fast, Moses," Owen say. Though a less primitive threat than Dominica, he too was feasting his eyes.

"Jeannie and I are old friends," I say coldly.

"Are these your cabin mates?" Jeannie peep inside.

"Let's go," I said abruptly, and hold her arm and pulled her long.

As we ascended I ask, "Is it all right for me to go up there?"

"As long as a first-class passenger is with you," she say, "or if you're invited up. They are very strict about it."

We got up to Deck A and went to the cabin. It was luxurious, needless to say. Bob was scattered about on the bed. He really look in a state. He was still dress as for dinner, but the suit was crumple-up and creased. His face wasn't white, or pale, but rather ashen. He was sweating. A thin trickle of saliva meandered down his chin. His eyes was shut, but he was moaning.

Jeannie move to him and say, "Bobbie, here is Moses."

He open his eyes and stare around vacantly. At last he focus on me and there was a flicker of life.

"Moses?" His voice was weak.

"Yes, old boy," I say softly. He was like a wax mummy, with his hands crisscross on his chest.

"Did you bring the priest?"

"He's delirious," Jeannie whisper, "he keeps asking for a priest."

"What do you want a priest for, Bob?" I ask.

It look like his few words exhaust him, he just keep on swallowing the sour bile that must of been rising in his throat, then he say: "I want to confess. I am dying."

"Oh Bobbie," Jeannie say.

"Come now," I say. "It isn't as bad as that."

"I'm dying, Moses. I—I—" his eyes roll in his head, and he lay there like in a stupor.

"It could be something he ate. What did you have for dinner?" I ask Jeannie.

"Coq au vin," Jeannie reply.

But it couldn't be food poisoning: if they had any contaminated victuals on the ship they'd serve it to Deck C passengers. To make sure I ask her if any others up here were ill.

"Not that I know of," she say. "In any case I haven't made any friends, they seem a stuck-up lot. Maybe he'll be better in the morning?"

That thought didn't occur to me: like he was dead already, and not with that restful countenance that comes to a departed one who has made peace with God, but all the features of his face was twisted up in agony and angles of shapelessness, as if he dead a violent death.

"Let's try and get him on deck," I suggest. "A bit of fresh air might revive him."

I bent over the prostrate figure and gently raised him. He was too weak to offer any resistance, but as he came upright, with his head dangling against my breast, I felt him give a sudden heave, and a torrent of sour vomit came gushing out. It come out with such force that it sort of ricochet when it hit my face, so not only begin to trickle down the rest of me, but bits shot off in all directions, and a scrap of half-digested chicken catch Jeannie in the eye, as she was bending over to lend a hand. The irony of it was that Bob himself, as he slip from my grasp and collapse back down on the bed, escape the geyser completely; even the saliva that was drooling from his mouth was rub off on me.

"Oh, oh, oh," Jeannie cry in dismay.

I back off from the bed, stumbling blindly as I tried to wipe the obnoxious mess from my face. "The sink, Jeannie, the sink! Lead me to the sink!"

I felt her hand hold me. She turn me and push me into the bathroom.

"Where is it?" I was blind and fumbling about.

Suddenly a cascade of water fell on my head as she turn on the shower.

I suppose it was the best thing to do. I stripped naked, making a bundle of my sodden garments and throwing it in a corner. I stood under the shower and allowed the cleansing waters to splash on my head and course all over my body. I used Jeannie's round Pear's soap, and afterwards sprayed myself all over with everything she had in the little cabinet against the wall. But the smell of human vomit is the worst smell to get rid of. Though camouflaged with creams and lotions and perfumes and even Johnson's Baby Powder (Bob used this) the sour, sickening odour still seemed to hang about me.

I wrap a towel around my waist and emerged.

Jeannie was distressed. Bob showed no improvement. He lay there in a coma, his eyes and mouth open like a idiot. Jeannie was sitting in an armchair next to the bed, holding his hand.

"What's to be done, Moses?" she appeal to me.

"We'd better get the ship's doctor. You go, Jeannie. Just tell any of the officers you see and they'll have him here."

She went and came back with the doctor in no time. He look half-pissed—a lot of these ships' docs have nothing to do but dish out seasick tablets or a dose of Epsom salts. But I will say this much for him, he did not look askance at my presence, as if he accustom to seeing a black man with a towel round his waist in every cabin on Deck A.

"What seems to be the trouble?" he ask brightly.

"Look at poor Bobbie," Jeannie say.

"Seasick," he say promptly, without touching Bob or coming any nearer.

The sound of a strange voice brought Bob to life. "I confess my sins. Hail Mary full of grace. . . ." He could not continue.

"H'mm," doc said. "If he's like this in such calm weather, he's in for a rough time."

"Ought he to be in the lazarene, under observation?" I ask. "He looks awful to me. I've never seen him like that."

Doc laugh. "There's nothing to worry about, some people just cannot travel by boat." He turn to Jeannie and take some tablets from his pocket. "Give him one or two of these every four hours or so. At least they'll sedate him and make him sleep."

"Is he going to be all right, doctor?" Jeannie was woebegone, wringing her hands.

"Of course. I'll come to see him again in the morning." The old doc was cheerful, not at all as if he was treating a patient on his last legs. "How are you feeling yourself?" It look like he was more interested in Jeannie.

"I'm fine, I'm enjoying myself."

"Good show." He nodded. "You can call me any time. Good night."

He gave me a smile as he left—or it might of been a smirk, I'm not sure.

"Maybe you should give him a tablet now," I tell Jeannie.

"I'll give him two." She fetch a glass of water.

Between us we lift Bob and try to prop him up on the pillows. I have to hold him while Jeannie administer the tablets. The moment I let go he slump back down into a miserable heap. Jeannie tuck the blanket up to his chin.

We look at each other.

"This is a fine state of affairs," I say.

"I don't know how I'd have managed without you, Moses. What a great pity you are not up here with us."

"I'll come whenever you need me."

She deliberately misconstrue my words and blush. "Would you like some champagne?"

"Well," I say.

She went and press a button on the cabin wall. In less than a minute a steward was knocking. They got these first-class menials well-trained, I can tell you. He didn't bat an eye when he see me.

"You called, madam?"

"Could we—may we have a bottle of champagne? It isn't too late, is it?"

"Our service is twenty-four hours, madam. I will bring it immediately."

So said so done. Not even Bob, at the peak of his efficiency when he was my lackey, moved with such alacrity.

"Poor Bobbie," Jeannie say as we quaffed, "he would have enjoyed this."

"Yes," I agree. "I feel guilty, almost as if we was celebrating his debility."

"Aren't we?" She eyed me coyly over her glass.

I cleared my throat. "I don't deny the situation opens up great possibilities," I say. It's an ill wind what blow nobody any good.

When it come to opening the door when opportunity knock, or make hay when the sun shine, or beat the iron when the fire hot, my brain become nimble and pellucid. That, couple with my philosophical nature and the lessons I have learnt in the harsh school of reality, veritably make me ten foot tall. But I want to make it clear from the beginning that I did not gloat or wallow in earthly pleasures and pursuits of the flesh at the expense of my friend Bob. Every morsel of delight was tinged with a little sorrow that he, too, was unable to share my enjoyment; every dalliance and sensuous satisfaction left a bit-ter-sweet taste in my mouth, for I am not one to kick a man when he is down nor take advantage of a handicapped oppo-nent. The way I see it, Fate was rewarding me for all my misfor-tunes and hardships and mishaps. And it is a good moral for us to remember, that when a man back against the wall and all seem lost, there is Someone up there who looks after us, and ekes out a little consolation to bolster us and give us the strength to cope with things.

However, it must not be thought that the situation was not without complication, far from it. For one thing Bob's *mal-de-mer* might be tentative, and he might rise from the dead unex-pectedly, full of vim and ire. For another, I was trespassing on Deck A, a gate crasher, literally an undesirable. Imagine if I, with such laudatory sentiments and intentions concerning Brit'n's reputation, found myself in the embarrassing position of being slung out on my arse like a vagrant sneaking out of a restaurant without paying his bill: worse still, to be clapped in irons and spend the rest of the voyage in the ship's hold with Galahad's deep freezer!

When Jeannie and me got up next morning—we slept on the carpet, the pile was so high and thick that it was as if we was laying down in a field of wheat or barley, and had was to raise up on our elbows to see each other—I decide to discuss things with her.

But my first thought, naturally, was for my friend. "How is he?" I ask.

"Who?" Jeannie yawn and stretch luxuriously. It was the first full night she and me spend together, and when I say full I mean full. She wrinkle her nose and ask, "What's that smell?"

To tell truth during the passage of the night neither of us notice it, but now that she mention it I sniff and get a whiff of stale puke.

I did not have to reply; she suddenly remember and leapt up, nude but not yet golden, and went to Bob. "He's still in a

deep sleep," she say. Some time during the night she did get up
and give him another dose of doc's tablets for safe measure.

But we did not talk right away. Some people say that no
matter how glorious the night, when you wake in the morning
and knock a refresher it is nonpareil. I agree.

Afterwards I say, "We can't spend the day on the carpet,
Jeannie. We got to sort things out." She give a long sigh.
"Whatever you say, Moses. You are captain of the ship." She gig-
gle.

"If Bob doesn't recover, you'll have a bad time."

"Oh yes!" She sounded happy at the prospect.

"And you know I shouldn't be here. It'll be terrible for you
too if they found out."

"They won't," she promise.

"We have to be careful, though. I have to work out exactly
how we can reap the maximum benefits with the minimum
risks."

"I'm sure you'll come up with some bright ideas, Moses,"
she gave me a little kiss. "I leave everything in your hands."

"I better go now," I say, rising.

"Oh gosh, what about your clothes!"

I hadn't thought of that. My suit was a wet, crumpled bundle in the bathroom.

"I'll have to wear something of Bob's. We are the same size."

"Look in the wardrobe. Take what you like. Later I'll get the
laundry to clean your suit."

I feel like a criminal putting on Bob's clothes, but there was
no help for it. He had no bloody right to puke all over me.

"When will I see you?" Jeannie ask. "Shall I come down, or
will you come up?"

"I'll see after breakfast. Stick around outside and look out
for me."

I went down to 13B with heavy steps, reluctant to return to
that dismal world, but hopeful that I would see a way to take
advantage of my good fortune. I made up my mind that if anyone asked me any questions, I would tell them to mind their
own fucking business. Even Walter, who it appeared was out of
my class, albeit white.

As it turned out neither Walter nor Owen said anything, but Dominica could not contain himself.

"Some people really lucky! They hardly get on a ship before they pick up a nice piece of white pussy! They spend the night out, and come back in different clothes! I wish I was so lucky!"

I ignored him.

"Like you had a hard day's night, Moses," he come direct now, taunting me, instead of addressing everybody like his first speech. "Let me know the cabin number, man, that's the least you can do."

"It's beyond your reach."

He make his laugh. "Man, I thought you was crazy, but you got method in your madness."

"If anything, you are the one who is mental," I get in the last word.

All three of them was lying down on their bunks, waiting for the come-and-get-it gong. Walter was reading a Ismith Khan novel about Trinidad what he get from the library; Owen had his eyes shut but he wasn't sleeping, and Dominica was scratching vigorously between his legs.

It was some innate sense of caution which brought me to the cabin. At first my thoughts had wings, wildly flapping, and I imagine myself shifting to the top deck to look after Bob and protect Jeannie. But it wasn't feasible to risk giving up my berth. I couldn't trust them tablets Bob was taking: it was just my luck that he might get up bouncing and frisky like a spring lamb. I had to play it by ear. But you can see that the very uncertainty was exciting and intriguing in itself. It look as if the voyage really be bon.

I ate a hearty breakfast, during which my three companions were bemoaning the fact that there didn't seem to be much to do on board.

"What're you going to do, Moses?" Walter ask. "I'd like to talk with you about Trinidad."

I didn't want to be aloof and preoccupied, in case I had to fall back on their company. "I think I'll just saunter about the ship," I say. "I'm not bothered about passing the time yet."

"What're you going to do?" Owen asked Dominica.

"I am going to try and find a Jeannie, like my friend Moses," Dominica say. "Man, I can't survive this long trip without a piece of puss." He was scanning the dining-room while talking, looking for possibilities.

"They've got notices by the purser's office, about things we can do," Owen say to Walter.

I left them to their own devices, and went on deck. I wasn't exactly tingling with anticipation, but I was feeling good. I take some gulps of fresh air, and look out on the sparkling ocean, wondering if my kismet was going to be favourable today. I say a prayer for Bob, that he would remain in bed for the rest of the voyage and have a good rest, which he would need for the fun and frolics in Trinidad. I wonder what time the doc was going to visit him, I didn't want to go up there until after he come and gone, when I would learn what was in store.

I gave him another ten impatient minutes, then wended my way up to Deck A. When I reach the top of the ladder I see a officer patrolling on sentry duty. Just my luck. I couldn't make out Jeannie among the passengers I could see.

The officer saunter down the deck towards me. "Good morning," he say cheerfully.

I stood my ground. As long as I stayed behind the barrier it was all right. "Just browsing," I say.

"That's fine, as long as you don't cross the barrier."

"I'm looking for a friend," I explain.

"He won't be up here. Try Deck C."

Just then I spot Jeannie coming. She had on a pair of green slacks and a red halter. She look fresh as a daisy as she trounce up and my heart fell, thinking all was well with Bob.

"It's all right, officer," she flash him a sweet smile, "this is a friend of my husband's."

"Oh, in that case," he open the iron gate and let me pass.

As we move off I tell Jeannie, "You see what I mean, you should of been here waiting."

"I couldn't come before," she say. "The doctor has just been."

We went into the cabin. Bob look as if he shrink; the coverings on the bed was so flat like he had no body, only his head showing, and one hand dangling which he attempt to raise when he saw me. His eyes was a little incoherent still.

"How do you feel this morning, old boy?" I went by the bed, but not too close, just in case.

"I am dying, Moses," he whisper. "I am sure of it."

"Don't say such awful things, Bobbie," Jeannie say in a broken voice.

"What was the doctor's verdict?" I ask her.

"He told Bobbie he must take care of himself. He said as soon as he felt a little better he should try to get out on deck."

"Listen, Moses," Bob whisper, "are we far from land? Can't they make an emergency stop and put me ashore?"

"You'll be all right, mate. We'll look after you. Have you had anything to eat? What about some nice fatty bacon, and pork sausages swimming in a thick gravy?"

He retched. But just a little greenish-yellow bile come up out on his lips. Jeannie wiped it away with a tissue. "Don't mention food to him, Moses. The doctor prescribed plain dry toast and crackers. I had them brought up, but he won't touch it. Will you try?"

She brought the plate for me. "See if you can get him to take something."

"Come on, Bob, you've got to keep your strength up," I chided him tenderly. "Think of the great times you are missing!" I dangled a piece of toast before him, but he turned his head and clamped his jaws together. I held his chin and forced his mouth open, and shoved in some toast.

"Don't hurt him, Moses!" Jeannie cry.

"He's got to have something in his stomach to throw up," I say.

He couldn't get rid of it unless he chewed, so his mouth began to move slowly like a ruminative cow. He was tricky, though. He stopped chewing and pretended it was gone, but I knew he hadn't swallowed it.

"That's good," I say encouragingly, "now swallow it like a good boy, Bob. Go on."

I watched his Adam's Apple but it didn't move.

"Get a glass of water," I told Jeannie.

She brought it with three tablets. I force his mouth open again and tossed in the tablets, like a stoker stoking coals in the old steamships. I poured in the water cautiously, until his mouth was full, then I shut it abruptly.

"You'll suffocate him!" Jeannie cry as he struggled feebly. But I did not let go until he gulped and swallowed.

"That's a good boy," Jeannie say. "Now shut your eyes and go to sleep and have a nice, long rest."

Bob made a loud sigh which would of alarmed me if it did rattle, and shut his eyes. Jeannie winked at me and say, "In a minute we'll be off."

He open his eyes. "Off where?" he mutter.

"She said you'd soon drop off," I say quickly.

"Don't leave me alone, Jeannie."

"No fear, old thing," I say. "One of us will be with you night and day until you recover."

"Let me know when we sight land, Moses."

"Okay. Don't worry about anything."

"Why are you wearing my clothes?"

It look as if them three tablets revive him rather than sedate him. I glanced uneasily at Jeannie as I reply, "I ran short. You don't mind, do you?"

"You mustn't talk too much, Bobbie," Jeannie say. "It isn't good for you."

But he ignore her. "Were you here last night, Moses?"

"Of course. Jeannie sent for me as soon as you took ill."

He appeared to consider this, and tried to continue, but the tablets began to work at last. He mutter something or other I didn't quite hear, and shut his eyes.

We stay quiet for a minute or two to make sure he fall asleep. Then Jeannie ask brightly, "What're we going to do today?"

"We must not be reckless, Jeannie," I say. "First things first. The situation is tricky."

"You can come and go freely now," she say. "I informed them that you were our chauffeur and handyman. You don't mind?"

"Good show," I tell her, "but we mustn't be seen on the deck together."

"I'm not going to be cooped up in here," she pouted.

"We'll have to take turns. Bob would jump to conclusions."

She threw her arms around me. "You were never one to look a gift horse in the mouth. Fortune favours the brave!"

Maybe she was right. Being so bad-lucked all my life, maybe I was getting the wind up when I should be carefree and gay.

"But fools dash in where angels fraid to go," I remind her. "I'll stay on duty, you run along and stretch your legs."

It is the third day of our voyage, and poor Bob's indisposition. The wind is fair to moderate, the sea calm, the barometer steady, we are logging about fourteen knots. Jeannie and I awake on the carpet, and instead of taking our constitutions on deck, we improvise some exercises right there. We shower and change. It is now time for Bob's medicine and Jeannie doses him with a handful of tablets.

Bill, the steward, brings in fresh Continental rolls, lamb's kidneys, grilled kippers, ham and eggs, and a steaming jug of Jamaica coffee. We put aside a slice of plain toast for Bob in case he feels peckish when he awakes. While we breakfast Bill discreetly and unobtrusively tidies up the cabin.

"I will take the first spell," I tell Jeannie.

"It's a shame we can't be together," she say. "What can I do on my tod? Bobbie's fast asleep."

"I don't trust them tablets," I say. "Let's don't be greedy, Jeannie. We shall have some great times, I promise you."

After she went I took up a Naipaul novel I found in the cabin and became immersed. I'm not sure how long it was before Bob groaned and opened his eyes. He made an effort to sit up but fell exhausted on the pillows.

"Take it easy, old man," I say. "How are we this morning?" I sat on the bed.

He look at me for a few moments, focussing. "Where's Jeannie?"

"She's taking a break. She sat up with you all night."

"I don't remember." Then he said, "You shouldn't let Jeannie wander about the ship alone, Moses. You know what she is like."

I didn't like that at all. It was not only a long speech for a man in his condition, it was cogent.

"You better have some more tablets, Bob," I say.

He shook his head slowly and carefully. "No. They make me sleep too much. Were you here last night?"

"Of course."

"I called for you and Jeannie several times."

"Them drugs make you imagine a lot of things, Bob. We was here all the time, playing gin rummy and watching over you. I myself hardly had a wink of sleep since you took bad. Would you like to try and eat your toast?"

"Yes."

Maybe he would puke or collapse if he ate it, I thought, holding it to his mouth.

"I can manage." He took it from me and began to munch.

"That's a good sign, Bob," I say, as if pleased. "But don't exert yourself: you have been terribly ill."

"I think I'm past the worst," he say.

How evanescent are a man's dreams and hopes! How fleeting his moments of happiness! As the colour came back to Bob's cheeks, so the rosy hue of the future palled.

"Is there any more toast?" he ask.

"No," I say firmly. If one slice was so efficacious, he might want to get out of bed if he had another. "I'm still hungry," he say.

"Don't push your luck. You might have a relapse."

"You're right, Moses." He began to breathe deeply now, and to shift about in the bed, testing his wings. He passed his fingers through his hair, and asked for a hand-mirror. When I gave him he looked at himself, twisting his face and rubbing the stubble on his chin.

Suddenly he asked: "What are you doing up here?"

"We told them I was your chaffeur and handyman," I explain, and added: "It's undignified, but I suffered it for you."

He liked that, he made a weak chuckle.

The more his spirits rose, the more mine fell. I began to get sullen and full of self-righteous indignation. "I suppose you won't want me around much longer, now that you are on the road to recovery."

"Stick around until Jeannie gets back," he say generously. Then: "How long has she been away?"

Just then the ship's bells on the bridge strike twelve o'clock.

"Good lord!" I exclaim, "is it that late? She's been gone for hours!"

"You don't think she's fallen overboard, do you?"

"Nonsense."

"What's keeping her? You'd better go and search for her, Moses. I'll hold you responsible if anything happens to her!"

"Don't excite yourself. The poor girl has probably fallen asleep in a deck-chair."

But he insisted, and to tell truth, I was glad to get away to have a word with her in private and warn her Bob was on the mend. Also, as the bubble was about to burst, it might be possible to have a compensating quickie with Jeannie: we could hide in a lifeboat and do it.

I search all over Deck A, ignoring askance glances and stony stares, before I had the common sense to put myself in Jeannie's place. What would she do if she was free as a bird, hobnob with the first-class passengers, or cast about for some excitement and action on the lower decks?

I scoured Deck B, which took less time, being as it was mostly blacks. Surely she wasn't down on C, unless she was making a tour of the engine-room?

I was just passing 13B to question the engineers when the cabin door open and Jeannie and Dominica step out.

She did not even have the grace to blush. She just rush to me crying, "Moses! Has Bobbie worsened?"

"He's asking for you," I say gravely, as if he was on his deathbed.

It was cold comfort to see her dash up the stairs in a panic.

"How do you make that laugh of yours?" I ask Dominica.

I have heard it said that environment, likes clothes, maketh the man. I leave it up to you to question the veracity of this homily. For my part I believe that what's writ is writ, and circumstances that are predestined are not to be baulked by a change of dirty underwear nor shifting from a black ghetto in London to a ship in mid-Atlantic. None shall escape: indeed in fleeing one situation for another it is often a case of out of the frying pan

into the fire. So it must not be felt that my cool reaction to
Jeannie's debauchery in 13B was a result of any worldliness or
abilities to keep my head when all those about me are shitting
their pants. It is just that I am easily reconciled to the thrusts
and parries of Fate. If all the men in the world was a pack of
cards, and you shuffle the pack, I would come out the joker.

Dominica was smug. He did not strut or flaunt, but every
now and then, during the next two days or so whilst I confine
myself to Decks B and C, he would give me a wink, or make his
laugh without any speech.

I did not waste time mooning. I had no intention of belit-
tling myself by going up to Deck A. They knew where I was and
they could bloody well get in touch with me if they wanted to. I
strolled about the deck, mostly, as there wasn't enough chairs to
go around, and by the time breakfast was finish everybody make
a scramble to get them. But it look as if some unspoken system
was in operation. Not only was the chairs earmarked for certain
passengers, but even square inches of deck space were settled
into. Sometimes there were altercations, like: "Aye, mister, you
sitting in my chair!" or, "Shift up a little, you occupying my
space." But there was never any great squabble, the trespasser
usually obeyed the unwritten code. This organisation must have
taken place shortly after we put to sea, for by the time I got
around to it, there was no available chair or space, and I had to
keep on the move like if I was on patrol. The onlyest time I
could sit down was if one of the chairs belonging to the three
other occupants of 13B happen to be vacant, and the moment
the owner appear I had was to get up.

One morning only me and Dominica was there.

"I haven't seen our friend for a while," he venture.

"I wasn't aware that we have mutual ones," I lift an eyebrow.

"Ah-h-h, you know bloody well who I mean," he say. "You
know the cabin number?"

"Didn't you find out?"

"We didn't have time to talk much. Is true she married?"

"I don't want to discuss it with you," I say.

"What you want to talk about, then? Pussy is the best topic."

"I don't want to talk about anything, Dominica," I say. "I'm
quite happy just resting here with my own thoughts."

"I got my eye on that thing from Barbados." He jerk his hand in the direction of a girl sitting a little way from us, talking to another girl. "But I could never get she alone, the two of them always together. You want us to tackle them?"

"I'm not in the habit of molesting people," I say.

"Ah-h, you full of shit, Moses. It's no use me alone go. You going to spend the whole trip walking about the decks?"

I suppose he only wanted to be friendly. After all, we wasn't only in the same boat, but in the same cabin. I didn't see what use Dominica could be to me, though.

When Walter and Owen join us I had to get up and sit on the deck.

"What about a game of ping-pong, Moses?" Owen ask. "I just beat Walter."

"Not for me," I say. "I get enough exercise walking."

"I could stand you boys a drink," Walter say. "I won twenty quid in the bingo last night."

I went along with them to the bar, as there was nothing else to do. I don't mean to say that nothing was happening, but for other people, not me. There was always little groups laughing and drinking, or playing cards and dominoes, and I hear it had some gambling game about how much knots the ship cover each day. But me, with my capacity for high life, couldn't find any pleasure in such mundane activities. The truth is, and I freely admit it, I was suffering from withdrawal symptoms. Though I left it up to Bob and Jeannie to contact me, it took a great deal of grit and determination to stop myself from going up the ladder and requesting permission from the officer of the deck to visit. But apart from my pride, I had an evil suspicion that Dominica was trailing me to find the location of Jeannie's cabin: in my perambulations several times I saw him coming and going.

As I sipped Walter's free drink—and they carried on idle chatter—I wondered if Bob was still abed but stubbornly resisting any call for assistance. After all, white people have pride, too! I made up my mind that after lunch I would make some attempt to breach the silence.

As fate would have it, when we was lunching, the steward brought a parcel and a note to the table.

"Which one of you blokes is Moses, the handyman and chauffeur?" Of course, he did not include Walter. I winced. At least they might have spared me that.

"I am," I say, and he handed me the note. "Will you excuse me?" I say to the others as I tore open the envelope eagerly. I heard Dominica laugh and repeat: "Chauffeur and handyman!"

I read: "You are cordially invited to wine and dine with us in our cabin at 8 this evening. Formal wear. Use this note to gain entry. Bob."

Inside the parcel was my suit, freshly laundered: I wondered if he had been waiting for it to come back from the cleaners before extending the hand of friendship.

"Good news, Moses?" Dominica ask.

I just got on with my lunch.

At one minute to eight I was presenting my pass and duly admitted. I had come to the reunion with an open mind.

Bob was a changed man. You would never of thought that a couple of days ago he nearly kick the bucket. Though the ship was rocking with a sickening swell that kept most passengers off the decks, his demeanour was that of a seasoned seafarer. He laughed as I held on to the door making my entry.

"Here comes the jolly tar," he sang out, "no colour reference intended!"

"I'm glad to see you well," I say.

"I'm going great guns, aren't I, Jeannie?"

"Yes, Bobbie," she say, pouring me champagne. She had on a long frock but the cleavage tween neck and navel more than compensated for the covering of her lower parts. "I thought you had deserted us."

"It must be dreadfully boring down there," Bob say. "What do you do to while away the time?"

"Oh, we have bingo, and other things," I say lamely.

"Did you hear that?" Jeannie cry out excitedly. "They've got bingo! Better than playing bridge with your stuffed-shirt friends. You've got to let me go down with Moses sometime— promise, Bobbie!"

"I'll get you to learn bridge if it's the last thing I do," Bob say grimly.

"Oh, I hate it, I hate it. All that rubber and finesse and dou-ble and re-double, when I could be eyes down for a full house!"

"Nine-oh, blind ninety!" I chuckled, egging them on.

"Cut it out, Moses," Bob say. "Jeannie's enough of a problem as it is. I'm hoping she'll pick up some cues on deportment and behaviour on this voyage."

"All that la-de-da and doh-ray-mee," Jeannie sneer.

"It's good for you, Jeannie," I say earnestly. "Culture and breeding is important."

"I wish you were here to encourage her," Bob grumble.

"I wouldn't mind Moses teaching me," she say, "I'd rather listen to him."

"Than you," I say.

"Pardon?" she say.

"I'd rather listen to him than you," I explain.

"Oh," she say. "More champagne?" She topped up mines and then Bob's. "Why don't you let Moses give me lessons?"

I daresay she was only being facetious, but I saw Bob frown thoughtfully, and my heart leapt at the wild hope.

"Lord knows I haven't the patience," he said. "Do you think you can?"

"Can what?" I ask innocently.

"Teach Jeannie some fineries?"

"Oh, that." I brushed it aside carefully.

"I'm serious. But no hanky-panky, Moses. You and I know how we stand with each other."

"That's a fine thing to say in front of me," Jeannie complain.

"It will only be for one hour," Bob say, "from ten to eleven in the mornings, while I continue bridge lessons with Franklin." (I learnt afterwards that Franklin was a bridge fiend, like that Egyptian actor fellar.)

Well, I suppose one could skim the cream off the milk in an hour. He went on to say that he wouldn't pay me anything, being as I would have an hour's luxury in first-class surround-ings, "enough to brace you for the rest of the day below decks."

That little matter settled, and having opened a bottle of whisky for Bob as he was getting high, we buzz for the menu and when it come by Bill and he wink at Jeannie surreptitiously and depart, we fell to discussing what we should eat. I thought it a good idea to order what they had the evening Bob succumb, as, if it were not directly responsible, at least it might of been instrumental. But Coq-au-Vin was off.

"What do you get down there?" Bob ask.

"Oh, the usual immigrant fare," I say.

"Pigfoot and peas-and-rice?"

"That's usually available."

"That's what I'm having." He said it decisively.

Jeannie was shocked. "Oh Bobbie! Is that what you really want?"

"That comes from mixing whisky with champagne," I mutter, but they didn't hear me.

When Bill came Bob tell me to order and went into the bathroom.

"Bill," I say, "can you indulge a whim?"

"Eh?" he say. Then, as Jeannie back was turn, he lean forward and say, sotto voce, "You got a good thing going here, mate!"

"The Master would like to sample something from the second-class table. Do you think you could get him some, er, trotters, with the peas-and-rice mixture?"

"Yeah." He was making notes. "That's for you. What're they having?"

I didn't argue with him. I give him the rest of the order, and told him to get some pepper-sauce to go with Bob's dish. I remember that some of the passengers was complaining that it give them the runnings.

By the time the food arrive Bob was well away with the Scotch. Jeannie was very hungry. I poured the wine and she lift the high silver covers from the platters, and aromas filled the air. The both of them was just about to fall to when I say wait.

"What for?" Jeannie ask, fork halfway to mouth.

"Grace. We should say grace-before-meals."

"Oh God," Bob say.

"That's not enough. You want to teach Jeannie the right things, don't you?"

"Mary, Mark, Luke and John, lie-on," Bob mumble, and began to eat.

I gave up. Jeannie was so busy eating she didn't notice Bob, but I was fascinated to see how he tackled the pigfoot, stopping every now and then to swill some whisky. I urged the pepper-sauce on him spitefully, and had the satisfaction of hearing him complain of tummy aches and gripes before I left.

The ship roll like hell that night. I did linger on at Bob's, hoping that if he didn't have a recurrence, when the cabin floor tilt it might pitch him against a bulwark and break his head or something. But apart from the pepper-sauce working it look like he was capable of keeping Jeannie company.

I did get some satisfaction before the night was out, though. Just as I was turning in the bow of the ship went up in the sky. As it come back down Dominica was hurtled out of his top bunk and landed up against the door with a tremendous bang. His string of oaths was a lullaby to me.

The next morning I turn up punctually for my tutoring duties. This time I wasn't going to daydream and savour: Bob hardly left for his bridge lessons than I slipped my hand up Jeannie's skirt.

Gently, but firmly, she remove it.

Like a fool, I was more tantalised by this unusual lack of co-operation, and ventured my trembling hand down her blouse and gave her left tit a little anti-clockwise twirling that I knew switched her on. Instead, she removed my hand and gave it a little smack, like what you give a child when it reach for the last cake on the table.

"Now now, Moses," she say, "there's a time and place for everything. Let's get on with the cultural instructions."

This novel, teasing titillation only served to heighten my delight. Nothing dismayed, I guided her hand to my fly where my private parts were exerting a terrific pressure for freedom and action. Instead of aiding and abetting the poor thing, she gave it a pull and a twist like a primitive trying out dentistry on a native in the jungle.

"Jesus Christ!" I yell, leaping back. "That hurt, Jeannie!"

"So it should," she say.

"You want to incapacitate me?" My private part was limp and sagging like a balloon after Christmas.

"I think we should make a start, don't you?" she say.

"Yeah," I rallied. "If you want to do it on the bed, why the hell you don't say so?" I began to take off my trousers.

"Stop!" she cried.

"What the arse wrong with you this morning?" I say, getting vex now.

"What does R.S.V.P. mean at the bottom of an invitation card?"

"How the fuck do I know?" I say irritably.

"Responday see voo play," she say brightly. "Didn't you really know?"

"Okay, okay, so what? Let's get cracking, we haven't much time left."

"Indeed. Sit down and behave yourself. Tell me if this frock is suitable attire for morning wear on board."

Perhaps I was being a bit precipitate. Being released from the humble environments of Shepherd's Bush and finding herself among high social company must of given her delusions of grandeur and hauteur. Personally, I did not think that Jeannie could aspire higher than collecting old and rare coins, but there was no harm in humouring her.

So I sat down. "I do apologise for my randiness."

"Accepted."

"Fun and games could come after."

"We shall see," she say. "If I'm going to be a lady, I cannot afford to let you take liberties."

I stifle a snigger. "Stand up and walk around a little, let me see what that frock looks like."

She stood up and throw back her shoulders and throw forward her bust: I curbed the temptation to make she put a book on her head and balance it while she walking.

"It'll do. When you are travelling on a holiday cruise, we can relax the rules a little. But it's a bit too early for so much make-up, isn't it?" I thought maybe it was because Jeannie did not want her mascara and eye-shadow ruined that she was playing hoity-toity and hard to get. It have a lot of women like that, who spend hours before mirror-mirror-on-the-wall trying to beautify their faces, and do not want no panting playboy to undo their efforts.

Howsomever, time was pressing. While I indulge Jeannie in

her fancies Bob must of already made a few rubbers and grand-slams and on the way back to boast to Jeannie.

"Isn't it time to drop this charade and get down to some practical demonstrations?" I ask.

"Such as?" Jeannie try to lift an eyebrow.

"The art of love-making as practised by the upper-classes," I say. "I can show you how Casanova or Romeo and Juliet did it."

"What a clever rascal you are, Moses," Jeannie laugh, "employing such ploys and ruses! Honestly, you take the cake!"

Heartened by this reaction, I was just about to start slicing the cake when Bob return.

"Hello," he say, "what progress are you making?"

"None at all," I throw up my hands in disgust. "I'd of been better off learning to play bridge."

And indeed, Jeannie kept me at bay for the rest of the voyage. By the time the ship hit tropical waters, I was back to square one.

When we sighted the tips of the Northern Range dappled in morning sunshine, did I stand at the rails with conflicting emotions to get my first glimpse of my native land after the years? When we pass through the Bocas into the Gulf of Paria, did I look up at the lighthouse on Chacachacare, and did I note the verdant little islands as we entered the harbour? Did I take a deep breath and sigh as the brilliant sun etched the houses and other buildings scattered about the hills around Port-of-Spain, and did I imagine myself falling on my knees and kissing the dear soil?

None of that shit. I was sound asleep, having drunk myself into a stupor the night before. When I awoke I could hear a lot of activity going on outside, but none in the cabin, and when I look around I see that nobody else was there. Only me and my luggage remaining. You would of thought one of the bastards who was my cabin-mates would of had the decency to give me a shake. When I was travelling on the tube in London, if it reach the terminus and I notice anybody asleep I used to give them a little shake and tell them journey's end. I didn't even left the ship yet and already I was sampling alien culture.

I wash my face and scrub my teeth. Sometimes you driving
to some destination for some purpose, but you don't want to
reach, you wish the drive could go on and on and don't finish.
Now the carefree days was done. Once I left this ship it would be
really saying bye-bye blackbird to Brit'n. If I was one of the crew
I could go ashore and have a good time and come back and sail
home. I try to work up some spirit as I get dress, thinking I was
going to plant the Union Jack on the land like Raleigh or one of
them fellars and get some new subjects for the Queen.

Bob come in and say, "Jesus Christ, Moses, we thought you
had gone and left us!"

I grunted.

Bob was in wild elation. I think he had a feeling he was
going to charge ashore and grab the first native he see in a grass
skirt and throw she down under a coconut tree. And afterwards
snap his fingers and a black waiter would come beaming with a
tray full of rum and bananas, like what you see in the television
ads.

"Hurry up, man," he say. "Jeannie is waiting. We must be the
last ones to leave."

We went through all the landing formalities and stepped
ashore. A steel band was playing on the water front, greeting the
tourists. Jeannie was thrilled. "Look Bobbie, isn't it wonderful?"

"Let's look for a taxi and get out of all this confusion," I say.

Suddenly there was a loud yell above the hubbub.

"Oh Chr-ist! Moses! Aye, Moses! That is you, boy?"

"That stevedore yonder is calling you," Bob say.

"Just ignore him." I held my head straight and urged the
others on.

"You bitch! You come back Trinidad and pretend you don't
know me?" The raucous shout was fainter now, thank goodness.

"Why didn't you stop, Moses?" Jeannie ask as we got into the
taxi.

"I'm not having anything to do with old acquaintances.
Once the news gets about that I am in town, they will all want
to hang on and sponge on me. I am having none of that."

The taxi driver ask: "Where to, sir?"

"The Hilton," I tell him. "Drive up St Vincent Street, and

turn left around the Savannah—I want my friends to see some of the sights."

"You must of been away a long time, bach," he say. "You can't go up St Vincent Street, is one-way. Why you don't just leave it to me?"

"Let's go straight to the hotel and settle in, Moses," Jeannie say.

That settle it, and good thing too, for it was like a oven in the car, even though the windows was open. When we get to the hotel we had to drive on top of it as it build on top of a hill, and the lifts take you down to your room. When we check in right away Bob and Jeannie start to get kicks at this little novelty, saying "Bottoms up" and "Come down and see me some time." For my part it only accentuate the withershins state of my affairs.

We went to our respective rooms, to meet later and plan activities.

But what activities had I to plan? I was tired, irritable and depressed; I just left my things on the floor and lay down on the bed wondering what the arse I was doing here thousands of miles from my tried and trusted surroundings, in a upside-down hotel?

I am sure it could not of been more than ten minutes' grace before Jeannie knock and enter.

"Moses, I was disappointed I never got my lei."

"Your what?"

"You know, the garland of flowers they put around your neck. I told my mum I would send her a petal."

"Go away, Jeannie, I want to think."

Bob came in and I really get vex. "I thought I'd have a few minutes at least to sort myself out," I snarl.

"It's Jeannie, she wants to be up and about."

"I'm sure the hotel has the usual amenities for tourists."

"Oh, I don't want to see Jamaica without you, Moses," Jeannie wail.

"I think I understand how Moses feels," Bob say. "Why don't you go back to the room and wait for me?"

"Okay," she say, "but don't be long."

When she went I suggested Bob should go too.

"Oh, come on, shake off your lethargy," he say. "You are back in your homeland. You were always saying how rosy things are here, now's the chance to show us."

"Why don't you and Jeannie go on a conducted tour?"

"You want to look up your friends and relatives, is that it?"

"Yes," I say, wondering who he meant.

He nodded. "I felt the same way when I went back to the Midlands after all that time in London."

"You didn't cross a whole ocean, though. The comparison is ridiculous."

He didn't take offence. "Of course. So we leave you alone, say, until this evening?"

"I don't look forward to it."

"Yeah, you do need some time by yourself, I can see that."

He went to the window and looked out. I could tell he was wondering if he and Jeannie should throw caution to the winds and venture out, if there be wild beasties and monsters there.

"Oh well," he say, "see you later," and went away at last.

The visit wasn't altogether useless, though: I got to thinking in truth about family. Other fellars have it jammy, at least with brother or sister if their Pa and Ma dead, that they could come home to, who would hug and kiss them and bring out a bottle of rum to celebrate the return of the prodigal son, and if they haven't a fridge rush out to the shop by the corner to get some sweet-drinks and ice, at the same time spreading the joyful news in the neighbourhood. They might even chase down a fowl in the yard and slaughter it and have a tasty meal apot before you finish your first drink. And you will give them all presents, corkscrews and little penknives with Trafalgar Square or Buckingham Palace on it, or some London smog in a bottle, like what American tourists like to take back to the States to show how unpolluted the London air is. Simple, basic pleasures they may sound, but even that was denied me.

Up to this moment, I have never told a soul the truth about my past, that I was born an orphan, and left to my own devices to face the wicked world, deposited on the doorsteps of a distant cousin in a old wicker basket, and nearly get tote away by the dustman and dump in the *labasse*. It was childless Tanty

Flora, living alone, who took me under her wing and gave me the name Moses and brought me up, and told me the facts of life when I came of age. Tanty was heavy on religion and saving souls, and used to preach by the wayside every Friday night. I remember I had to get the flambeau ready for her—fill up a rum bottle with pitch-oil and make a wick with a rag—and she would light it and put it down on the pavement to represent the Light. It does not shame me to confess my lowly origin: Christ himself was born in a stable.

I move to the window and sat down looking across the Queen's Park Savannah, remembering, as I did, that Tanty Flora used to vend oranges around there for a living. Up to the day I left London, she never write me, and for all I know she must of dead by now and gone to limbo.

In this state of reminiscence and dim memories, as I look at the blue slopes of the Northern Range behind the Savannah, and my eyes fall down to wander over the *squibbly* grass struggling for life and greeness in the remorseless sun, I see a old woman sit down on a box near the pavement, selling oranges. She was so lifeless, and motionless, that I didn't notice she at first: I thought it was a bundle of rubbish or something, until her hand, in an outward sweeping movement, divorced itself from the lump to make its own outline and break space—probably shooing away a fly or a mosquito. Like you, I pooh-poohed the idea that it might be Tanty Flora drowsing in the sun. Yet, I felt a little uneasy; I sat upright, staring though it was impossible to make out any features at that distance. I start to ponder on reasons why it couldn't be or why it might be, and then I thought, what the arse, it least it was something to do instead of mooching about in the room.

One of them crazy taxi drivers from St Anns or Maraval nearly knock me down as I was crossing the road, and even though he was in the wrong he look out the car window and curse my mother's arse. It was only a short walk from the hotel, but I was dripping wet with perspiration by the time I got to the edge of the Savannah. One thing you may of notice about me is that I take some time to get moving, but once started, you can't see me for dust. So rashly I went straight up to the vendor—I was planning I would buy a orange if it wasn't Tanty, to alleviate the intrusion.

But it was Tanty all right—you and I might logicise about odds, but what has that to do with Fate? I could tell by the mole on the left side of her nose, and when she look up at me there was no doubt.

"Tanty," I say crossly, "you are a fine one. I write you all the way from London, and up to now I ain't get a reply."

She look at me blankly, and a little uneasy. St Anns, where they keep the mad people, wasn't far from here.

"You don't recognise me?" I try again.

"No." She was coming to life now.

"Look good," I say, turning my head this way and that.

"Who you?" she frown.

"You don't remember Moses who went to England to make his fortune?"

"Moses? You Moses?" Eyes piercing now.

"Yes, Tanty Flora."

"You come back to Trinidad?"

"Yes."

"When you come back to Trinidad?"

"This morning."

"This morning?"

"Yes."

"Let me look at you good." She do this, eyeing me up and down from head to toe, making little sounds of doubt and surprise, then she put out her hand and touch me.

"I getting old and addled. How I know you could be Moses, still alive after all these years?"

"You self still alive and kicking," I say.

It got some people in Trinidad, they live through fire and water to a ripe old age. They seem to thrive on trials and adversities that would batter you and me up and knock we about so we get grey hairs before our time. Instead of shrivelling and drying-up they mellow into longevity like a evergreen tree when we ready to call it a day. And when they dead I don't think they dead like other people. They just evaporate, or energise like Spock and them fellars in *Star Trek,* and disappear.

"Tell me something you remember from when you was a little boy."

"I don't remember nothing, Tanty."

"What song I used to sing to put you asleep?"

I rack my brains. It have an American TV game, *Name That Tune,* and they hardly begin to playa demi-semi-quaver before some eager-beaver yell the name. Was it Brahms' Lullaby? Mighty Lak' a Rose? Rockabye Baby on the Tree-top?

She give me a clue by singing the first line: "Go to sleep, my little piccanny. . . ." And when she stop I still hearing her voice, and now I remembering how she used to sit down in a old rocking chair and put me in her lap and rock me to sleep.

"Brother Fox is going to spank you if you don't," I sang, and water come to my eye. "Slumber on the bosom of my loving mama Jenny. . . ."

Laugh if you want. I don't care. That's the way it happen. I may be hard-boiled and black, but tender is the night, and I am not abashed to confess that poignant moment in the sunlight.

"Moses! Is really you!"

"Yes, I come back, Tanty."

"And how you know where to find me?"

"I was looking out the hotel window and remember you used to sell orange round here."

"Over there? You staying in de-Hilton?"

"Yeah, with some friends. Why you didn't write me, Tanty?"

"Well, well, well. *Eh bien oui!* Moses come back to Trinidad, this morning, from England, and staying in de-Hilton!" She connect up the facts slowly. "And you see me from the hotel window, and come over here, in the hot sun!"

"Yeah. How are you, Tanty?" I didn't know what else to say.

"So boy, tell me!" Having admitted my existence she was all animation now, and I geared myself for the hug and the kiss and the welcome home. But she just went on, her eyes lit up, a thin sheen of sweat on her face, "Tell me something, boy! How is She Majesty the Queen? You seen the Coronation? You come by plane or by boat?"

Questions was part of Tanty's conversation, she did not

expect any reply. "Well boy, I glad to see you. *Too* glad. So you staying in de-Hilton?"

I guess she found it hard to believe I was staying in the most expensive hotel in the island. She kept looking across the road as if she was seeing it for the first time.

As I had to say something, I say, "So you still selling oranges, Tanty."

"What to do, boy, what to do. Oranges in season. When it's not orange, is pommerac or sapodilla. How long you going to stay, Moses? You better get out of that place"—she indicated the hotel—"it must be costing you a pound and a crown! That's for the white tourists—them. Why you didn't write me you was coming? I would of prepare for you. You want to suck an orange? Is navel-orange. You get navel-orange in England?"

I began to rue my impulsive dash from the hotel. Not that I wasn't please to see Tanty, but it was as if out here by the Savannah I lose my identity and become prey to incidents and accidents: you remember that sanctuary thing I tell you about in London when I went for my passport, well, I feel the same way about de-Hilton. I wish Bob and Jeannie was with me, they would of sustain me with their presence, even make light of the encounter and push on to something else.

Tanty had some oranges peel already. She slice one in half and sprinkle a little salt on it and give me. The juice literally sprang out and I began to suck it, as if the oranges had been picked that very morning—nothing like the squibbly ones imported in London.

"Listen, Tanty. I can't stay long. I will have to come and see you. You still living in John-John?"

"Yes. You remember the place?"

"I'll find it."

"You sounding strange, Moses. You learn to talk like white people?"

"God forbid."

"You don't sound Trinidadian to me no more, though. Maybe as you been away so long."

"Yeah, that's it." I wanted to blow the scene, but with decorum. I took out my white handkerchief and wipe my lips, and look for some place to deposit the sucked-out orange.

"Just fling it," Tanty say.

"Where?"

"Just fling it in the Savannah."

"They don't have little dustbins saying 'Keep Trinidad Tidy'?"

"They try that, boy, but the rogues and vagabonds mash them up."

I fling the orange over my shoulder. I was ready to leave, but somehow it didn't look right just to walk off and leave Tanty.

"How much for all them oranges?" I ask.

"All of them?"

"Yeah."

"Six cents for one."

"I'll take the lot."

"You mean all of them?"

"Yeah."

"But what you going to do with so much orange, Moses? Give them to your friends?"

"I don't really want them, Tanty. I just want to give you the money so you could go home and finish work for the day."

"But I like to work, Moses. I got nothing else to do if I go home now."

"Go on, you could sell them tomorrow."

She didn't like the idea, I could see that. It jerked her routine. But I wanted to get away. I pulled out some notes.

"Here you are, three pounds. That should more than cover it."

It was the worst thing I could of done. She struck my proffered hand away and the notes scatter on the pavement.

"I don't want your money!"

"I offer it in good faith, Tanty—" I began.

"Good faith, huh! You come back here on your highfaluting horses and trying to bribe your way into my good graces! Not a word from you all these years, for me to know if you alive or dead!"

"I was busy, Tanty," I say lamely. "People got no time to write letters in London. They have to work hard all the time." I picked up the sterling.

"And offering me *balbo* money too!"

"I haven't any TT dollars—you could change it in the bank?"

"You think I have any bank account like a millionaire? I never been in a bank in my life. And I wouldn't take it if it was pounds instead of dollars!"

It look as if even humble street vendors were cognisant of sterling's instability. . . .

"Well," I cleared my throat. "I didn't mean to upset you. It was just a gesture of good-will. The English pound is still valuable in spite of what you hear." I looked around helplessly, feeling trapped.

"You come back here with bad money, and bad manners, Moses," she say. "I hope you not doing anything dishonest."

I turn halfway to the road, hesitating. "I sorry to leave you with hard words, Tanty."

"You going back in there," she gesture again, "with your white friends?"

"Nothing wrong with whites," I say sulkily. "I live with them for years. You shouldn't believe all the bad things you hear about them."

She stood up now and put her hands on her hips. It remind me of when she was a wayside preacher. "We got no time for white people in Trinidad, Moses, them days is gone forever, praise the Lord. Black is Power now," and as she say that, she sort of make a circle in the air with the sharp knife what she peel the oranges with, a delicate, confident action, nothing like the angry fist in the air, but threatening enough for me to back off.

"I'll come to see you soon, Tanty, promise. It's funny we should meet this way," and I make the Dominica laugh.

I didn't wait for any more; I braved the traffic and got back to the sanctuary of the hotel. The first thing I did was to knock back a couple of heavy rum-punches to steady myself and think of my next move.

As I was rattling the ice in my third glass, sitting at a table watching the tourists gambol in the swimming pool—it was out in the open, and it had big umbrellas shading the tables—a young man approached me.

"Excuse me, are you Moses?"

"Yes?"

"I'm a reporter, Lennard, from *The Guardian.* Could you spare some time to talk?"

I sat up. A reporter from *The Guardian*! All the way from London!

True, this Lennard was black, but so was Othello, and Martin Luther King.

"But of course," I say. "Have a seat. Would you like a drink?"

"Thanks," he say. "A double rum-punch."

I flagged a waiter and gave his order and said, "You're a long way from home."

"Not really. I live up St Anns."

"Oh. You've been here a long time, then? You've come to cover the Carnival?"

He laugh. "I'm talking about the *Trinidad Guardian,* man."

"Oh."

"You been away so long you forget we have a *Guardian?*"

"I was thinking of the English paper."

"I just want a little interview, about how you feel to be back in your native land."

It did not surprise me in the least that Lennard knew of me, or that he wanted a story. All my life I have been hounded by the Press, albeit I have this innate modesty for publicity or any form of self-advertisement. I remember the very day I stepped off the boat-train in London, a reporter wanted to hear my views, and I pretended I was too busy with my luggage. And once in Oxford Street, a television unit was doing interviews, and a guy come up to me with a mike to find out how I felt about a National Front rally, and I turn my back on him.

"I'd like to help you if I could," I say. "What do you want to know?"

"Let me tell you the idea I have. You don't mind if! call you Moses?"

I wave a hand.

"I want to do something big on you. Right from the beginning, what made you leave Trinidad in the first place, your early experiences in England, your reactions to living in a white society, and that sort of thing. And of course, what made you decide after all this time to forsake everything and return to Trinidad."

"I don't know where you got your information from," I say, "but to start from the ending, it remains to be seen if I remain or not. As it were."

"Oh?" He frown, and pull a air-letter from his pocket and checking up on some information there. "Galahad wrote me that you were here for keeps."

"Galahad?" It was my turn to frown. "You know Galahad?"

"He's a good friend, we went to school together. You and him was good friends in London too, not so?"

"In a manner of speaking," I say.

"He told me you were never really satisfied or contented with the conditions that immigrants have to put up with, that for years you have been active in protest and rebellion. Is that true?"

"Let me see that letter from Galahad!"

"No." He put it back in his pocket. "He didn't want me to mention his name. Forget about him. It is you I am interested in. This story could make the centre-spread in the Sunday issue, I'll get a photographer to take a few pictures."

"What story?"

"About your experiences. Let me get you another drink." He swivelled and called a waiter.

It struck me then that I was being a fool and taking the wrong attitude. Was this not a golden opportunity for me to defend the old country from all the calumniations and rumours of doom and disaster? Had I not honorarily delegated myself to the mission of correcting all the false reports and hearsays, that the children of Brit'n did not play spoon-and-potato races no more because potatoes was expensive?

I was immediately excited. "Look Lennard, about that centre-spread—"

"I'm not certain about that," he interrupt. "I'll have to talk with the Editor. And it depends on how much you co-operate. Galahad warned me that you might be difficult to get along with, and that you have a lot of funny ideas."

"What I have to say is worth more than a centre-spread," I

tell him. "By the time we are finished you will be eligible for a Pulitzer prize in journalism. My story will make you famous."

"We haven't started yet. Let's talk about things and then we'll go into all that."

"Well, first and foremost, I want all the communications medias in the whole island to be involved in this. In fact, let's say the whole Caribbean."

"I want a scoop," he say sulkily.

"My story is too big for one man, Lennard. But you'll be the kingpin, I promise you. I won't talk to anybody else without your permission. You scratch my back, and I scratch yours. You know the old saying."

"All this is getting us nowhere," he say. "You haven't spoken a single word that I can use."

"Softee, softee, catchee monkey," I say.

He laugh. "Look Moses, cut out all the shit and let's talk man to man. Give me some facts." He take out his reporter notebook. "What year did you leave Trinidad immigrate to Brit'n?"

"I did not immigrate to Brit'n, let's get that straight for one thing. She called me during the war to do my duty as a Commonwealth citizen and British subject, and I rallied to the cry."

"You mean you went as a Serviceman, then? What, the Raf?"

"No, not the Raf."

"What then? The army? The navy?"

"No."

"Emm-eye-five?"

"Don't joke about, Lennard. I just went, because it was my duty to be near the scene of battle. They also serve who only stand and wait."

"All of that means you immigrated, however you want to put it."

"Don't misquote me. That's what I don't like about you fellars who do reporting. A man say one thing and you put down another. Perhaps we better get a tape recorder which you can play back and don't make no mistakes."

He turn his pencil upsided down and make an erasure in the notebook. "Okay, okay, we'll come back to that later."

"Not later. We better have an understanding now. The best way to go about this business is for us to have a kind of general talk about the idea, and agree what we going to do. You don't think so?"

He put away the notebook and take a sip of drink. "Okay. Let's just rap, if that's what you want to do."

"You should still take notes, though. You might miss something important."

"That doesn't seem likely."

"As you like." I shrug. I had to feel this man out before I tell him anything about my purpose. You would be surprised how many black people gloat and wallow to see Brit'n on her knees begging for mercy. Suppose Lennard was one of these militant blacks who out to put the white man in his place, whose sympathies lay with and in this Third World they talk about, and would spike my statements as soon as he get back to the office? I had to sound him out to know if he held liberal views or if he was going to deride and laugh Dominica laughs when he heard what I had to say.

"I suppose you hear a lot about the deplorable economic state of affairs in England?" I began.

"It's common gossip," he say. "We ran a story about Londoners queuing up for bread like in the war days the other day. I don't blame you for getting out while you could."

"Those stories are grossly exaggerated, Lennard," I say. "You can take it from me that Brit'n is still a great and powerful nation."

"The economy in the whole world has gone topsy-turvy. Even here in Trinidad. So what are you trying to say?"

"It's true we haven't escaped unscathed, but I assure you if we had kept out of the Common Market, like Enoch said we should of, the tills in the Stock Exchange would be jingling merrily."

He laugh. "I like the way you're saying 'we'; as if you're an Englishman. Galahad was right about you."

"After thirty or so years of winters and summers, I think I am entitled to express an opinion."

"If you are so conscientious, you should've stayed and faced the music. Which brings us to the important point of why you left."

I dodged that. "The thing is, Lennard, not why I am here,

but that I *am* here, and I can give you a truthful picture and put a stop once and for all to all the sensational nonsense that you people publish. The whole world jealous of Brit'n, you know. A man only have to streak in Piccadilly Circus and the next thing you know they are saying that the British Isles is a nudist colony."

"I must say you're funny. But not original."

I was beginning to get irked. "Look Lennard, newspaper reporters are supposed to be credited with a certain amount of intelligence and perception. Did you come to de-Hilton to amuse yourself because of Galahad's letter, or to get a story for the centre-spread on Sunday?"

"I'm not amused," he say. "We've spent the last half hour together and I haven't got enough for a classified ad."

"You're not listening, I've said a few mouthfuls, but you refuse to take notes."

"Maybe I'd better come another time," he say, "give you a chance to reorient and shake the dust of London off your feet."

"You give up quickly," I sneer. "*The Guardian* is not the only newspaper in the island. I am sure if I go to *The Bomb* they will explode my story on the front page with banner headlines. I have certain facts and figures you won't be able to get from any-body else."

I don't think he was going to throw in the sponge, but it seem as if he was losing interest. He was too useful to me, just the sort of contact I needed to establish my object.

"Let's have another drink and assess what we've got so far," I suggested.

He said he did not object to another drink, and I turned to beckon a waiter.

I saw Jeannie approaching, wearing only a big dark pair of sunglasses. At least it look like that, for she had on a flimsy flesh-coloured bikini that was an eyeful even for the hardened Hilton staff. Shameless hussy, I thought.

She came straight to my table. Lennard knock back his chair scrambling to his feet in anticipation.

"Moses," she say, "will you swim with me?"

"Go away, Jeannie," I say testily, "can't you see I'm having a Press conference with this gentleman?"

"That's-quite-all-right," Lennard say, the words coming out so fast they trip over one another.

"I'm sure I'm sorry for the interruption," Jeannie say, "but Bobbie's got sunstroke and won't budge from the air-condition unit in our room."

"It isn't always as hot as it is today," Lennard say conversationally, "it's much cooler in the evenings, it's the best time of the day, really, my name is Lennard, I'm a senior reporter from *The Guardian*, would you like a drink, please have a seat, you're not interrupting anything, is this your first trip to Trinidad?"

"Please to meet you, I'm sure, Lenny," Jeannie say.

Cor. In less than a minute, at a first meeting, after a dozen words or so, it was "Lenny."

I cleared my throat. "Why don't you run off and play, Jeannie?" I suggest. "We're just making some headway in our discussions."

"What'll you have to drink, Jeannie?" Lennard ask her.

It was me who throw in the sponge. But it was only Round One. There are more ways than one of catching a fish. Having made sure that Lennard took the bait of Jeannie, I allowed him a little flirtation, by proxy, as it were, and elicited a promise from him that we would meet again in the near future and get down to brass tacks.

Jeannie was so charming that it was difficult to get rid of him, and useless to bring up our former topic of discussion. It was only when he was paged to the telephone that I saw my chance and skedaddled off with Jeannie.

That very day, once it was seen that I was a boon companion to the delectable Jeannie, I started to be treated with a certain deference and priority, not untinged with jealousy, by the members of the hotel staff. Even by myself, I only had to appear on the scene and the head-waiter would whisper a word or make a signal and they would all come scurrying to serve me. A rumour went around that I was some sort of Dignitary from England (which was not far from the truth, in a way) who had come to witness the Carnival celebrations, and furthermore, one whose credit was good with the Bank of England. As a result of all this pampering and attention I spent the next few days taking a well-earned rest in the hotel, leaving Bob and Jeannie to fend for themselves. But I don't think they went out often. Poor Bob suffered greatly from the heat, and was always to be found in the precincts of an air-conditioner, wheresoever it happened to be, making sure it was working efficiently. Indeed, his close inspections made the staff think he was a salesman, or an executive, belonging to an air-conditioning company. And strangely, though Jeannie was his spouse, they did not extend the same warmth to him as to me. I suppose I have a natural mien too, a certain way of carrying myself that bespeak sophistication and worldliness, qualities that Bob could never possess no matter how diligently he tried to learn the ropes. He opined that maybe it was because Massa day done in Trinidad and black people were in vogue since the island was free of the fetters of colonialism; in any case, he did not exhibit any open resentment at my preferential treatment.

One morning we were breakfasting on ripe pawpaw, orange juice, fresh crispy hops bread, a delightful concoction of roasted saltfish, onions, tomatoes, lime juice and sweetoil, covered with slices of avocado pear. Bob was fascinated.

"Is that avocado?" He was accustom to them shrivel-up little things you get in London, and could not believe the size, and texture, and the pale green blending into buttery yellow. He helped himself to a slice to eat it like starters, like English people, but I stop him.

"Eat it all together," I explained to him and Jeannie, and showed them how. "It is called 'buljol' by the locals. The main ingredient is salted cod, what they used to feed the slaves with."

"I'm not touching it," he say. "They should ban such reminders of those horrendous days." But he looked around and saw all the white tourists digging in. "Do they know the history of their breakfast?"

"Oh, stow it, Bob," I say. "Don't let your sensitivity mar your appetite. It's delicious. Besides, you should fortify your belly with a good breakfast, the amount of drinking you get through before lunch."

He took a taste, and was soon busy eating.

"What are you doing today, Moses?" Jeannie ask. "It's about time we started doing things together. I'd like to go downtown to pick up a few things."

"Let's go to one of these beaches," Bob say, consulting a handout for tourists. He liked to show off his knowledge as he was genning up on the Caribbean even before we left London. "We have Maracas Bay, Mayaro, Manzanilla, Toco, Balandra Bay—looks like we have to stick a pin, unless you got any ideas, Moses?"

"They're all good beaches," I say, "though in the South the sea is murky because of the Orinico river in Venezuela shedding its waters in the Dragon's Mouth." I could show off too.

"Are we so close to the Mainland?" Jeannie ask.

"You can go across in a rowboat," I told her. "If you look out of your window you can see the mountains of Venezuela."

"I know all that," Bob say, "but where are you taking us? Are you going to loaf about the hotel forever, until your money runs out?"

"I like it here," I say. "It's safe and secure."

"Fine company you are turning out to be, Moses," Jeannie say, "you stick in the hotel, Bobbie investigates his ancestry, and I am left to amuse myself."

"You've got your coin collection," I say. "Besides, I am making notes on a story for Lennard."

"Why don't you forget all that shit, man?" Bob say. "You are fucking things up from the start."

Jeannie frown. "It's too early for such language, Bobbie."

But Bob went on, "Don't you start me off by being cheeky."

"If I may suggest it," I say, "how about organising a schedule? Days we spend together, and days when we each attend to our own business?"

"And where do I stand in this schedule?" Jeannie ask.

"You go with me wherever I go," Bob say.

"Oh, you are both being horrid this morning," she say.

"The only thing have to remember, Bob, when you go out, is that I am on home territory, whereas you and Jeannie belong to the minority white groups. So you have to watch your arse."

"You are not indispensable," Bob say coldly. "Perhaps your

natural instincts have come alive, and you want us to pay you to show us around, like an official tourist guide."

"You are insulting now, Bobbie," Jeannie reprove.

"Let's show him. We'll arrange to rent a Hertz car and drive about to places ourselves."

"There are less gruesome ways of committing suicide," I warn. "You take your lives in your hands when you drive on the streets here. They don't have no breathalysing tests either."

But Bob get up, his face shining with perspiration even though it was so early and we was indoors. Before they went off Jeannie pat my hand and whisper, "We'll see you later, Moses, when he cools off."

I sip my coffee, realising that I could not go on like this, I had to make some sort of plans. I tick off ideas in my mind: (a) Get together with Lennard and do my story and establish my objective of making the population cognisant of Brit'n's worth; (b) Go up to John-John and visit Tanty, and take her some gift; (c) mooch about the city reviving such memories as I had.

It wasn't much of a design, but I just had to get moving. I went to my room and took another shower, and changed into a light pair of sharkskin slacks and a white cotton sportshirt, and checked my sterling, for I was determined to negotiate with the pound as long as possible as part of my campaign.

I phoned Lennard at *The Guardian*.

"When are we going to work on that story?" I ask.

"How is Jeannie?" he ask.

"She's spending the day with her husband," I say pointedly.

"Oh."

I repeated my question.

"I'm going to be tied up today, Moses. The editor wants me to cover an important political meeting at the Red House."

"Well, what about this evening, then?"

"The meeting may drag on, with a lot of filibustering. The issue is important, it's whether to reconsider the decision to outlaw the words 'coolie' and 'nigger.'" His voice dropped perceptively with the last three words.

"I'm not interested in all that. I could reshuffle my activities and be free tonight?"

"Em . . . do you think Jeannie will be free then?"

As I did not answer, he went on, "How about tomorrow?"

"Do you mean Jeannie or me?" I ask coldly.

"Don't be like that, man. What about tomorrow?"

"You've mucked up my day, Lennard. I am a busy man, I have to allocate my time preciously."

"The editor is very interested in your angle, it's rather individualistic, he said, to have someone contrary to world opinion."

"I thought he might be. It's more important than any bloody politics to mess up the Queen's language, if you ask me."

"I'm sorry, I really can't make it today. I'll call you tomorrow, okay?"

I slam down the receiver in annoyance, but before I could lose my vim I was elevating up to Reception and asking the girl to get me a cab.

"A cab, sir? You mean a taxi?"

"Yeah." I glare at her.

"There's usually a few waiting outside," she twist her head to the entrance.

I went out and was immediately accosted by a coolie—I mean Indian—driver, who was sitting in the car with the door open to prevent being fried in the heat.

"Where to, sir?"

"Just drive me downtown," I say, with some vague idea of buying a present for Tanty, instead of farting about the hotel.

De-Hilton is on a little tree-covered hillock, a curving road leads up to it, and as we was swinging the first corner at about sixty a big delivery van was coming up hogging the road.

Both drivers stop. The Indian one toot his horn. The delivery man, a burly Negro wearing a American baseball cap, toot his horn. The Indian toot again. The Negro toot a double-toot. The Indian lean out the window.

"Back off, man, what wrong with you?" he ask.

"You back off and let pass," Delivery say.

"Stop making joke, man, I got a passenger, you can't see?"

"I got an important delivery for de-Hilton. You come around the corner like a madman."

"You should of blow your horn coming up the hill."

"I blow."

"I didn't hear."

"Well back off, man. Pull aside and let me pass."

"Pull aside my arse. I got the right-of-way. It easier for you to back off than me, too besides."

"You only causing unnecessary delay and holding up the traffics."

The Indian turn to me in the backseat. "Who right, mister, he or me?"

Once the taxi stop the heat did accentuate and it was like I was boiling in there. "I don't know, I wasn't looking, but it seems we're going to be here all day unless one of you gives way," I say reasonably.

Delivery get out of the van and come across to the taxi. He push his hand through the window and collar the Indian. "You moving or you moving?" he ask.

"I got this mister as a witness that you collar me!" my driver cry, and turn to me. "You witness, mister? You see how he assault me for nothing? We was coming round the corner slow as a snail and this man was charging up the hill."

Behind the van a stream of traffics was building up, and drivers was tooting their horns. The sun was really hot. Birds was whistling in the foliage about us.

The Indian was trying to tug-off the hand but Delivery hold on like a bulldog, and say, "Move this kiss-me-arse taxi out of the way before I wash you down with licks."

"You witnessing, mister, you witnessing? You see how he threatening me now? It's people like him who give taxi drivers a bad name. Ten years now I been driving and this is the first time I ever have any trouble."

I got out of the car and slam the door hard. Behind me the Indian whine, "Wait mister! This man got to move! I want you to bear witness!"

I strode down the hill in a will-o'-the-wisp of heatwaves shimmering off the asphalt, thinking that I shouldn't let such a little thing upset me, there were starving millions in India and a spaceship had been sent up by the Americans to circle Venus.

"What's the hold-up there, mister?" a black woman call out

to me irritably about six vehicles down. Her tone hinted that whatever it was, it was *my* fault.

"Two irresistible forces have met," I sang out, "and nothing's giving."

She stared at me suspiciously and with disgust as I went sauntering down the hill.

Distance is relative. To a Trinidadian walking from de-Hilton the shops in Frederick Street might seem endless, but to a Londoner like me, who walk countless miles either from missing the last bus or not having the fare, it was just a stroll. If wasn't for the hot sun I might of enjoyed it; I minimised the perspiration by my time and making one-today-one-tomorrow steps. White people really lucky, because science say white does repel heat, whereas black does attract it. That's the true reason why some black people wish they was white: to keep cooler, nothing racial.

I reach down by Park Street, and went in a parlour to have a glass of mauby to cool off. It was one of the local refreshments I was yearning for—a tall glass of mauby, with shave-ice, made frothy at the top with a lay-lay stick.

"A tall glass of mauby, please, with plenty shave-ice, swizzle it up nice and frothy," I say to the girl attendant in a green and white uniform.

She laugh. "Mauby! We don't sell mauby, mister."

"How you mean you don't sell mauby?" I ask.

"We got milk-shake, Cokes, Pepsi, orange juice, sweet-drinks and ice-cream, but we don't sell mauby."

I look around the establishment. It wasn't like the kind of parlour I remember in the old days. It was all spick and span, a few people was sitting at tables, and it had some more girls behind the counter to serve customers, and a cash register machine. It even had machines dispensing the drinks she mention. And no flies was buzzing around.

"How you mean, no mauby?" I ask again. When I was in Trinidad everybody used to drink mauby.

"Nobody don't drink that any more. You got to go by the market, or look for one of them small parlours in a sidestreet." She look at me suspiciously, as if she explain too long and unnecessarily, then ask: "Where you from?"

"London."

"Oh." She turn to another girl and say, "This mister asking for mauby!" and the both of them laugh as if is a joke, and even some of the others in the shop.

"Okay, okay, give me a Coke," I snap.

"You got to get a ticket from the cashier," she gesture to the woman behind the cash register.

"A ticket?"

"I can't serve you without a ticket." I went to the cashier and ask for a ticket. Please.

"What for?" she ask.

"The girl say she can't serve me without a ticket," I explain.

"What for?" she ask again.

"I just told you." I was beginning to get a little hot under the collar.

"What it is you want?" She talk like she was talking to a dummy.

Behind me another customer say, over my shoulder, "Two pack of Anchor and a box of match," and pass a dollar to the cashier, who give him a ticket.

"You understand now?" she ask me.

"I'm not a fool," I say. "The system is that you pay first and take your slip to one of the attendants for service. Isn't that right?"

"Yessir."

"Supposing I don't like the service or what I pay for?"

"Complain to the management."

Another customer come from behind and get attention while I still standing there.

"Where I come from, you get service and satisfaction before you pay," I say loudly, for all of them to hear.

"Please move out the way until you decide what you want," the cashier say.

"Things are different in England," I stood my ground, thinking I might as well start to put the facts straight. I addressed them all. "In England, people are trustworthy. They leave their money on the pavement in full sight of the public and not a soul touches it. Do you mean to say that it have so many thieves coming in this parlour that you have to pay first before you eat or drink anything?"

"He must be drunk," someone say.

"Or else a drug addick," another say, and everybody laugh.

"Go in Woodford Square if you want to make speeches, mister," a third suggest.

I could see that I would have a hard time as Jesus with the Pharisees spreading my gospel in Trinidad. But I wasn't daunted. It was only because the manager of the parlour come out to see what was going on that I left—he look too much like a chuck-outer for me; and the whole set of them look illiterate, anyway.

I start to walk down Frederick Street, and it look like the whole of Port of Spain decide to do their shopping for the carnival that particular morning. Thousands of people and vehicles was plying, and I did not have to use my legs to move forward, I was pushed and jostled along in the crowds of sweaty pedestrians until I find myself land-up at the corner of Queen Street like a piece of flotsam and jetsam. I do not know if you have ever had that experience of becoming a bubble in a seething mass of humanity, where your life is not your own and you are powerless to direct your movements. To boot, it is not to say that the current was pushing everybody down Frederick Street, but some more thousands was fighting to come up, and you could imagine the cross-currents and eddies, the swirlings and maelstroms. It was God, or caprice, what shipwreck me on a tiny two-bee-four spot on the pavement against a store window—in the eyelet of the hurricane, so to speak.

The Cathedral clock near Woodford Square begin to toll twelve, and I saw one or two Catholics make the sign of the Cross on their breasts, and heard them mutter, "God bless the holy hour." Tanty used to do that too, I don't know why.

As I thought of her I remember about the present I wanted to buy, and I wonder what to get. It's funny how this does always be a big problem for a lot of people. I didn't want to go into any of them shops: if the outside was so bad it must be pandemonium inside. Perhaps I should buy her a orange plantation, or a house around the Savannah where all the aristocrats live. Then I thought maybe I better see her first and find out what she want herself instead of giving her something she mightn't like and make her suck her teeth or fling it back at me like she did with the pound notes. But then, what the arse was I doing here, the hot sun directly on top my head, so I stood on my shadow? Like if the sun choose my head instead of all the other heads in the street: even standing motionless, I could feel perspiration trickling all over my body. I began to get my trio of adversities—restlessness, depression, and irritability, not necessarily in that order—and asked myself if I was a mad dog or an Englishman?

I gave myself a stern talking-to. *Come on, come on man, what is all this shit? What about all the things you miss when you was in England, besides a glass of frothy mauby, which out of fashion anyway? Are you not now, at this very moment, among your countrymen, and do you mean to say that you do not know one single soul, male or female, or a juvenile, or even a tot, in all these crowds? Are there really no friends to look up, no particular spot or place in this colourful city which you remember?*

Alas, the answer was negative, and made more so by a mighty dread to disturb the pattern I had lived abroad: I was scared stiff to refamiliarise myself with anything, I should have kept my arse quiet in de-Hilton, safe and secure among the foreigners and visitors. Still, the little monologue had the effect of making me determined to move, at least physically, from one corner to another, even without destination, and I turn to walk and bounce right into Dominica.

"Why the arse you don't look—" he began, before recognition dawned for both of us. "Hello man," he say then.

I grabbed his arm—yes, like a drowning man clutch a straw. "Dominica," I say, using a tone that belied my words, "I hoped I would never see you again."

He laugh. "What you doing in this crazy crowd?"

"Just browsing, looking up old places and old friends. And you?"

"I'm going to meet some friends for lunch."

Lucky man. He had friends already. "Oh. You got off the ship all right? You got a place to stay?" I make lame conversation to keep his company.

"I'm staying with some friends."

"Oh. You know your way around? How you like Port of Spain? You not afraid you get lost in all these people?"

He laugh. "After London, you can't get lost anywhere in the world, boy."

"That's true, boy. That's a hot shirt you wearing. Where you buy it?"

"I got to go, Moses. If I cut across the square here I come to St Vincent Street, right?"

"No, man, that is Abercromby Street. You want me to show you? Where you have to get to?"

"It's okay, I could find it." He make to move but I was still holding his arm.

"You seen any of our cabin mates?" I ask shamelessly.

"No. But I got their address. You want it?"

"Yes man, sure. Yours too."

"You got a pen?"

"No."

"Shit." He take out a little notebook and write down the address on a page and tear it out and give me.

I look at it. "Your writing hard to understand." I had to release his arm to hold the paper and he turn to go. "Wait, you don't want mines?"

"Oh, okay, okay."

"Write it down."

"Just tell me, man, Moses, I in a hurry."

"I'm putting up at de-Hilton."

"Okay."

I don't believe he even hear me: he was looking for an opening in the crowds to pass through. As he move I cry desperately, "Wait, Dominica!"

"Oh shit, man, Moses, I in a hurry."

"Do you know who's also staying at de-Hilton? Jeannie!"

I am not a guiltless person, I have beams in my eyes, but I swear to God that never before in my life I ever descend to using other people's names for my own purposes. I pray that she would forgive me. My remorse was such that I hang my head in shame and did not look at Dominica as he turn back.

"Did you say Jeannie?" he ask vibrantly.

"Yeah," I say wretchedly. I couldn't lie now: two wrongs don't make a right.

He glance at the Cathedral clock. "I don't have to meet my

friends until one o'clock," he say. "If you not busy, what about a drink?"

"Yeah, sure, man." Might as well be hung for a sheep; I even throw a friendly arm around his shoulder.

"I was in the Angostura lounge last night, it's not far from here, by the foot of George Street."

We join a cross-current and get to the other side, dodging the traffic. Drivers must of been observing an amnesty, none of them curse our mothers' arses.

As I wended my way up the hill to John-John that evening— a craggy bit of hillside with brokendown houses where reputedly the worst and poorest elements of the city dwelt, albeit there was a superb view of the harbour on this side and the rolling hinterland on the other—for the first time I begin to feel as if I come back home in truth. It was in this section of Port of Spain that I grow up, pitching marbles in the dusty backyards; rolling a hoop or bicycle wheel without the tyre; climbing mango trees and thiefing fruit in season. But there was changes, a lot of the hovels was replaced with bungalows, and the roads was not so rocky, and there was electricity and run-ning water for those who could afford it. Tanty live right at the top—you had to go up a narrow lane, climb twenty steps and continue a spell before you get to her home. Them very steps get me in trouble one day when I was small, rolling my roller— the rim of a car wheel this time; the bloody thing get away and went helter-skelter down the steps and knockdown a little boy, and Tanty give me a good cut-tail for the accident with a stout limb she break from a hibiscus fence.

There was improvements in the old dwelling, I could see electric light burning, and though the balata posts and founda-tions was still the same, another room was added, and the little shack where she used to cook was now attach to the house.

I climb up the six wooden steps and knock.

"See who that is, Doris," I hear Tanty say inside.

Whoever this Doris was come and stand behind the door. "Who that is?" She call.

"Me, Moses."

"Who it is, Doris?" Tanty ask.

"He say is Moses," Doris say.

"Is Moses?"

"So he say."

"Oh, don't open, let me make sure is Moses."

I hear Tanty move inside and she poke her head out of a window at the side of the door.

"Moses!"

"Yes, is me, Tanty."

She turn her head and tell Doris to open the door, that it was Moses in truth.

"We had to make sure who it is, boy," Tanty say when I went in, "it got so many bad-minded people does go about molesting women for nothing at all."

She hug and kiss me as if she really glad I come: not like the other time by the Savannah. "Let me take a good look at you!" She hold me off and even make me turn round to look at my back. "You put on some weight! Your head starting to get grey! But I didn't expect you!" She turn to Doris. "This is Moses, Doris, that I was telling you about!"

Doris was sitting down by an electric Singer sewing machine. All about the floor was scattered bales of velvet and silk and satin of various hues.

"We making some Carnival costumes for a John-John band," Tanty explain. "But sit down, sit down!" She clear a space and draw up a chair. "I talking too much. You had anything to eat? You hungry? What they give you to eat at de-Hilton? Look at him, Doris! My little Moses who went England and come back a big man!"

She take a break and put her hands on her hips, shaking her head and smiling, and it give me a chance to size up Doris.

I caught my breath as I did. I will say one thing for the pot-pourri mixtures of races that populate the island, sometimes out of the brew you get a species call high-brown, and the females of that concoction is some of the most beautiful creatures in the world, a glorious composition of sperms and ovaries that create the best of the first, second and third world. Doris remind me of that saying, a thing of beauty is a joy forever. My heart was pounding as I wait to be formally introduced

to her, but as this did not forthcome I step over a bale of velvet
and push out my hand.

"I am Moses, of Shepherd's Bush, London," I say, "an
Ambassador of Her Majesty's Service."

Doris laugh. "Is that what you playing for Carnival?"

"No, Doris, it must be true," Tanty say. "That's why he living
at de-Hilton."

"What sort of job is that?" she ask.

"It entails a great deal, you will be able to read the details
yourself when my story appears in *The Guardian*. But I hope I'll
have the pleasure of telling you personally as we extend our
acquaintancy."

I hoped for a lot more than that, too: I feel as if I was under
a spell gazing at this paragon.

"Doris was a waif like you, Moses," Tanty say. "The poor girl
was living with a step-mother who used to beat she every day
for nothing at all, and she run away. I find her walking about by
the Savannah and bring she to live with me."

"If wasn't for you, Tanty, I would of kill myself," Doris say.

"Thank God it never came to that," I say, gazing into her
eyes. She drop her head shyly from my gaze and toy with the
machine. "Is that the Carnival costumes?" I ask.

"Yes. We got a big job, to make twenty for the band."

"That's a lot."

"Twenty? The band have more than a hundred people in it!
Other seamstresses making the rest."

"Well, I haven't seen Carnival for a long time, I guess it must
be change up a lot."

"How long you been away in England, then?"

"Before you was born, Doris," Tanty answer for me. "But
look how I standing here and not offering the boy a drink or
anything! I have a little rum, Moses, that I keep for illness. We
don't have no visitors here."

"I was looking for a present for you, Tanty, but I didn't
know what to get," I say.

"I don't want anything, boy. The less you have, the less you
worry. It make my heart glad to see you, and that you come to
visit me, that's enough."

She went in the kitchen to get the drinks. I draw up a chair and sit down near to Doris as she went on sewing. "Is it all right if I call you Doris?"

She laugh. "What else?"

"You like living with Tanty?"

"She is all the mother I have. But you treat she bad. You never write one single letter for she all these years. Still, God is good—she win a sweepstake some years ago, and spend all the money fixing the house and putting in a few things."

"I should of really bring a present," I say. "I feel bad."

She stop sewing and look at me serious. "You come back to Trinidad to help Tanty out, Moses? You going to stay and get a job in Trinidad and help out?"

I shift uncomfortably in the chair, wanting so much to get into this girl's good graces. It might look as if a lot of things was happening to me for the first time in my life, but by Jove, it really look as if I get catch by the short and hairy, for a strange bewitchment fall upon me from the moment I enter the door. The ever-ready, instant repartee fail to come.

"You want me to stay, Doris?" I blurt out, and I verily believe, that had she said yes, I would of been well and truly doomed, but instead she look at me with a shrug and say, "It got nothing to do with me. But that's what Tanty hoping for."

"Er, well, the way how you ask me that, sudden-so."

"It's just that I feel I know you, because Tanty tell me all about you."

"I hope she say good things."

"You don't have to answer my question if you don't want to. I know the answer already."

"Okay, tell me then."

"Here today and gone tomorrow," she reply promptly. "I told Tanty she shouldn't worry with you and have any false hopes."

"It look as if you judge me already, Doris," I say. "It look as if you make up your mind not to like me even before we meet up here tonight."

"It's true though, ain't it?"

"You wouldn't like a man to give an answer when he was not sure, would you? You know I got property in England?"

"And no doubt you got a white wife too."

"I'm not married, if you want to know."

"I don't care if you married. Why I should care?"

Tanty came back with the drinks, and ask: "What happen, you and Doris having words already?"

"I did nothing to upset her, Tanty," I say. "She just resents the fact that I went away to England to better myself."

"Listen how he talk, Doris!" Tanty exclaim. "Just like white people! Keep on talking, Moses, I love to hear you!"

"I could talk like we when I want to. It's just that I am a man of many parts. I suppose even that she vex about."

"I went to school, you know," Doris said, biting off an edge of thread from the sleeve of a costume she just sew. "Big words and accents don't impress me in the least."

"Come on Doris, have a little drink with Moses and get out your bad mood," Tanty say. "I will have a shot myself, I feel a fresh cold coming on. I only got mauby to chase with, Moses."

"Mauby!" I cry, "I was downtown searching for mauby one day."

"Really?" Doris ask, with some interest.

"Of course! You think I forget mauby, and crab-and-calaloo, and that nice corn-cucoo Tanty used to make?"

"You can't get those things in London?" she ask, as if she really want to know.

"Not the real stuff," I say. "You get mauby extract in bottles, but it can't compare at all."

Tanty say, "You must come one day and let Doris make a good calaloo for you, Moses. She won't spit in the food!"

"Don't tell Moses about that, Tanty!" Doris jump up from the sewing. "Please!"

"Why not? Is a good joke!" Tanty giggle like a small girl.

"Don't listen to her, Moses," Doris entreat. "She always making up stories."

Tanty lean towards me. "Doris work for some white people round the Savannah as maid and cook. And every time they humbug her, she does spit in the food she cooking for them!"

I rub my face, not sure how to react to this. They say in Mexico that before he get slaughtered Montezuma take his revenge by putting a *zeppy* on the water, and when white people drink it they get the shits. Looking at it from this historical angle, what is a little spit compared to all the years of slavery and gruesome tortures that the white man mete out to the blacks? I know some people who does dig the curdled snot out of their nose, give it a brief appraisal, then pop it into their mouth. We all of us have our little foibles and failings.

So it did not diminish Doris one whit in my eyes, but she herself took it hard, running into the kitchen, and wouldn't come back until Tanty went to fetch her, with a shot of rum, which was gone when they return.

First I had a taste of the mauby before contaminating it with alcohol, and it brought back a host of memories, for it was my favourite drink in this very house; it was only when I went to England that I took to hard liquor. Doris was more relax now, as Tanty reminded me of my younger days, recalling many an incident I had completely forgotten. She herself did give up the wayside preaching when Doris come to live with her, but if there was any religious meeting in the neighbourhood she went, "for without the Light one lives in Darkness, Moses."

"Let's make a toast, Tanty," I say, raising my glass, by this time containing more rum than mauby.

"God bless you for coming home, Moses," Tanty suggest.

"And God grant me my fondest wish," Doris say.

"What is that?" I ask.

"It's a secret. Even Tanty don't know."

"Well, my toast is that whatever your wish is, may it come true," I say, and we clink our glasses and drank.

"Moses," Tanty say, "why you don't join the John-John band and play mas? You well used to like your Carnival bacchanal before you left Trinidad!"

"Huh," Doris say, now back at the machine sewing, "Mr Moses going to sit down in the Grandstand in the Savannah with his white friends, and wave and clap his hands when the bands parade."

"I haven't really thought about it," I say truthfully. "Are you playing, Doris?"

"A born and bred Trinidadian like me, and you asking if I

playing?" She laugh. "Not with a band, though. I might just jump up by myself. I can't resist when Jouvert morning come."

"If you're going to be alone," I begin, but she stop me.

"Who say so? You think I haven't any friends? I might jump up with Francis."

"Who is this Francis?" I ask, crestfallen.

"Francis is her boy-friend," Tanty say.

"It's a pity," I say. "I was thinking of getting Grandstand seats for you and Doris, or even hiring a car for the whole Carnival so you could drive around instead of staying out in the hot sun."

"What sort of Carnival that is?" Doris suck her teeth. "I want to play, not look."

"And I prefer to sit out on the pavement with my friends, like I do every year," Tanty say. "I does have a good time with them."

"You inviting Francis too?" Doris stop sewing and watch me.

"Fuc—" I begin, turning it into a lisp, "four people won't be comfortable, I don't think."

She just smile to herself, as if my answer satisfy her.

"What time you got to get back to de-Hilton, Moses?" Tanty ask, "don't think I chasing you! Is just that we got to get these costumes finish by tomorrow-please-God, and I want to give Doris a hand. We could still talk and work, and if you want, you could stay the night."

"Huh," Doris wasn't missing a word, "you think Moses will leave his simmons mattress and air-condition to sleep here on the floor?"

Yes yes! I wanted to shout, *I would sleep if you hang me up on a nail in the wall, just as long as I know Doris is near!*

But what I say is, "Well, I don't want to keep you all back. I did promise my friends I'd have a drink with them before too late."

"Stay little longer, Moses," Tanty say, but I could see she didn't really mean it, and already she was sorting out a bundle of the things Doris complete.

So I said no, I'd better get along, but stood still for a few moments, wondering if Doris would say anything, even good-night, but she was more concentrative than ever on her work. It was only when I edge away and reach the door I hear her say, head still down as if she talking to the machine, "When you coming again, Moses?" And again, just as I was about to say I am at your beck and call, Doris, she spoil my chance by going on, "To see your Tanty, I mean?"

The best I could do was say, "Tomorrow," feeling like a straight-pin resisting magnetic North as I get further from her.

"Good, Moses," Tanty say, "we will expect you, and make preparations."

I shrug. "Don't fuss, Tanty. I would be happy just coming and talking with you and Doris for a little while." And then, much louder, "Well, good-night Doris, pleasant dreams," but she was having some trouble with the machine and didn't hear.

"I better see you out, Moses," Tanty say, and come out on the verandah with me. She begin to wring her hands and say she sorry they was so busy; she feel bad that they didn't cook anything for me; they had to finish the costumes or they wouldn't get pay; I should be careful going down the hill before some John-John grapple me and cuff me up and thief my money.

"Tanty," I ask when I get the chance, "who is this Francis?" "Oh, him," Tanty flick her wrist like shooing a fly. "Is just somebody Doris go out with sometimes."

"She must have a lot of boy-friends," I say lugubriously.

"Who, Doris? Not true, Moses. She hardly ever leave the house, no matter how much I encourage her to go out and enjoy herself. And as for Francis, it's only because he treat her with a little respect that she talk to him, it ain't having nothing in it."

"How I could be sure?" I ask.

"She won't lie to me, and she tell me everything, boy." She lower her voice. "I even know what her secret wish is for. You want to know what is for?"

"What is for?" I ask.

"To married a decent man and get out of Trinidad. It's only because of me that she still here, though God knows I won't stand in she way if she get a decent one. But when I say decent, I mean decent, Moses, not nobody sinful who would swell up she belly and leave she to fend for sheself."

I said good-night to Tanty thoughtfully and left.

The sky was full-up of stars, and the air was fill with music of steel bands practising for the Carnival. I stump my foot on a junior boulder and didn't feel it. A anopheles mosquito sting me on my nose and I donated my blood without protest, so deep was I in thought, so deep the night.

I used to hang out in Piccadilly Circus night after night, by the Eros statue, contemplating women from all over the world, and the little cherub Cupid never shoot me with his bow and arrow. The bastard wait until I come quite to Trinidad, up on John-John hill, to fire at me.

If I did know that arrow was coming I would of duck instead of getting fuck, but it hit me square and fair in the middle of my heart.

I drifted into de-Hilton on wings of song. Dominica was having drinks with Jeannie and Bob. How swiftly he had moved, thirsting for white pussy! Some men would try to get it instantaneously without any of the preliminaries decent folk associate with the attraction of a male to a female; they know nothing of the bittersweet, tantalising anticipation, the despair and the zeniths of true love; you would never catch one of them plucking the leaves of a clover and saying she loves me, she loves me not. While we lovers are serenading or writing sonnets, or listening to gypsy violins by candlelight, they are pawing and grabbing and breathing heavily to gratify their bestial lust, displaying an abhorrent lack of finesse.

I pitied Dominica as I floated to their table. If he only knew the wonderful sensations and delightful emotions that a decent man in the throes of true love could experience!

"Oh Moses, we've been waiting ages for you," Jeannie greeted me.

"You look as if you done your drinking already," Dominica say, laughing after his words for a change.

"Yeah, you seem in a daze," Bob observe, "what's the matter?"

"Nothing any of you will understand," I say.

"It's all that bad rum we drink this afternoon," Dominica say. "I only sobered up after I pour a bottle of soda-water over my head. It's the local remedy for a hangover."

"I must try it some time," Bob say.

"You will have to take a bath with it to sober up, Bobbie," Jeannie say, and the three of them laugh.

They was in gay spirits, as everybody around was; a steel band was playing on the other side of the swimming pool, and tourists was dancing, some of them with locals they make friends with: very pleasant and pleasing it is to see blacks and whites coupled and dancing: it is to be hoped that the Last Waltz will be thus, or at the least, if dark shades are apartheided, that a steel band would supply the music! Also, some nocturnal swimmers was horse-playing in the pool. Overhead, the night was so starry, that if all the people in the world start counting, they would dead before they reach a hundred!

Jeannie and Dominica went off to dance.

"He seems a likeable chap to me," Bob say. "He wants to make up a little band to play Carnival. What sort of day did you have?"

"Oh, it was all right," I toy with my drink, hugging the new emotion of Love close to me, feeling as if I was seeing Tanty's Light for the first time.

"We had a smashing time in Maracas," Bob say. "If all the beaches are as nice, we should sample them all. You're right about the driving though. We narrowly escaped a nasty accident coming back over the mountain road; we were inches from the edge of a precipice, forced there by a drunken driver who tried to overtake us." He took a sip and ask, "Are you listening to me?"

Not having ever been in love before, I was savouring this bewildering state of bemusement that I found myself in. I didn't know if I should be happy or if I should be sad. Was this what I had come to Trinidad for? Was it writ in the stars that this to be my destiny, and that after all my wanderings and adventures I was to sit in a rocking chair with my slippers on, while a string of little piccaninnies playing around me? That orange grove I was thinking of buying for Tanty—it wasn't such a bad idea, when you come to think of it. The few square feet of fallow ground I own in Shepherd's Bush might fetch a handsome price on the market with one of them real estate speculators, and I could realise a capital to invest in a hundred acres or so of arable land, where Tanty and Doris and me could not only plant oranges and other crops, but maybe raise a few head of live-stock. That wouldn't mean we would have to live in the coun-try—we could have a townhouse round the Savannah and just visit the estate when Doris felt like it—perhaps we could install Tanty in charge there, give her a nice little bungalow to live in. We might have a couple of cars, but I wouldn't like to drive, nor let Doris, we might employ a teetotal chauffeur if we could find one, come to that.

"Moses."

"Eh?"

"You're looking sleepy, man. The night is young."

"Bob, if I put the property in London up for sale, what do you think it'll fetch?"

"Christ, man, what new craziness niggles you now?"

"I'm serious."

"I've no idea. That whole section of Shepherd's Bush is due for demolition by the London County Council."

"I think I should ask Galahad to put out a few feelers."

"Look, if you're worried about how he's managing, why don't you contact him?"

"Yeah, I think I'll send a cable."

"What's wrong with the phone?"

"Of course." That was the quickest way. I might even be able to give Doris some news tomorrow.

I went to the nearest available phone and put through my call. The phone ring a long time, but I was lucky, when it answer it was Galahad himself, with a sleepy, "Yeah?"

"Is that you, Galahad?"

"Yeah."

"It's me. Moses."

"Jesus Christ, it's two o'clock in the morning!"

"Never mind that. Listen carefully—"

"I got a bird with me, Moses, call back later."

"I want you to find out the state of the market—"

"Hold on, hold on, let me light a cigarette."

"I'm not talking from Notting Hill, you know. This call is expensive."

"Okay, okay. What's this about the market in Notting Hill, they run short of pig-foot in Trinidad?"

I stifle an oath. "I want you to get an idea how much the property would realise if I sell. I want you to find out right now."

"Right now?"

"Perhaps that's unreasonable. As soon as you can."

"I can hear steel band music in the background. They warming up for Carnival?"

"I want you to call me back with the answer. You got that?"

"Man, you sound as if you been drinking some bushrum. Like you can't wait for the Carnival!"

"Treat this as urgent, Galahad. I am going to hang up now."

"How much you asking for the place? I might be able to negotiate a private deal."

"I am going to hang up now, Galahad."

"Hold on, hold on! Where you staying?"

"At de-Hilton."

"Whee! Jeannie and Bob too?"

"Yeah. Goodbye for now."

"Wait man, give me a quick word with Jeannie!"

"She's dancing with Dominica."

"Who?"

"I am hanging up in ten seconds from now."

"Listen, I have certain expenses here—"

I didn't even give him the ten seconds, I slam the phone down. I don't suppose many people get kicks like that with a trans-Atlantic call, sweating as the pips pip and the money mount up. And I make another observation, that people who are not in love are cruel and heartless to those who are; they would do their endeavour best to break the magic spell, they are jealous and envious to see anyone walking on cloud lucky seven, and remind you of rent and mortgage, lung cancer and Oxfam, or whatever tragedies and disasters happen to be topical. Worse still, they would convince you that it is all for your own good!

Still, better couldn't of been expected of Galahad, even if he did know the state of my mind.

I don't remember much about the rest of that night. I know I drank a lot, in order to keep up with Bob, and some time as the night wore on Jeannie developed some nasty migraine and Dominica kindly offer to escort her to her room as Bob and me was busy conversing, and the two of them trotted off.

Bob had this freaky idea that they should invent a portable air-condition unit, so you could tote it around with you in the hot sun, and I was pointing out that it was not feasible nor practical.

In the midst of the argument I become aware of quietness about us. The steel band was gone, the dancers was gone, most the lights was out, and the onlyest living person I could see was the night waiter, audaciously sprawled over a nearby table instead of standing by to attend to our needs. (I made a note to see the Manager about that.)

"Looks like everything's packed up," I tell Bob.

"Let's have a last night-cap, then," he say, hailing the waiter.

He got up slowly and drag his feet to us.

"Sir," he say gently, "the bar was close more than an hour ago."

"How come we've been drinking all this time, then?" Bob ask with surprising shrewdness.

"That was from a bottle that Dominica paid for before he left with Madam, sir, with his compliments."

I did not dream of Doris when I went to sleep, though I tried hard to, maybe too hard. But when I get up, she was first in my thoughts, and I savoured strange and new sensations. Lovers are in a class by themselves, we are ridiculed by others who are not under that old black magic, or who cannot think of the opposite sex without getting a hard-on. Our protective feelings, our gentle considerations, our yen to everything for a sweet smile or a light touch of the hand—even for the loved one to drop her handkerchief and be the lucky man to retrieve it—what has happened to all these beautiful and lovely emotions in this world that we live in today? Are people really so bitter and hardened and disillusioned, that they are blind to the flash of a humming-bird's wings in flight, to the heady, intoxicating perfume of the hibiscus, to the sun setting in colourful splendour over the green mountains of Venezuela?

The telephone ring and I automatically reach for it.

"Hello, Moses?"

"Yeah, I'm busy—"

"This is Lennard."

"Who?"

"Lennard, man. We suppose to meet."

"Yeah."

"I'm waiting upstairs. You coming up?"

"Yeah, I suppose so. I just get up."

"It's almost midday."

"Okay. Give me a couple of minutes."

I showered and dressed in a plain white cotton shirt and a light pair of blue slacks. I stood by the window for a moment, wondering if Tanty turn up for work by the Savannah, but the traffic was heavy, and the noon-day shimmers from the asphalt made my vision wavy: the most it did was remind me to get a pair of sunglasses.

Lennard was drinking rum punch, but I chose one of those exotic, non-intoxicating drinks you see advertise on the television, with droplets of icy water on the outside of a tall glass, and inside have a concoction of red cherries and green berries and orange juice and a yellow slice of pineapple, all floating around with crystals of crushed ice, and covered with grated nutmeg. It look good though it taste like shit compare with an ordinary glass of Tanty's mauby, but it was impressive to sit back and stir the mixture now and then with two long straws and look about idly, like the tourists was doing.

Lennard say, "I discussed the project in depth with the Editor this morning."

"What project?"

"Your propaganda to lift Brit'n's sagging economic image."

"Oh, that."

"Yeah. But there's a hitch."

"Of course."

"He thinks it is a great idea, but he wants us to relate it somehow with the carnival, which is topical now."

"I disagree. Carnival is a pretentious masquerade, man, and my theme is a solemn, serious, patriotic one. How can we mix the two?"

"That is what you and I have to resolve."

"I'm sure the *Bomb* would explode my story—"

"Cut the shit, Moses. Surely a man like you could figure out a way? I myself have an idea, but we'll have to hurry."

"What's your brainwave?"

"If you can compose a calypso with your theme! That will have maximum effect at this time."

"Bah." I took a sip, drawing hard on the straws as they were full up of little bits of tropical fruits. "Even if I could, there isn't enough time."

"I could arrange to give it the widest broadcast at the shortest notice. I have my contacts."

"Bah."

"I will help you with the words and construction."

"I'm quite capable of constructing my own compositions when I have to," I told him coldly.

"Okay, let's give it a whirl now."

"You mean here and now?"

"Exactly. If it doesn't work we'll have to think of something else."

I laugh. "You expect the Muse to come so easily?"

"Here's biro and paper." He produce them. "I've got to interview somebody else in the hotel. Have something to show me when I get back, even if it's just to give me an idea if it's possible."

He went off. I took a draw on the straws and they make a sucking sound as all the liquid was finish. I order another, and while it was coming twisted the straws in my hands, twining one around the other and making odd designs. Just to show the bastard, I was mad to actually compose something.

I do not know how much time pass, nor how it pass. It was only when I feel a hand on my shoulder that I started as if from a dream, and saw my new drink untouched, and Lennard leaning over me.

"Let's see what you've got," he say.

"I didn't write anything," I say, "you're back already?"

"What's this, then?" He took up the piece of paper and read aloud:

"Her eyes are like two pearls of dew
To you that may be nothing new
But when my Doris eyes alight
They rival stars that shine at night
And when her lips part in a smile
You wonder where she got that style
Oh Carnivals may come and go
But this one thing I surely know
She is the greatest calypso."

I was pleasantly bemused. "Did I write that?" I ask him.

"Jesus Christ, Moses!" he say, letting the sheet of paper fall from his fingers.

I took this as high praise. "Well, it just came, sort of inspired. If I had more time—"

"Jesus Christ," he say again. "We will give up this idea."

I raise my eyebrows. "Of course it's only a rough first draft. You can't expect miracles at a moment's notice."

"Forget it," he say shortly. "Forget the whole project, unless you can come up with a connection with Carnival."

"That's only the first verse," I say.

"I'll give you until tomorrow to come up with an idea, Moses, otherwise we're going to kill the story dead."

I grab the sheet of paper off the table. "I'll send it to the *Bomb*," I threaten.

"You couldn't do better," he say, and now he was actually jeering. "If they explode it it will sound like a fart."

"You call yourself a reporter," I jeer back. "You only hang around de-Hilton looking for a piece of white pussy. I'll get Jeannie to give you the cold shoulder."

"She's gone with her husband to visit the Pitch Lake in La Brea," he say. "Is there anything else you'd like to know?"

"Yeah. Whatever gave you the idea you could be a journalist?"

"You've got one more day, Moses. Lay off the booze and prove your mettle, otherwise I would have to agree with Galahad that you are full of shit."

He walk off before I could thumb my nose at him. For spite I order and drink a double rum punch, fuming and exasperated, to put it mildly.

I took a posy of red roses for Doris when I went to see she and Tanty that evening. Tanty thought it was for herself and start to thank me, but I took them into the kitchen where Doris was preparing the meal and gave them to her with a flourish.

"Roses are red, violets are blue, flowers are sweet, and so are you," I recited the lines I make up as I was coming up the hill to John-John.

"Nobody ever gave me flowers before," she say, her eyes alight and sparkling like two pearls of dew, and she cover her face with the posy and smell the roses, and then she burst out laughing and say, "You too fresh-up with yourself, Moses!"

"Let me put them in some water, Doris," Tanty say, and she took them away.

"Did you have a nice day?" I ask Doris.

"Oh, so-so," she say. "Nothing like you, living like a big-shot in de-Hilton." She dip a wooden spoon in a pot of calaloo and take out some and blow on it to cool it and taste it.

"You got crab in that calaloo?" I ask.

"You expect me to make calaloo without crab?" she say. "You get crab in England?"

"Yeah, but nothing like our big blue-back ones." I subtly emphasised the "ours."

"You got calaloo bush?"

"Some West Indian shops import it. You could get a lot of things if you shop around."

"What you done today?"

"Oh, nothing much. That chap from *The Guardian* came to see me."

"You going to get your photo in the papers?"

"I suppose so." I pat my lips as if bored.

"Moses, how come you stay so long in England and you didn't married a white girl?"

"I didn't fancy any of them."

She laugh. "You mean you couldn't get any!"

I laugh too. "I could of married any time I like."

"And why you didn't?"

"Just because I think married is a serious business."

"That's why you didn't?"

"Yes."

"So you mean to say you would never get married?"

"What's all this about married? You tell me why *you* never married."

"Men only after one thing. And if you give it to them, they go and look for another woman."

"Not every man is like that, Doris, even if you had any unfortunate experience—"

"Huh! No man ever touch me, Moses, let me tell you! And no man going to either, unless we join together in holy matrimony!"

"Amen!" Tanty chime in, coming back. "But why you two always quarrelling?"

"This Moses think I give myself like a fowl in the yard!"

"Nothing of the sort," I protest.

"You suggest it, anyway. That's just as bad."

Tanty say, "He wouldn't of brought you flowers if he had bad thoughts about you, Doris."

"Thank you, Tanty," I say.

"Maybe so, maybe not," Doris say, cooling down.

Tanty ask her if the food finish and she say yes, then ask me if I wanted a drink before we eat, as Doris buy a bottle of Barbados rum especially for me.

"Don't tell him any foolishness, Tanty," she protest, "I buy it because I prefer it to Trinidad rum. You think I would waste my money on the likes of him?"

We went into the drawing-room and Tanty serve the drinks. "You been to any of the calypso tents, Moses?" Tanty ask.

"Moses don't know what that is," Doris say. It might sound as if she nettling me all the time, but I know that Caribbean girls have that way, that if they like somebody, they tease them all the time.

"Of course I do. It's where you go to hear all the latest calypsoes composed for Carnival." As I say that I remember I had my poetry in my pocket. It was to be expected that a philistine like Lennard would snort and guffaw at my efforts, but I had saved it for just such an opportunity. Nothing venture nothing gain. "I was trying my hand at writing one this morning," and I took it out and looked at it.

"Let me see it," Doris say.

"No," I say weakly.

She grab it from my hand and begin to read. It is possible for a rosy hue to suffuse the face of a high-brown, unlike mines, and one did on Doris face. She laugh to hide it. "This is not a calypso, Moses!"

"I know. My mind must of been on something else," I say slyly.

"What it is, Doris—read it loud," Tanty say.

"It's not for you," Doris tell her, and to me, "You want it back?"

"You want to keep it?" I ask hopefully.

"All right." She pretend she was doing me a favour, but I could see she was tickle pink, and she stuff the paper down her bosom.

"But why I can't see it, Doris?" Tanty persist. "Is not some rudeness Moses write?"

"I will show you later, go and bring some ice, Tanty, and dish out the food, let's eat." When Tanty went in the kitchen she say, "You too fresh-up with yourself, Moses. I didn't ask you to write no poetry for me."

"You like it, Doris?" I hung on her reply.

"U'mm," she say. "I didn't know you could write poetry too."

"I could write a million more better than that." My throat was getting husky. I lean forward and dare to take her hand. For a thrilling moment we touched, then she give my hand a hard slap.

"Keep your hands to yourself, Moses!" she cry. "We only know each other for one day!"

"Twenty-four hours, ten minutes, and twenty seconds," I say. "I feel as if we know each other all our lives, Doris. It's as if I come alive for the first time."

She laugh prettily, and I try the touch-hand again, but she seen mines coming and jump up. "I better help Tanty to lay the table," she say, and dance her backside out of the room, knowing fully well I was watching.

I could tell she was not indifferent or cool to my advances; there was a song in my heart. I continue to watch as she set the dining-table; she was humming one of the new calypsoes make-up for Carnival; now and then, as she place knife or spoon or fork, she would give me a quick glance, coy as anything, that stylish half-smile playing about her lips, and when she bring the vase of roses and put it in the centre of the table, she push out her tongue at me like when little children playing, and she lean over the table, and I caught a fleeting look of the tops of her breasts when her cotton blouse get disarrange.

Talk about kicks. If I had to spend the rest of my life just sitting and watching Doris lay the table, I would of done it.

We had a happy meal, the three of us, as even Tanty look as if she suspect something was in the wind between Doris and me that she wasn't averse to. In fact, it appear she was doing all she could to encourage the liaison, plying me and Doris with drinks and fussing over us like we was children, and when she find the wishbone of the stew chicken in her plate she give Doris and me to make a wish, and I do not have to tell you what I wish for. Furthermore, Doris herself when I start to tackle the blue-crabs in the calaloo, broke off the big *gundees* which had the most meat in them, and crack the shells with the bottom of a dessert spoon and extracted all the sweet, succulent flesh for me, which is a thing not many women do for men. And furthermost, after the magnificent meal—I don't know why they say you only peck at your food when you in love, because I eat like a horse—what should good old Tanty suggest but that I take Doris out to the calypso tents, you two young people go out and enjoy yourselves, I am too old for that sort of thing, but don't bring she back too late, Moses, else I would frighten some hooligans attack you, it not safe in Trinidad these days to stay out late, I don't know what this place is coming to; Doris, why you don't change that and put on the nice pink cotton blouse and green skirt?

Aye, that was a happy night, the happiest night in my life, because although it had others which were more intimate, it was the first time I take Doris out, and there was a kind of innocence and breathlessness and pristine quality about the whole excursion which I never ever experience again. So much so, that when I try to remember it, it is like the poetry I wrote for Doris, I can't remember how or when or why or what or where the lines come from, and similarly, the events of that blissful night remain wistful and tantalisingly on the edge of my memory, and I would rather they stay there than brutalise them by taxing my brains to remember. I do recall holding Doris's hand as I floated down John-John with the city lights twinkling below us, and the sea a sheet of star-lit gold in the distance. I do recall getting the best tickets we could at the calypso tent at the foot of St Vincent Street—it always have a few pricey seats remaining—and how she laugh and titter as the calypsonians come on one by one and sing their ballads—The Incredible Hulk, Lord Starsky, The Wood, Tom the Atom, and a new group, the Astronauts, to mention a few. Some of the calypsoes was really spicy and juicy, with references to the sexual act and the private parts of males and females, and all sorts of amoral intrigues, and these was the particular ones all the white tourists in the audience was waiting for. But because they couldn't quite catch the local *picong* and insinuations and allegories, they would wait until the black people give them the cue before they titter and guffaw too.

Afterwards we went round by the Savannah and had two fresh water-coconuts from a vendor with a donkey cart who open them up with two strokes from a sharp cutlass, and we had the soft jelly too, eating it with spoons make from the husk of the nuts. And we had half-a-dozen oysters each from a vendor on the pavement who open them fresh and shake a little pepper-sauce on each.

All of which might not sound eventful in itself, but any activity, if performed by one caught in the throes of love and accompanied by the beloved, is transported from the commonplace to the realms of high ecstasy and joy, and vaguely, at the back of my mind, I was trying to find rhymes for "coconut" and "oyster" to write another poetry in commemoration.

And if you think that is wishy-washy and unrealistic, how about when I take Doris back to John-John and she allow me to kiss her hand good-night? The steel bands in the neighbour-hood was serenading we, and not with no rudeness calypso either, but something from the classics, a little night music, as it were. She said she got to get to know me better before I grant you any kisses, Moses, but you may kiss my hand if you wish.

And that's how I know our love was the real thing, for in London, you only have to give them girls a bun and a cup of tea and they want to push their tongues down your mouth to tickle your tonsils.

Having Jeannie in the same hotel meant that I had no need for an alarm clock. No matter how late she went to bed, or how hard the pace of the night's frolics, she was up fresh as a lark and full of beans. Naturally this was a pain in the arse for Bob, by necessity a late sleeper, and when he drove her out she had this habit of nipping over to my room for a chat or just to sit around and twiddle her thumbs until it was time for break-fast.

I was awake the next morning when she come, though. What wake me, disturbing the sweet dream I was having of walking up the aisle with Doris, was Lennard, who come in the dream just as I was going to tell the minister I do, and stop the ceremony, saying it was too late, my time was up.

I couldn't go back to sleep after that, thinking that in truth today was D-day and I did forget all about him and his ultima-tum. I was racking my brains to think of something when Jeannie come and sit down on the edge of the bed, in a red cot-ton halter—no bra—white shorts—no panties—and sandals. She must of seen I was in a brown study for she keep quiet for a minute or so, and when she could bear it no more she burst out, "Moses, have you got any local coins?"

I had been persisting to trade in sterling whenever possible, flaunting my wallet thick with Bank of England currency, but inevitably I got change in Trinidad money. I got the habit of piling it all upon the little table next to the bed, and I gesture there now when she ask.

She examine the lot and shake her head. "I've got all those in my collection already. I'm after the old ones, like what they used before Independence."

"You won't get those coins now," I say, "and in any case, they were just like the old English coins before decimalisation."

"I know. I'm after one of the old pennies, like this one." She hand me a coin and I take it without interest and turn it about idly in my hands, still worrying what to tell Lennard. It was a old penny and the thickness was worn, but it had King George the Fifth head on one side, and on the other Britannia sitting down in her helmet and gown, balancing a ornamented shield with one hand and holding one of them forks with three prongs in it, like what masqueraders playing Devil does use at Carnival time.

I throw it on the table among my pile. "Them pennies pass out of circulation," I tell Jeannie.

"Yes," Jeannie say, "they are only mementoes of when Britain ruled the waves and was a great world power. Don't mix it up with the others."

I sit up and sort it out of my pile, Britannia face-up. It was at this precise moment, as my eye fall on that symbol of the British Empire, that I rub my chin thoughtfully and get up slowly and holding the penny gingerly, I went by the window and hold it up to the sunshine, taking a good look.

I have said that life is a funny thing so many times that I shall say it again. You have only to study my life to know what I mean. Look how I chance upon Tanty Flora by accident. Look how I fall in love with Doris at this late stage after having harems of international beauties at my beck and call. And look at me now with this dilapidated penny in my shaking hand, as if is one of the Crown jewels!

I curb my excitement with difficulty, though I feel like doing a jig of joy or prance about the room in wild elation. I merely went over to Jeannie calmly and peck her cheek. "You are an angel in disguise," I say. "If I had Hall's wine, I would give you a glass."

"Whatever it is, you can show your gratitude more than that," she stretch out her arms, not even curious.

I move back gently. "May I keep this coin?"

"What for?"

"I'll tell you later."

"It isn't valuable or rare, I can tell you."

"It's worth something to me."

"Oh, all right," she shrug. "Just don't lose it."

"Why don't you be a good girl and toddle along now?" I say. "I've got to shower and change."

"I'll scrub your back."

"Not this morning." Incorrigible Jeannie was going to be a problem. "I've got things to do. But I'm very happy that you came."

I went into the bathroom and strip. I stand under the shower, tingling, thinking about the idea I had, magnifying it into possibility and practicality. Jeannie come and pull the curtain and stand there, having discarded the halter to exhibit her magnificent breasts, truly golden now.

"Bobbie's going out this morning to trace his ancestors," she say.

I start to hum one of the calypsoes I hear the night before.

"You'll get wet with the spray," I point out.

"I'll take off my shorts," she say, taking them off.

"You want a shower?" I ask.

"I might as well now," she say, starting to come in.

"Well, just give me a minute to get dry." I grab a towel and wrap it round my waist and step out of the bath.

Jeannie step in and pull the curtain. "No peeping!" she laugh.

I start to dry myself—not rubbing briskly, that's for cold climes, but just sapping up the excess water off my skin, leaving some moisture to cope with the day's heat—well, half an hour or so, anyway. I hoped that Jeannie was getting the message, and I was just putting on my shorts when she call out if I wasn't coming.

"I've got a busy day ahead, love," I say tactfully.

"It'll only take a minute to scrub my back," she call, "a quickie."

"I've already dressed, I'm afraid," I say, hastily donning the rest of my clothes.

She pull the curtain back. "What's the matter?"

"Nothing Jeannie, really." I give myself a supreme test by not averting my eyes as she stood there naked.

"What have I done to offend you?"

"Nothing, absolutely nothing. Please try to understand. Sometimes a man, even me, got things on his mind. You know how wholehearted I like to be with you—it'd be an insult otherwise."

"Well, it must be something funny with that blasted penny, then." She start to dry herself. "What're you going to do with it?"

"When I'm sure, I'll tell you," I say. "Let's go see if Bob is having breakfast. No hard feelings, eh?"

"No hard feelings!" She peal laughter at my unconscious pun, and make a grab at my private parts.

One thing with Jeannie, she does not bear a grudge, and it is part of her charm. I wondered what she would say if she knew that it was because I was in love that I resisted her lures: no pushover, I assure you. I couldn't help feeling a little proud of myself.

When we went up I tell Bob immediately that I was sorry I could not spend the day with them. As it turn out they did make friends with a white couple in San Fernando en route to the Pitch Lake, and they was coming up to town for the day and all of them going to the calypso tents in the evening.

"I still want to see some obeah and go to Arima to see the last of the Caribs," he say. "When will you have time?"

"The Carnival will be such a surfeit of pleasure you may desire nothing more," I say. "Besides, you've got to get along with researching your ancestry, haven't you?"

"Yeah. But we ought to go somewhere together soon. The only time we see you is in the hotel."

After breakfast I phone Lennard and told him I got it.

"Got what?"

"The idea we're after."

"What is it?"

"I can't explain on the phone, man! Get over here as quick as you can."

"You sure, Moses? Don't let me waste time. The Editor—"

"So sure that I won't only eat my hat, but we can drop the whole thing!"

"Okay, then."

"You better bring a photographer too, Lennard."

"Time for that when I hear what you have to say." He hang up.

I pace about the lobby waiting for him to turn up, tossing Jeannie's penny and catching it; once I miss and roll off and I fling myself after it because it was so precious.

Restless as I was, Lennard was even more so, he stride up and greet me, "I'm on my way to an important assignment. Let's talk quick."

"Cool your water," I say. "Relax, let's have a drink."

"One drink, Moses," he warn, "and only soursop juice for me."

When we sit down he begin to drum his fingers. "Come on, start talking."

"First, take a look at this." I hand him the coin.

He look at it and say so what.

"Not that side. Look at Britannia on the other."

He look and ask: "Well?"

"You dig?"

"Dig what?"

"She. Britannia."

"If you got anything to say, say it, Moses."

"You know our theme of uplifting her fallen image?"

"Yeah, yeah, Go on, man."

"And your Editor say we got to link it with Carnival?"

"Yeah."

"I-am-going-to-play-Britannia-for-Carnival!"

It would be nice to say you could have heard a pin drop after that portentous pronouncement, but of course it is impossible in the location where we was. Nonetheless, only a dolt would of said that Lennard was not bowled over—even thunderstruck is not too extreme to say—though whether from derisive mirth or awesome astonishment was the question. One good thing he wasn't laughing: he just keep looking at the symbol on the penny, which goes to show that I have a higher IQ than him, for the significance and potential of the idea was instant with me, whereas his bird-brains could not cope with it.

"I said I-am-going—"

"I heard you."

"That's it, Lennard. Take it or leave it. It's a whooper, a brainstorm, and if you and your Editor can't see the sensations that masquerade will cause, the both of you can go and fuck a keyhole."

He look up. "Okay, I'm still here, ain't I? What made you think of it?"

I wave a hand. "Don't ask quibbling questions. That's neither here nor there. It's money, right? And money is behind all the calumniatory stories about Brit'n. And there's that woman, sitting on her arse for centuries. I will make her step out of that coin and do her duty. Look at that three-prong fork, man!"

"The idea is good, I grant you. But there are snags."

"What snags?"

"Britannia should be white and feminine to be authentic."

"You talking shit now. Carnival is a masquerade and an impersonation."

"The truth is I don't think you are capable of pulling it off, Moses. It is too big for you."

I gave him a Dominica laugh. "You want to chicken out, you mean."

He jump up suddenly and my heart fell. "Okay, Moses, you have earned yourself a reprieve."

"You mean—?"

"Exactly. First, you'll have to get yourself organised. There is very little time. If you can do it, if you can get all the things—there are so many 'ifs' I wouldn't bother to tell you. And before any commitment, you will have to have a dress rehearsal. I might even persuade the Editor to come. With a photographer."

"What rehearsal?"

"To prove you're serious. Playing mas isn't playing the ass. It got men who plan their bands and costumes years ahead, and employ draughtsmen and other technical experts to advise them, and spend months doing research in the libraries and archives."

"I could see this working, Lennard," I say earnestly. "Don't throw cold water on it."

"Well, it is all up to you. Keep in touch and let me know about developments."

"How about some advance publicity? Just my photo, perhaps, even passport size, with my name underneath?"

"You got to show me that you mean business, Moses. Anybody could have ideas, it's results that count."

"I will surprise you."

"You certainly will."

He was moving off when I remember my penny. "Aye, man, give me back that coin!"

He toss it as he went, and it slip out my hand as I try to snatch it and fall on the table. It roll around and spin, and spin, place your bets, ladies and gentlemen, and I swear she was smiling when she land face-up!

That call for another double-Scotch—I was already celebrating with whisky. The good omen start me daydreaming. The way I saw it, I was killing a few birds with one stone. Firstly, there was the satisfaction of expounding my theme and aiding Brit'n. Secondly, I would get my photo in the papers and don't let Doris down. And thirdly, which should really be firstly, I would get Doris to make my Britannia costume and we would work together to make it a success. I had a deep sense of joy and gladness as I realise I was fulfilling my two most important desires at one time. Britannia on one side, Doris on the other, and yours truly in the centre. We three was not a crowd!

Aye, how easy it is to dream, and how pleasant! People love to talk about the things they would like to do, the places to visit. Men envision making love to the most beautiful woman in the whole world. Women thumb through mail catalogues and bedeck themselves in all the clothing and glossy fineries and jewelleries advertised there, and furnish their homes with antique furniture. Employees dream of sitting in the manager's chair; the manager dreams of a cruise on his yacht; the yachts-man dreams of becoming a millionaire; the millionaire dreams of becoming a multi-millionaire; the multi-millionaire thinks wistfully of the time when he didn't have so much money, and would trade the lot to wake up with a piss-proud in the morn-ing! Verily it is said, that the less you have, the more you have, and it is a happy man who is content to play a penny for Carnival, instead of a million-dollar bill like Gregory Peck in that film. Great oaks from little acorns grow, but not from sit-ting on your backside drinking double Scotches, for another maxim is action speaks louder than words.

I dash out of de-Hilton and trick a taxi-driver by flagging him down in order to cross the road to the Savannah. Tanty was tending a customer and I wait impatiently, wet as a racehorse what just win a race.

"Leave all that, Tanty," I say without greeting. "I will buy the whole tray of orange."

"You come back with that stupidness, Moses? I tell you already that money isn't everything. If I stop working, what I will do for the rest of the day?"

"You will go downtown and buy some things for me, Tanty. I am going to play mas, and I haven't got much time to get organise."

I give her instructions and details while she look at me speechless for once.

"That's too much for me—one to do, Moses. I best get Doris to come with me. I think she got half-day off today."

"Great."

"And we have to measure you up for the costume."

"I'll come up to John-John this evening."

"And it going to cost you a lot of money."

I pull out my wallet and gave her some fistfuls of fivers. She back off the sterling, but I told her it was the best money in the world.

I went back to the hotel. I went to the receptionist.

"I need a few things," I told her. "I want a ruler, a geometry set, an exercise book and some drawing paper, and a English history book around the period when Britannia rule the waves. You got all that?"

"We got nothing like that sir," she say coolly, "you got to go to the shops."

"Get them," I snap, "unless you want me to talk to the Manager. This is de-Hilton, and I am a paying guest. Put it on my bill, and send everything down the moment they arrive."

I didn't have to look back to know she was staring at me as I stalk to the lift.

Just before I enter my room I put up the DO NOT DISTURB notice on the door.

Measure up Moses, Doris," Tanty say, handing her the tape.

"I rather you do it, Tanty," I say. How could I have Doris jamming up a tape all over my body, under my arms and between my legs, without losing possession of my senses? Bad enough to have her in the same room.

I had had the image of Britannia photographed off Jeannie's penny and blown up to lifesize—after a chat with the Manager of de-Hilton and reminder that my credit was good with the Bank of England he would of booked me for the first passenger trip to the moon if I wanted. (Surely some enterprising masquerader would do a Neil Armstrong or a Moonman?) And when I brought it to John-John, with the drawings and designs I had worked on, Doris tack it up on the wall near to the sewing machine. She and Tanty had got all the clothing materials, and make arrangements for craftsmen in the neighbourhood to get cracking on the helmet and the shield and the trident, money no object. Indeed, but for the assistance these women gave to the whole project, God alone knows how I would of manage. Doris herself remind me of the simplest thing—you can't see the tree for the forests—which was that we had to make a big circular hoop to round off the whole image of the penny.

"Also, Moses," she say now, writing down my dimensions on a little scrap of paper as Tanty measure me up and call out the

lengths and breadths, "we" and I want you to note the "we"—
"will have to put you on a platform with wheels so you could
move."

Compare to me, Doris prove herself not only good for her
looks, literally, but practised an efficiency and an enthusiasm
that show me it was a lucky man who manage to espouse her: I
had was to pull up my socks instead of repeating I-didn't-think-
of-that like a one-phrase parrot.

The time had come—albeit a little premature—for me to
tell Doris the story of my life, so while Tanty was cutting some
cloth, and she was taking a breather, we went out on the little
gallery in the front of the house, and lean over the banister.

"I don't know why you want to come out here, Moses,"
Doris say. "Mosquitoes going to kill we."

"I just wanted to tell you something," I say, and told her
about my motives for playing Britannia.

"That's what you call me out here to tell me?" she ask.

"Not really," I say, slapping a mosquito *dead* that bite me
even through my shirt.

"What else, then?"

"Well, well," I stood up there in the gallery in John-John,
and for the first time—maybe second or third—I was at a loss
for words, so delicate were my feelings. Also, my ardour to open
my heart was being cooled by the night breeze and the mosquitoes that was now ganging up and attacking in twos and threes;
to boot Doris make a joke and say they like my blood more than
hers. But above all that, to be quite honest, it was some primitive instinct, even stronger than my newfound emotions, that
bade me be wary and don't rush in like a fool where angels fear
to tread.

"If you got nothing else to tell me we best go back inside."

Did I detect a note of coldness in her voice, or was it disap-
pointment? What could I say to save the day?

"I spoke on the phone all the way to London, to my friend
Galahad who is looking after my interests. I ask him to check up
how much I would get if I sell my estate."

"Like you staying in Trinidad, then?"

"There's a good chance of that."

She make a female version of the Dominica laugh. "Yes," she say, "like how it have a good chance that cock have teeth," and turn to go inside.

I put out a restraining hand. "Doris," I say.

"Let's go in, Moses," she say quietly, "I got a lot to do if you want to play mas."

The moment was lost. More so when we went in and Tanty say, "Mosquito must of made you hop out there. You should use citronella oil for them, Moses."

And Doris herself start to get busy with tools and materials, while Tanty oiling the sewing machine.

"What can I do?" I ask, feeling helpless.

"Just sit down and talk with we while we work," Tanty say. "Tell we about England. Is true the people does live under the ground like manicou?"

"I don't feel like talking, Tanty," I say, wondering what was passing in Doris mind.

I didn't wonder long. "You could go, Moses," she say. "We don't need you. You only distracting me. Go and drink with your white friends in de-Hilton."

"If I go, it will only be because I want to consolidate certain ideas about my masquerade," I say.

"Whatever the reason, just go." Like she was driving me out. "Give us a chance to work in peace."

"Well, okay then, I'll see you tomorrow."

"Oh no you won't. Don't come back until you are summoned." She was even throwing phraseology at me now.

"Oh. When, then?"

"It might take two or three days. Or it might take a year. Or it might not finish at all. We'll see. Maybe. It depends. There's a good chance."

I swallowed. "How will you let me know, Doris?" I ask timidly.

She turn now and put her hands on her hips. "Do you think you are the onlyest one who can use a telephone, mister Moses?"

Intuition told me it would be disastrous to delay my departure. The course of true love never did run smooth, and somehow or other I had made a balls of things, and the situation would only worsen if I stay. I admit, that for all my big mouth, it look like if I meet my match.

"Good night then, Tanty," I say.

"Good night, Moses. Don't forget to get some citronella oil, though I don't know if it have mosquitoes in de-Hilton."

"Good night, Doris." She didn't answer; pretend she was too busy, so I went on, "You'll call me, then," and she still didn't answer, and I move to the door, and say, "Make it soon," and I open the door, and say, "I'm going now," and when I get outside I kick myself.

And a horde of mosquito, as if they was just waiting for me to come out, descend and keep me company all the way down the hill in poetic justice: I was so upset I just let them help themselves.

Birds chirp. Bluejean, keskidee, pick-o'-plat, poor-me-one, semp, cravat, even corbeaus chirped; the onlyest one I didn't see or hear was humming-bird, though Trinidad is the land of it. The sky was blue no arse—it had some clouds, but you could tell they was only jokers, that rain was the last thing in their minds, they was only gambolling and playing pass-out with the hot sun, all shapes and sizes of them. The vegetation around us was thick and jungly and full of philosophy, for it was dog eat dog and the survival of the fittest going on in that bush, and the stringy little trees and shrubs and lianas grab-hold of the big, towering balatas and immortelles for a tow in the rat-race for sunlight, and whilst we was coming to the beach in Manzanilla, the Hertz run over a big mapippire snake that was crossing the road; the car bump over it like it hit a rock or something, it was so big. But the vegetation on the beach itself consisted of coconut trees and sea-grape trees; the formers like a hedge planted along the coast, and leaning towards the sea as if they want to cross the Atlantic and reach Africa; the latters scatter in-between the formers, not as tall but short and spreading, with thick, shiny leaves like the rubber plant. The sea was blue and beautiful, and the breakers was breaking a good way out, and then rolling in full of spume and spray and frothy like mauby when it swizzle with a lay-lay stick. Some of them finish off and start up another wave before they get to the beach, and when they get there, they spread out sideways and try hard to reach up to the coconut hedge, and when they can't, the water start to go back to the sea, but many times a fresh wave coming in push it up the beach again, and you have to wonder if these waters in the shallows will ever go back to the deeps—plenty philosophy here too, for it look like the new breakers would never give them the chance, all of them pushing from the ocean to reach land after the long voyage across the Atlantic. It have a little kind of fish with big bulging eyes what does play and skip about in the shallows along the coast here: if you try to catch them it not easy. They float up with the dying wavelets and appear to be left stranded high and dry, but the moment you try to catch one it make a wiggle and jump back where it could swim and get away.

When we first come all four of us—Jeannie, Bob, Dominica and myself—unite and try to catch one, but couldn't.

At the moment, Bob and Dominica was playing cricket with sea-coconuts on the beach—these are hard little nuts like golf-balls, washed up by the tides and currents, and you could always make a bat from a dry coconut branch—and Jeannie and me was lolling under a coconut palm, I with my head in her lap, she sitting with her back against the trunk, and facing the beach, so she could warn me to sit up when Bob coming back.

I had taken advantage of the interlude Doris force on me to accompany the others on this jaunt. I thought it was a good idea to get away from all my problems and headaches and breathe some fresh air—when the breeze reach Manzanilla on the east coast of Trinidad, it's the first land it touch since it left Africa. So we loaded the Hertz with a variety of local goodies and eats and drinks and a big plastic bag of party-ice, and set off early that morning, for it take a good two hours or more from Port of Spain, unless you drive crazy like the natives. Of course, we had all jump into the sea the moment we arrive; now the heat had evaporated the water off my skin and I could rub dry salt off my body, though I didn't in case of mosquitoes, and also because some old wives say it good for your health.

As I lay there with Jeannie I was peaceful and relaxed, listening to the surf and those birds I tell you about, and the breezes in the coconut fronds. Jeannie too was temporarily out of passion, which was remarkable if only because we was chasing our drinks with coconut water, and a popular calypsonian say that coconut water good for your daughter. Be that as it may, a quiescent Jeannie was something else, as the saying goes, and I was really enjoying the absence of human voices as she motherly ran her fingers through my hair. Well, sort of trip along through the kinks and whorls, then. But being a woman, how long could she sustain silence?

"Moses," she say, "you and me haven't really spent much time together since we came to the tropics."

"You and I, Jeannie," I correct lazily.

"What?"

"Never mind." The sunlight was filtering through the coconut fronds, casting a trellised design which lightly shadowed us.

"A little birdie tells me that something is bothering you. You have become withdrawn, almost melancholy, which is so unlike you."

"I have a lot of things on my mind, Jeannie," I say.

"Is it Galahad and your house in London?"

"No."

"Is it nostalgia for England?"

"No."

"Is it the heat?"

"No."

"If you're running short of money you can keep that penny I lent you."

You may of noticed another charming thing with Jeannie, she sometimes come out with some little gems, quite innocent and unaware. Like now, she did not mean to be funny, I am sure it was because she thought the coin had some antique value that I wanted to hold on to it.

"Jeannie, can't we just sit like this, and enjoy the scenery and the sounds of nature?"

"No, because my wedding ring is stuck in your hair and you

have to shift your head." She gave a little tug to show me and it hurt. I had to change my position and take it out myself. I was now sitting up next to her.

"Let go for a swim, I'm getting hot again," she say.

"It's nice and shady here."

"I don't mean the sun, silly!"

Maybe the coconut water was working after all. "You are too energetic, Jeannie. You should rest your libido sometimes."

"What's libido?" She wiggled her legs as if she suspected I meant some rudeness.

"Go and swim with Bob and Dominica, I just want to stay here and think."

"They have wandered off," she report. "After cricket they took up golf, and now they're out of sight. Please come, Moses."

"Oh well."

She did not wait for me but ran on ahead and plunge in.

"Don't go too far out," I call, "the current could be treacherous here."

"Come over here, where it isn't so shallow," she shouted, "it's nicer."

I make a few strokes and join her. Jeannie grabbed me, laughing. "This is wonderful, Moses. Teach me to swim."

"Cut it out, Jeannie," I say.

We were a little more than waist-deep-higher when the waves passed—and she put her arms around me and pressed her thighs against mines.

"I want to do it out here, Moses," she say. "I've been dying to."

"Do what?"

"This," and she French-kissed me midst the breakers.

"Don't, Jeannie," I said after a while. But her hands were already below the surface undoing her bikini pants.

I don't want to go into a long harangue trying to justify my actions. After all, I am merely an ordinary virile man, and in my particular circumstances I truly believed that it would have the cathartic effect of completely clearing my brains so I could face up to the future and make certain decisions. A secondary reason being the novelty of the experience for Jeannie herself.

It wasn't easy to get it in, though, though Jeannie co-operated heartily. It took some underwater manoeuvring and timing the waves before we succeed: I felt as triumphant as an astronaut locking his space capsule to the mothership.

As we bobbed and weaved as one, now, and just about to come, I gasped, "I hope you got the bikini pants?"

"No," Jeannie panted, "you've got it."

"Shit," I said, "you had it."

"It must have slipped away, Moses, but never mind about that now!"

"We got to find it!" I snarled as I uncoupled in frustration.

"Oh Moses, oh!" Jeannie cried, but I dived to search with my hands and feet. But in all the churning and swirling that was going on with us and the waves, it was a hopeless task.

I surfaced after a few tries and yell at her. "Why the arse you didn't keep a hold of it, Jeannie? Now we are really in the shit." I looked along the beach and my heart lurched as I see the golfers coming, in the distance.

"I've got another in the car, but that isn't much use, is it?"

I did not spare a moment. I galloped out of the sea, lifting my legs high and awkwardly over the waves, and did sprint to the Hertz. I spotted it on the back seat, grabbed it in a flash and sped back.

"Hi, Moses!" I heard Dominica yell.

I galloped into the ocean: the fucking waves was against me now and I had to battle them, diving into each as it sought to topple me head-over-heels; all turmoiling now instead of gambolling, but for all that, I kept my head, and hold on to the bikini like chewing stick on to a hot piece of iron, as a noted calypsonian say.

"Put it on quick, for God's sake." I gave it to Jeannie.

I held her shoulders to steady her as she bent and tried to get into it. A horrified expression crossed her face.

"Oh my God, Moses, you brought the bra!"

I did not panic. I said, "You can't make it work like a pants?"

"That's impossible," she cried: close to crying too.

"All right, keep cool. Stay out here, Jeannie, don't come any nearer in. When I leave you, splash about and wave to Bob and Dominica as if you were having the time of your life."

"What're you going to do, Moses?" she wailed.

"I don't know," I said honestly.

By this time Bob and Dominica were hailing out to us. I waded ashore to them.

"You guys must need a drink after all that birdies and pars and handicaps," I said. "Let's go and fire one."

"I'm more hungry than thirsty," Bob say.

"What's keeping Jeannie?" Dominica ask, making a visor on his forehead with a hand and looking out to sea keenly.

I tell you one thing with Caribbean people: they may be black, but they don't lack pertinacity and perspicacity; I could read Dominica like a book, he suspected some mischief was afoot, and I was more concerned with drawing his attention away from Jeannie than worrying about Bob.

"Jeannie wants to be alone for a while, Dominica," I said firmly.

"It look like she in difficulties," he say; the foolish girl was overdoing the splashing and waving.

"Don't you recognise highjinks when you see them?" I sneered, and held his arm firmly and dragged him along to the picnic spot, with Bob following.

"Why don't you shin up that short tree and get us some fresh nuts, Dominica?" I suggest easily. "I'll fetch the rum and glasses."

"You shin up and I'll fetch," he say.

"You mean you can't climb that short coconut tree?" I scoff.

"He can't play cricket or golf either," Bob say. "He's just fucking useless."

"Okay, okay," Dominica grumble, but he begin to climb.

I waited until he pass the point of no return and turned to get to the car. Bob make to follow me.

"You stay here and catch the nuts, Bob," I told him. "If they fall on the ground they get bruised and the water's not so good."

"They are too heavy to catch, Moses."

"Just put out your hand and break the fall," I snarl, getting rattled even more now.

I don't know how much time all this took, it appeared ages to me but I guess it couldn't of been more than a couple of minutes or so. I made races to the Hertz, made sure I got the bikini pants this time, stuffed it down my trunks, and sped down to the sea in a direct line so I wouldn't have to pass near to Bob under the tree.

As Jeannie and I emerged and began to walk up the beach towards them, Bob call out as we get near, "What the hell is going on, Moses?"

"Dominica was right," I was prepared for questions. "Jeannie was in difficulties, she caught a cramp, it was lucky I saw her and went to her rescue."

"You all right?" Bob ask her.

"Yes, Bobbie," she say, "I wasn't out of my depth, but I was frightened."

Dominica came down the tree, skidding on his bottom and using his hands as brakes. He looked at me and winked. I suppose he must of had a good look of the proceedings from the top of the coconut tree. He kept on winking, you know how some people are when they feel they know your secret and want you to be aware of it, but I walked off to get the rum, and Jeannie came too, to get the eats ready, as Bob complained again of hunger.

We spread the food and drink on dry coconut branches, and began to eat. Bob tackled some of everything—the roti and curry beef and potatoes, the fried chicken and chips, the hot pies with various fillings, and then ripe mango-julie and sapodillas for dessert. Dominica ate less ravenously—he gnawed at a drumstick and was still persisting in the stupid winking, this time more to Jeannie, until she had to ask him if something was wrong with his eyes, whereupon he quipped that nothing was wrong with *his,* but something was definitely wrong with Bob's, and made his special laugh.

Sated and half-pissed, we lolled about, making small talk and discussing the Carnival.

"I'm afraid I won't be with you." I took the opportunity to tell them I was playing Britannia.

"How mean you are," Jeannie say. "You make your own plans and don't tell us a word."

"It was all sudden," I explain.

"What's this Britannia lark?" Bob ask.

"You'll see when the time comes," I said. "One is not supposed to divulge one's impersonation to anyone. I'm just telling you because I'll be busy attending to things."

"You don't have to worry," Dominica say. "I will make sure that Bob and Jeannie have a good time."

"I'm sure," I say drily.

"I knew you were up to something," Bob say. "Are you sure you're telling us everything? You've been acting funny with us, like you're hiding something."

"What would I hide from you and Jeannie?" I ask, all innocent.

"Come on, who feels like a stroll down the beach?" Dominica look at Jeannie. "It'll help to digest your food."

"Coming, Bobbie?" Jeannie ask, getting to her feet.

"Not just yet. I'll keep Moses company."

The two of them wander off, but with Bob around it didn't look like I would be able to get back to my original relaxation earlier on. Bob keep tapping the bottle and I drank too—his excuse was that the party-ice was melting fast, and he liked the coconut water we were chasing with more than the rum, really, but he couldn't have one without the other.

We talk some—about Trinidad—by now he must of seen more of it than me, and I do not mean of recent times only, for there are people who live in one place and remain glue to it, and before I went to Brit'n I was a Port-of-Spain man, having a natural urbane manner and temperament, and did not venture into the hinterland often. I never seen the Pitch Lake where Raleigh and his merry men caulk their ships with pitch when they came to look for El Dorado, for instance, and Bob and Jeannie did. The furthest south I ever been was San Fernando, attracted by one or two fetes, but drive back to the city right after, no matter what hour of the night. And to tell you the truth, this present trip to Manzanilla was the first time I ever come to that beach.

I ask Bob what he had been up to the times I wasn't with them, and that crank him up to talk about the ancestry business, which is a great, if not the greatest, English pastime. It has always amazed me how keen they are to be able to climb or descend the family tree, and trace their forebears back to the days of William the Conqueror or Hereward the Wake and those other quaint chaps. There are a lot of Englishers who would swear blind that they have some dreg of royal blood in their veins, and the possibility is not so remote when you consider how them kings and dukes and earls of yore used to fuck the tavern wenches and such. To give an example, that girl what used to sell oranges, Nellie Gwyn or something like that, is recorded in the pages of English history, as is that brazen-faced tart who ride naked on a horse in Coventry. The lowliest farm labourer in some hamlet in the heart of the English countryside would be able to tell you of times circa A.D. or even circa B.C. when his great-great-great grandpa used to hunt the dinosaur or go clubbing for a long-tressed female and drag her off to a cave to make the initial stroke what start off the whole business. So many commoners try to jump on the royal bandwagon, that it is to be noted that Royalty and that ilk relegate their sexual intercourse to close circles in order to make sure of the highest percentage of blue blood, and if some renegade dare to make a stroke out of class, he got to abdicate or get ostracise or give up his (or her) chances of ever sitting on the Throne and ruling the British people. Even in this present day and age we have examples of this sort of thing happening, but it is not in my place to cast aspersions, though if you call name I will whistle. Whereas orphans like me are content to let the dead bury the dead and be thankful and humble for little happinesses and small mercies that God mete out, Englishers like Bob have an insatiable curiosity for the past. No doubt students of this topic could unearth several reasons for this, such as the hope that they can lay claim to some ancient land titles or bequeathments, or find out that they have the privilege to emblazon a Family Motto on a Coat-of-Arms, or even have the right to queue up with the poor on a Maundy Thursday for a handout from the Queen.

Whatever the facts, the fact remain that Bob had continued his investigations into the Caribbean side of his lineage, and was now boring me. I had to pretend I was interested and ask him if he find out anything.

"Is the trail getting hot?" I ask.

"Sort of," he say. "They don't keep tidy records of the past here, do they?"

"Of course," I say, "but every few years, when political corruption and graft and other unpleasantnesses reach a crescendo and the mark threaten to burst, somebody burn down the building what house the documents and records."

"One thing I'm certain of," he say. "Some time in the last century someone to whom I may be related sailed to these waters and set up roots. I'm determined to learn as much as I can, and I'm not very far from finding out."

"What bloody good would the knowledge do?" I ask. "Did he bury treasure or something, and left a hidden map for you?"

"You're incapable of appreciating the satisfaction a man gets when he learns the history of his ancestry, Moses. That's the difference between you and me—being civilised and primitive."

"That's a lot of shit, and you know it," I say. "Look at me, I don't even know who my father and mother was, and I do not lose any sleep over it. And further, compare my social and economic standing with yours."

"What you are saying is that you are just a fluke," he sneer, "a random bastard who adopted England as his home. No wonder you don't know if you're coming or going."

"Don't call me no fucking fluke, Bob!" I cried. "I got people who love me, boy. You only got parents in name. You come like a bleeding foundling to London yourself, and if I didn't give you hearth and home and friendship, you would be a bloody wino drifting about the East End begging for a crust, and sleeping underneath the arches in Charing Cross!"

I regretted my outburst and reproachfulness, though I was in the right. But it just goes to show you how uptight an Englishman could get when it come to this business of raising the dead—and rousing relationships instead, as it were.

That little sojourn in Manzanilla had the opposite effect to what I expect. Instead of fortifying me for the future it depress me with the present, for I itched more to be with Doris.

I reflected how wonderful it would of been if she and me alone had gone to the beach—the pick-o'-plats and the other birds would not of only chirped but burst into gladsome song, and the jungles would of been a Garden of Paradise instead of promoting prosaic philosophy.

What made matters worse was that as soon as we get back to de-Hilton the switchboard girl tell me that there had been a telephone call for me, that they had paged me fruitlessly, and that I should remember to leave my key at the desk when I was going out, else how could I expect the staff to know if I, sir, was in or out?

"Man or woman?" I ask as soon as she stop talking. She shrug. "It could of been either, sir. The line was bad, I could hardly hear the person."

"You'll have to do better than that," I say. "Telephone calls are vital to me. You should of ask the Exchange to trace the call or something."

All night long I tossed in bed, wondering if was Doris, they couldn't of finished Britannia's outfit so quick, so if it was Doris, maybe she wanted to tell me she was sorry for being so huffy the last time, or better still, ask if *I* didn't miss her, which would give me the chance to tell her how much, night and day, in the roaring traffic's boom, in the silence of my lonely room, like the song say.

I skulked about the hotel next day, every now and then passing by the switchboard operator to let her see that I was present and in good health, and exchanging a little pleasantry to keep things friendly between us in case she jam-up the lines for spite. As soon as the bar open I told her, slowly and precisely, that I was going to have a drink, and that I would not budge from that spot without telling her, even if I wanted to pee.

I was on my second rum punch when it came. The bartender was talking with a roisterous group of tourists who was going to hike over the mountains to Maracas Bay and wanted to know what antidotes to take for snake-bites, and if they could do it in time to get back for the evening meal. Though the phone was ringing loud the bastard was ignoring it until I shout at him.

I almost climb over the bar when he was answering, saying

who, who, in the mouthpiece like a fucking owl. "Hello, hello!" I
was saying even as he hand me the phone.

"Hello, is that you, sir?"

"Yes, this is sir!"

"I have your call for you. Will you hold the line, please?"

I hear some clicks and clacks, and then, "Hello, Moses?"

"Yeah, yeah!"

"It's Lennard here . . . hello, you there? Hello, hello?"

"Ye-a-ah."

"You got sore throat or something? Speak up man!"

"I hear you."

"Where you been, man, I try to get you yesterday . . . hello?
Did you hear me?"

"What you want, Lennard?"

"I hope you have been busy. The Editor is infatuated with
our idea—"

"Did you say 'our'?"

"I better come to see you, man, the line must be bad at your
end. You not going out?"

"No."

"I'll be there in half an hour. Okay?"

"Yeah."

"Okay, you got that? Your voice sounding hoarse. You pick
up a cold?"

"Yeah, yeah."

I was on my fifth drink, I think, by the time Lennard come.
His face was beaming as if he take over *The Guardian*.

"Things are going great," was his opening remark.

"Yeah?"

"It's plain sailing from now on, provided you do your part.
The paper will even subsidise us, so if there is any question
about money?"

I wave that away: I didn't want nobody to say afterwards
that if it wasn't for them I would of had to scrap the idea.

"Good. Spare no pains, Moses. What have you been doing?
Have you got the costume under control?"

"Yeah."

"Who's playing with you?"

"What you mean who playing with me?"

"You've got to have somebody to pull all that gear along, man, with you sitting down on the platform?"

"The platform will have wheels."

"And every now and then you going to get out and push?"

I didn't think of that.

"And what about music? You should have a steel band in the background. Don't forget this is Carnival."

"Look, Lennard, you only putting stumbling blocks in the way and trying to make a *pappyshow* of my idea. This has got to be a dignified mas, man. It got to have solemnity and pride, and pomp and splendour, like when the Queen coronating." But while I was talking a brilliant idea come to me. "What you could do, is get a tape made of that tune, Rule Britannia, Britannia rule the waves, Britons never never never shall be slaves, and every now and then I could switch it on to impress the people. How about that, eh? The idea just come to me, out of the blue."

"Yeah. You think you'll manage that?"

"Sure, you just get the tape." Ideas was coming one after the other in my brains. "Another thing, you should get the British High Commissioner to cooperate with that."

"Well, maybe. I am seeing to my side of things, don't worry. It's you I'm bothered about. When will you be able to do a full rehearsal for me? We only have a few days left."

"I'm expecting a call any minute now," I say, "and I will get in touch with you. But I still think we should have some publicity beforehand."

"The Editor is adamant about that," Lennard say. "Nothing doing until the Carnival."

"But what about my actual story, man? I thought it would go hand-in-hand with what we doing."

"He is more interested in pictures, Moses. Every picture tells a story. But we'll try and work in as much as we can in the captions."

"H'mm. I suppose we'll have to settle for that in the end."

"If you have any problems, call me. We are attending to all the other details, like getting you registered for the Individual Costume Competition, and all that sort of thing. There's a lot more to Carnival nowadays than you think, boy, but I wouldn't bother you with all that."

"You've set me enough problems as it is," I grumble.

"If Galahad gets here on time, he may be able to help you," Lennard say.

"What shit you're talking?"

"Haven't you heard from him?"

"No?"

"He wrote me he was trying to make it for Carnival on a charter flight with Brenda. Who's she?"

"Never mind who's she! What else did he say?"

"He said he was going to write you, to ask Jeannie to meet them at the airport. You want the flight number and date?"

"Fuck that," I say vehemently. "I got enough on my plate. The bastard didn't even have the decency to let me know."

"I've got to go." Lennard look at his watch. "Don't forget. Move fast. And don't let me down, I've pushed my neck out for you."

I snarl a goodbye to him, coming here like a bloody Jonah to throw me once more in confusion and frustration. I almost choke as I swallow a drink, thinking of having to cope with those two at a time like this. Then I thought why the hell should I? I would ignore their presence in the island, except to learn from Galahad if he had found out anything about selling the property—it was pretty obvious I wasn't going to hear from him now. But what about the property itself, who or what would he leave it in charge of? Did this development call for another trans-Atlantic call?

My answer to all this was to get on to my eighth drink. White people lucky, they have long hair to pull in despair, but the poor black man either get drunk or freak out.

I had a cold salad lunch at the hotel, with some slices of roast pork. It served to sober me a little—there was too much at stake for me to play the giddy ass and go a binge.

After lunch I crossed the road to the Savannah, to see Tanty and find out how things were going.

She was not there.

Only illness would prevent from turning out for work. All I needed was for her to drop dead suddenly and that would be the finishing touch to my career, not even playing a last Carnival before I succumb to the adversities of life.

I stood for a moment in thought, then hailed an empty taxi and drove as far as the foot of John-John. By the time I walked to the top I was sweating out all the rum and was sober, if not cold. (The secret of the heavy drinking that does go on in Trinidad is that you sweat out the alcohol in the heat.)

To my amazement, I see a roughly boarded-up shack had been erected at the side of the house, and I could hear hammering and sawing and other industrious sounds of great activity going on in it.

I hasten up the steps and knock and Tanty open.

"Moses!" she exclaim. "What you doing here?"

"I thought you was sick in bed," I say.

"But it all suppose to be a surprise! Doris was going to phone you later today when we finish!"

"You finishing today?" I ask. "Everything?"

"You best hads come in, as you here already." She turn and I follow her as she shout, "Doris! Is Moses!"

Doris come out of the kitchen. She did not greet me. She say, "I thought I told you I was going to telephone you when to come?"

"The hotel phone giving trouble, Doris," I say, which was true, for me anyway, "and it such a long time since I seen you."

"That's a lie to begin with, as you didn't know I was here." But she didn't say this as if she wasn't please I was lying, and went on, "It save me going out in the hot sun to look for a telephone, anyway."

"Come and see, Moses," Tanty say, and lead me to the side window, from where we could look down in the shack. Three workmen was there, busy as bees constructing the penny, and the accoutrements for Britannia. "Mind how you chipping that wood, Felix!" Tanty call to one of them. "If you break it I take it out your pay!"

I turn from the window. "Well well. I didn't realise I was putting you and Doris to such trouble. I don't know how I going to thank you."

"It's Doris you have to thank," Tanty say. "She ain't had a

drop of sleep staying up to sew, and she keep home from work today solely to get everything finish and ready to surprise you, Moses."

A lump came in my throat. If I had only known Doris was home, I would of been prepared. What had I done to deserve such devotion and loving labour, that this girl would sacrifice the chance to expectorate in her white employer's victuals, and lose a day's pay for the sake of a wastrel and good-for-nothing like me? I believe I would of plighted my troth there and then: I actually moved towards Doris, but she tossed her hands in the air as if absolving herself of all responsibility and say, "Tanty do everything, in fact that's the onlyest reason why I am home, I couldn't bear to see her killing herself out for you."

"Oh," I say. "If it is not asking too much, may I have a look at the costume?"

"Yes, Moses," Tanty say, "you best hads try it on, in case we have to make any alterations."

I follow she and Doris into the bedroom, and there it was, spread out on the bed, press to such a dazzling smoothness it hurt my eyes to look at it.

Doris left the room as I began changing, but Tanty stay to help me put the costume on. It fit me like a glove, the work-womanship was superb. If any Britons was around, they would of fallen to their knees.

"Come and see, Doris," Tanty call her as I stood in front of the long mirror on the dressing-table.

I sat on the buffet and strike a pose for Doris—not exactly hauteur, not exactly pride, but imperialistic, regal posture as on the penny.

"What you think, Doris?" I hold the pose.

"You look all right," she admit, moving around me. "Perhaps I should take the shoulders in a bit, and lengthen the arms."

"It feeling comfortable to me," I say.

"You don't know anything about it," she was taking in here and letting out there, using some straight-pins she held between her lips.

"We will have to spray you and everything over with copper

paint when the time comes," Tanty say. "But something missing, I can't think what it is."

"What could be missing, Tanty?" Doris ask.

"Aha, I know!" Tanty exclaim. "It's a hand-maiden! You should have a hand-maiden with you!"

"It don't have no hand-maiden on the penny, Tanty," I say, taking off the costume. "Hand-maiden?" I frown, thinking, and by Jove, it didn't sound such a bad idea at that, to have a hand-maiden wafting one of them big feather fans over me like the little black slave boys in them films, in all that hot sun. The more I think about it, the better it appeal to me. I begin to walk about excitedly as the idea expand, talking to myself. "Yes! I can see this impersonation having just the effect I desire of putting Brit'n back in her rightful position as a monetary power. We got me as the penny, and, aha! who else but Jeannie could be appropriate to be my hand-maiden? And who else but Bob to haul me through the streets? Gosh, this whole thing might even strike a blow for Race Relations at the same time, with a black man as Britannia, and two white people as his servants!"

I was in such a state of excitement that I grab Tanty and whirl she about in a hopping dance, but for some reason she tug loose, and not thinking anything I try to catch hold of Doris, but she give me a nasty cut-eye look, stamp her foot, say "Chuts!" with utter disgust, and storm out of the room.

"What have I done wrong now, Tanty?" I ask, deflating slowly.

"Oh Moses!" Tanty wail, wringing her hands, "you can't see for yourself? Doris thought you was going to ask her to play the hand-maiden with you!"

There are great stories in English Literature about men who make supreme sacrifices and risk the wrath of their loved ones as they go off to fight dragons or joust with a foe. As they don buckler and breastplate, as they slip into chainmail and gird gauntlets, and remember to lock the chastity belts before they go, their females are sobbing their hearts out, clinging to husband or lover. And in not one of them stories, has the hero relented his rashness and turned a deaf ear to the call of duty and honour, for such matters go beyond the bounds of personal safety and affections. What he do instead is he gently disengage himself from the clutching arms of his grieving wife or sweetheart, give her a little peck, tell her to be good and don't do nothing that he won't do, check up on the c-belt if he smart, and set off on his errands.

All I wanted to do was play mas, and have Jeannie and Bob help me for a worthy Cause and no other reason, so Doris should of take a leaf from one of those damsels' book and submit to the inevitability of the situation.

I tried to explain all this to her before I left John-John, to show her that we should not only think of ourselves but that we were doing a favour for the Mother Country, even told her that Bob was Jeannie's legal husband and I witness their wedding and they loved one another as passionately and ardently as I hoped someone would grow to love me. But I could tell she was really disappointed, she wouldn't listen, put her hands to her ears and cover them, and would not come to the door to say cheerio.

"I will try to comfort her, Moses," Tanty say, "but the poor girl thought you love her."

"I do, I do!" I cried. "But how can she understand how much I owe the country that took me in and nursed me all these years? I was hungry and they gave me fish and chips; I was thirsty and they gave me a cuppa; I was penniless and they gave me dole; I was destitute and today I am Landlord of a Mansions in West London. I was even awarded a prize once, Tanty, by the National Front, which is the very British they say against black people."

"A prize, Moses?"

"Yes, a one-way air ticket to Jamaica. If I had the return fare I would of gone, too."

Although it was a bad moment, I realise I couldn't leave without making arrangements for the rehearsal. "Tanty, I'd like to bring my friends tomorrow evening, if I may."

"Bring them *here*, Moses? What for?"

"We have to do some practice, and make sure everything is going to work okay."

"But I got no place to entertain white people, Moses!"

"You don't have to do a thing. We will bring lots of food and drink and whatever is necessary."

"Well, if you must, you must. But I don't know what Doris will have to say when she hear about this."

"Coax her, Tanty. Show her that what I am doing will make her and you proud, that I am not only thinking of myself."

"I'll try, Moses, that's the best I can do." I left, a determined if saddened man. Brit'n has a lot to answer for, I can tell you.

Bob and Jeannie return from a day-trip to the sister island of Tobago, after dinner. As Robinson Crusoe was supposed to be shipwreck there—they even have a cave he used to live in— he had hoped to pick up a clue, though for the life of me I could not see the connection between Crusoe and his ancestors. Still, he seemed happy enough, and told me the highlight of their day was a splendid lunch off fresh lobsters and crabs which they caught themselves, and the native boatman cooked for them.

I gave them a while to prattle on before I told them about my plans, and what I wanted them to do.

To my utter astonishment, Bob instantly raised objections and make excuses, and also cast aspersions.

"Look, old boy, we didn't come to Trinidad to help you make a giddy ass of yourself!"

"This is very sudden, Moses," even Jeannie, usually most harmonious with me, seem uncertain. "What sort of costume have you got in mind for me?"

"I am not asking for much, Bob, just your co-operation to ensure success. I am confident this thing is brilliant and that we have nothing to worry about."

"I don't know how you do it, but you're always coming up with some shitty ideas."

"Well! That's a fine attitude for you, a born and bred Englishman tracing his ancestry, to take. A golden opportunity to improve the image of your country, and all you can do is sneer and make disparaging remarks."

"At least I have been spending my time constructively," he say. "I am close to digging up a root of my family tree."

I turn to Jeannie. "Jeannie," I say, "surely you can see the merit and glory that will be ours? Surely there is some little corner of your heart that beats for old Blighty? We all have to play our parts, and do our bits."

"That fan you want me to carry, will it be heavy?" she ask.

"Light as a feather," I assure her, "and you won't have to tote it all the time, only for a few minutes when we are actually parading before the judges."

"Why don't I play Britannia myself," she ask, getting ambitious.

"Yeah, let Jeannie play Britannia, and you pull the contraption," Bob say.

I tried not to lose my patience. "It's my idea, and the costume already made for me. You and Jeannie, being white and English, will add colour and significance and dimensions. Jesus, here I was thinking that you two would jump at the chance to help your country, and instead you behave like blacks, finding faults and picking holes in everything."

"Whatever you say, it still looks like shit to me." Bob turn to look at the dancers and listen to the steel band music, as if he did not want to discuss the matter any further. "Hello," he say, "isn't that the reporter chap you told me about, Jeannie?"

Lennard was approaching. I was glad to see him. Perhaps he could convince them. He joined us and Jeannie introduce Bob, Lennard insisted on paying for a round of drinks.

"I forgot to give you the flight number for Galahad and Brenda, Moses," he say. "They arrive tomorrow."

"I couldn't care less," I say.

"What's this?" Bob sit up. "Are they coming for the Carnival?"

"Yes," Lennard say.

"Blimey, you never told us!" Bob say to me. "There's your problem solved, hand-maiden and slave at one blow!"

"Shit to that!" I actually pound my fist on the table and upset Lennard glass. "Those two will have absolutely nothing, but nothing, to do with it. That's final. If you mention it again, Bob, you and I will really fall out."

"Shall we dance?" Lennard ask Jeannie tactfully: also saving time.

Jeannie got up. "If that creature Brenda is being considered, *I* shall have the greatest pleasure playing your hand-maiden, Moses."

"What's this all about?" Lennard ask.

Jeannie was explaining to him as they went off.

"Aren't you going to meet your friends at Piarco?" Bob ask me.

"You can go if you want to," I say. "I've got better things to do. Also, Bob, can we drop the subject of Galahad and Brenda? I find it boring."

He went into a little huff, turning sideways and giving his attention to the dancers and the music. I nibbled at some titbits on the table—large scampi caught in the Gulf of Paria and fried in a batter of pepper and flour; olives stuff with pimento; a tiny potato-like vegetable called topee-tambo, and another called peewah—you peeled it and ate the creamy, orange-coloured flesh, and the nut if you had strong teeth; there were also some cutters—to help keep you sober—of cubes of roast pork which had been marinated in vinegar and bags of garlic, and some wild meat, lappe and agouti, curried but quite dry, so you could pick it up with your fingers fearlessly. And also saltnuts for the dainty. I should mention that I had the foresight to order these things in advance, to help absorb the amount of alcohol we were consuming. The tourists about us must of thought we was having our Carnival dinner in advance, but they were only light refreshments really.

When Jeannie and Lennard return he say, "Splendid idea, Moses, if Bob will play."

"Lennard's going to splash our names all over the newspapers Bobbie, with lots of pictures too!" Jeannie exclaim. "And I am to have a personal interview with him!"

"I'd also like a quote or two from you too, Bob," Lennard say quickly, "your impressions of the Carnival, and what you think of our island, that sort of thing."

Bob became alert. Dangle publicity before the Englishman and it's down, boy, down all the way. "Hump," he say, "Moses never mentioned Lennard was involved. When do we have our interview?"

"You never gave me a chance to come around to it, Bob," I

tell him, more than relieved that he was now more amenable. "This is a big operation that *The Guardian* is interested in."

"But we haven't got costumes?"

"You can just paint yourself black and wear a swimming trunks," I tell him.

He frown. "Does it have to come to that? The trunks is okay for the heat, but black paint!"

"The public will know you are a white man, Bob. And it will only be for some hours."

"And I?" Jeannie ask.

"My dear," I say, "you are no problem. A bikini would be just great."

She wanted to wear more—really go to town in some extravagant dancing-girl outfit, but Lennard and I talked her out of it. We argued about a few trifles, but the fact was they was roped in, and I told Lennard we would do the rehearsal the next evening. Another trifle came up, which was who was going to meet Galahad and Brenda at Piarco. The way the three of them look at me, you would of thought that I had personally been responsible for extending a warm invitation to that reprobative couple to the island. Bob said he would not put that past me, that I had been behaving very mysteriously in the past days and never divulged my thoughts; Jeannie said she would not of minded if it was Galahad alone but she just could not stand that creature Brenda; and Lennard protested that he had his journalistic duties, apart from various matters pertaining to our masquerade, to attend to.

The upshot of it was that there was no upshot, I left them in a huddle arguing about the reception committee and went to sleep, perchance to dream of Doris, if she would deign to be entertained therein after I put Jeannie in front of her. I only hoped that bastard Francis would keep away from John-John as Doris was just in the mood to go out with him to spite me.

I left de-Hilton right after breakfast the next morning, and as Fate would have it, first in the taxi queue waiting outside was my friend the Indian driver who did want me to bear witness in that altercation he had with Delivery.

"Morning boss," he say as I got in. "You going out early to beat the hot sun, eh? Where to?"

"The public library," I say, wedging myself securely in the back seat, just in case. "I'm not in any great hurry."

"I make a case against him, you know," he say conversationally as we set off, picking up our association as if it had never been broken. I was tempted to pretend ignorance or forgetfulness, but he sounded friendly enough, and the sun wasn't hot enough yet to make me fretful or irritable. Besides, I thought talking might make him concentrate on some safe driving, ironic as it was.

"Did you now?" I say.

"Yeah, man. The magistrate fine him twenty dollars for assault and battery."

"It didn't constitute a traffic offence, then?"

He laugh. "No, it always have that kind of confusion on the road. It was when he *bong-up* my eye after you left that I really get vex and decide to call the police. Look, the bruise ain't heal-up yet," and he swivel his whole head round to show me.

"Yes, yes," I say quickly. "Please keep your eyes on the road."

"Don't worry, chief, you safe with me." For a few moments he take my advice, then: "I was just setting a trap for him, you know. You notice how I was arguing with him?"

"You did exchange words," I agree.

"You know what I was trying to do?"

"Get him to back off so we could proceed?"

"No, man! That sort of confusion happen all the time!" He slow down to join the heavy traffic by the Savannah, and rest one arm relaxfully on the back of his seat and half-turned. "I was jockeying him to make him call me a coolie! That is what I wanted."

"Would that have cleared the road?" I ask, puzzled.

"Clear the road!" He sound as if I puzzle him now, and then, as if he understand, "Yes, clear the road for the magistrate to jail his arse in Carrera"—the local Alcatraz—"instead of only fining him twenty dollars!"

"I hope I understand," I say. "You mean it is a more serious offence to call you a coolie than to create a traffic hazard endangering lives?"

"That's *exactly* what I mean, boss. And I could of seen that even though you yourself black, if you don't mind, that you not from these parts, staying in de-Hilton, and would of made a honest witness; where you from, Africa? You don't sound like you from the States."

He was already changing the subject: in a quarter-hour drive with a taxi driver, he could cover a multitude of topics ranging from a rundown of local affairs and world events to his personal history, past, present and future.

"I am from London," I say, seeing no point in disillusioning him: rubbed it in, rather, by adding, "my good man."

"I thought so." He nodded. "It have a lot of black people living in England. I wanted to go myself a few years back, but we got six children and the wife don't like the cold. You ever meet that fellar Enoch Powell?"

"I never had the pleasure."

"I hear he make things rough for black people. It's a wonder somebody don't assassinate *him*. You want a little drive-around before we go to the library?"

"No."

"It had a bad accident by this corner yesterday between a Vauxhall and a Dodge. You going to the Grandstand in the Savannah to see the Carnival?"

"It's the best point of vantage, isn't it?" I counter.

"So they say. I playing in a band myself. Watch out for a band call Rhodesian Terrorists, I be in it. We almost there now, boss. It might be hard to stop right in front the library on account of the busy traffic, so you have to hop out quick if you don't mind, and you could pay me now to save time."

I gave him a pound note and waited for reaction. There was none, he did not make a fuss. He only said he did not know the present rate to convert it to give me change, and I was so pleased I told him to keep it.

"Thanks, boss. Whenever you want a taxi, just ask for me. Tell them you want Boysie to drive you."

I did not want to make a mockery of my impersonation, Carnival was one thing but my aim and intention was another, hence my trip to the library, to research. I even looked up great speeches in the Houses of Parliament, in case I got the chance to step out of the penny and address the tumultuous crowds. The Prime Minister of Trinidad and Tobago was going to be there and I hoped he would hear me, for they say his hearing is not all that good and he only hear what he want to hear. There would be many other dignitaries too—Lennard said the High Commissioner for Great Britain was sure to attend, with a party, and there would be representatives of communication medias from all over the world, so I had to put my best foot forward.

I lunched at a Chinese restaurant in Queen Street—not one of the fashionable ones, but the food was good. I had curried prawns and fried rice, with a salad on the side, and did not drink any alcoholic beverages, only a can of Carib beer, because of the heat. I phoned Lennard to let him know I would be at the library and they could meet me there when it was time to go up John-John for the rehearsals, but he wasn't at *The Guardian*, try de-Hilton, I was told, and when I did and got through, he said that Bob had gone to Piarco to meet the plane, and he was keeping Jeannie's company, and okay, they'd pick me up at the library.

As it turned out, only Jeannie came with Lennard, as Bob had phoned from the airport to say the flight was delayed, and that he was getting pissed and didn't think he could drive them back, but it was okay, as Galahad could drive.

Lennard drove us in his little Volkswagen to the foot of the hill and sealed it, and we ascended with the tape recorder and some bulky refreshments. The sunset was magnificent over the hills of Venezuela behind our backs as we went up, and steel bands was practising in the backyards.

I barely had time to make introductions when we arrive before Doris wanted to know, first thing, where was Jeannie's husband if she was supposed to be married; that if she, Doris, was married, she wouldn't go visiting no strange places without her husband to protect her. Mark you, her tone and choice of words was most civil and decorous, leaving nothing to be desired, but there was a bite and an edge to it which did not escape me. I hastily explained Bob's absence, and she seemed to accept it, but as I suspected she would, she kept up her starchiness all evening.

Lennard, too, was not very helpful in relieving the atmosphere of formality, he kept jamming up to Jeannie every chance
he got, his elbows brushing against her breasts, even blatantly
encircling her waist at times, as if he wasn't satisfied with the
goings-on that must of gone on in de-Hilton.

It was only Tanty's natural exuberance and kindness and
eagerness to please that clear the air a little.

I change into my costume, and Jeannie into her bikini, and
we all went into the shack, where so much loving care and work
had been lavished that all I had to do was pick up the trident
and step into the penny. The shield was nailed to my seat so I
only had to rest my hand on it.

Lennard clap his hands. "Okay, everyone. Let's have some
action."

"What you want me to do, Lennard?" Tanty ask.

"You just stand over there, Tanty. You're part of the audience." He swing to me. "Come on, Moses!"

"I'm ready," I say.

"He's ready, he says." He fling his hands in the air like an
exasperated. film director. "Do I have to do everything around
here? Do me a favour and get painted, Moses."

"I'll do it," Doris say, and she get the can and begin spraying
me all over.

"I hope this paint could come off, Doris." I shut my eyes
from the spray.

"Of course," she say brightly. "I'm sure Jeannie will be glad
to clean you up with some rags and pitch-oil."

"Am I to be sprayed too, Lennard?" Jeannie ask.

"I think not, Jeannie," I say, before he could answer. "We
want your white skin to show. Otherwise I would of preferred to
have Doris as my hand-maiden." I open my eyes to make sure if
Doris hear that, but if she did she show no sign.

"Okay, Doris, that'll do," Lennard say. "Moses, get in position, but don't do anything until I tell you. Jeannie, get behind
Moses with the fan, dear, that's nice, just relax until I tell you.
Keep out of their way, Tanty. Doris, you and Tanty stand over
there and be the audience."

These instructions was fired at all of we as if Lennard just get a Oscar from Hollywood for Best Director or something, and trying to show us why. All he lack was a Director's chair with his name on it and a megaphone, and maybe one of them visor-caps too, and we could have been shooting *Gone With The Wind*. He was prowling about the shack now, circling the platform, darting his head about. God knows why the arse he was doing all this, but I can tell you if he did keep it up much longer he would of got on my wick: luckily he stop, apparently finding a suitable angle, and shout: "Okay! You first, Moses. Strike a pose, hold forth your trident, rest your other hand on the shield, and look straight ahead as if you looking into the future."

I curb my rising temper and try to do what he say.

"No, no, no! Hold it. I mean, break it up. Doris, straighten his helmet, centre it between his eyes. Clever girl, that's it. Try again, Moses."

I give it another whirl, just to please him.

"Not like that!" he yell. "You not playing African Warrior, for Christ sake! Hold the trident with some dignity!"

I charge off the platform with the trident out in front of me like a pole-vaulter, aim straight at Lennard head. I hear Tanty gasp "Oh!" Doris "Ah!" and Jeannie "No!" but none of the three stop me as I catch his neck between two prongs and back him against the wall of the shack so hard it shake.

"This is only a warning, Lennard," I snarl. "Cut out all the shit, we not in M.G.M. studios."

"Okay, okay," he disengage himself from the trident, Tanty coming to help him. "I am only trying to create the kind of atmosphere that will bring out your best."

"I have studied my part," I say, "and I know what to do, and how to do it."

"Don't lose your temper, Moses," Tanty put an arm on me, and lead me back to the platform.

I was cooler now. The disruption did make the two girls draw together, but now Jeannie climb back on behind me.

"You can carry on, Lennard," I say, "but try not to be temperamental, please."

"Okay." He take up where he left off as if nothing happen. "I am not supposed to remember everything. Doris, where is the tape recorder?"

"Right here, Lennard," Doris produce it.

"It got to be out of sight. Put it under Britannia's gown so that it doesn't show. That's it, you can go back now. Moses, you think you could switch it on with your foot, sort of supercilious, and still hold your pose?"

"I'll try."

"Okay. Stand by for a complete run-through when I say now. Okay? NOW!"

I make my pose, and fumble to work my big toe out of the sandal to switch the tape recorder on. "Rule, Britannia" flood the little shack.

"Hold it, Moses, you're fine. Jeannie, dear, just hold the fan over his head and waft it. Great. Tanty, you and Doris are the audience, what do you think?"

"Moses look like the penny," Tanty say, "but Miss Jeannie look as if she laughing."

"Laughing?" I say tight-lipped. "I bursting my arse to keep some majesty in my pose and Jeannie laughing?"

"I can't help it, Moses," Jeannie gasp. "I've never acted before."

"Really! Anyone should be able to do what you have to do," Doris say. "The feather fan isn't too heavy for you, is it?"

"What do you think of Moses, Doris?" Lennard cut in.

"Quite frankly, I think Jeannie should play Britannia and let Moses haul the platform. That's the history I learn at school."

I bite my lip. "All this business decide already, Doris, who and who going to do what and what."

"I wish Bob was here," Lennard look worried. "You think he'll manage to haul that platform?"

"Try it, Lennard," I suggest.

He went to the front and hold on to the rope and tug. It didn't budge.

"There are chucks under the wheels, Lennard," Doris say.

"Oh well." He gave it up. "Let's have a break."

"Don't you think I should rehearse my speech?" I protest.

"Speech? What speech?" he ask.

"I got to address the multitudes, haven't I? I have been working on my oration all day in the public library."

"Oh Christ," Lennard say, "let's talk it over later. I'm tired and worn out."

"It will only take a minute, man!" I wanted Doris to hear my peroration: I was sure it would help her to understand better, but she herself now began to clean up the shack, as if she lost interest.

I got off the pedestal muttering to myself. Not only was I in Doris's bad books, but my altruistic motives for Brit'n were being denied—and the horrible thought came like the straw what break the camel back, that Galahad and Brenda must of touched down at Piarco by now.

"Open up some bottles of rum," I tell Lennard.

"Come, I'll help you," Tanty say, and the two of them went in the house. Jeannie follow them to change into something decent.

"Where's the pitch-oil? I got to get all this copper paint off. Will you help me, Doris?" I appeal to her.

"Why, certainly." She get a rag and soak it and begin to clean me. Don't think it was any nefarious Swedish massage, though, because pitch-oil is only kerosene, and the mood Doris was in, she was rubbing and scrubbing me like a dirty piece of linen.

"Doris," I say, "why are you taking this off-hand attitude with me, of all people? You do not know how desperately I need your sympathy, besetted as I am with so many worries."

"What off-hand attitude, Moses?" she ask sweetly. "This is how I behave all the time. And what makes you think you stand out in a crowd?"

"I want to have a serious talk with you," I say. "Just wait until the Carnival over, Doris, that's all I ask of you."

"Your Carnival will never over, Moses. You are playing mas all the time."

"What I have to say is just for the two of us, Doris, and the future." I tried to hold her hand, but she flicked it away contemptuously with the rag as if she didn't intend to.

Faint heart never won fair lady. I pursued my wooing. "One thing I can tell you now, without reservation, is that I have honourable intentions, and they always was ever since I met you."

"Of course," she say easily. "Just lift your arm a little—there, that's finished. You ought to have a shower before you join us."

"I cannot stand this disdain—and apathy, Doris," I pleaded. "You are near, and yet so far away. I would rather you rave and rant at me, or even pitchfork me with Britannia's trident if it will make you happy."

"If words was money, you would be a rich man, Moses. I think I should go and help Tanty, if you'll excuse me. I don't want your white woman to think we are inhospitable."

"Doris," I blurted, but she was gone.

There and then, I felt like running amok and mashing up all the bloody equipment and ripping the costume to pieces. In fact I give Lennard tape recorder a nasty kick and it switch on "Rule, Britannia."

But as the martial strains of music fill the shack, I saw my duty clearly and I was stirred, and stiffened my upper lip.

By the time we left John-John we had demolished two bottles of rum. I just could not bear Doris's iciness—oh, she skinned her teeth all right, and replenish the drinks and made sure we were not short of ice, and mauby to chase with, but she kept her distance with me. Lennard and Jeannie enjoy themselves, though their drinking was to heighten their pleasures, mines was to drown my sorrows.

Tanty wanted to know how we were going to get Britannia away from John-John, but Lennard said that was *his* worry, he would arrange to have the whole caboodle transported. By now my jealousy and rage at his usurping management of the project was replace with indifference—if he felt he had the aplomb and flair to play Britannia, he was welcome to the role.

When we was ready to leave I hazily remember some drunken attempt to drag Doris and Tanty along to de-Hilton with us, and Doris's polite "Some other time, but it's kind of you to ask," or some nastily polite refusal like that.

The hotel manager was waiting for me in the foyer when we lurched in. He was a little nervous.

"Your guests have arrived," he said, "they checked in under your name, assuring me they were expected."

"Indeed, you have my reassurance," I aim my words a little sideways so he wouldn't smell the alcohol.

"They wanted their own private suite," he was relieved now, "but I'm afraid that was impossible as we're filled right up for the Carnival. I could only let them have a double room—is that all right, sir?"

"Sure." I pacified the manager. Why should I spend all my life biting my nails or gnashing my teeth, even though a doss-down in some flea-bitten boarding-house in an unsavoury part of town was all they deserved?

I fling my arm around Jeannie and Lennard and the three of we do a kind of one-legged race to the bar. When is Cup Final in London you have to battle a barrage of boozers before you even glimpse the bar. When is Carnival time in Trinidad you are lucky to get a whiff of liquor, for the masses who want to fill up—that is why a lot of people go through the period in an alcoholic daze, knocking back as many as they could and accepting every offer, for though you may know *where* the next drink is coming from, you have to plan a strategy *how* to get your hands on it.

We jam-up against the rearguard of the thirsty mob, who was flagging the bartenders with various currencies and shouting the place down. We was about to take a respite when we hear a shout from behind us: "Ahoy there!" and turn to behold Galahad beckoning for us to join him and Brenda and Bob at their table by the pool.

He clap me on the shoulder with a string of his false sentiments and greeting to which I paid scant attention.

We sat down and resumed drinking amid animated chatter, everyone speaking at the same time and no one listening: Bob must of genned up Galahad and Brenda so they were in the picture and knew what was afoot.

I leaned back in my chair and appraised the party. Jeannie was wedged between Galahad and Lennard, trying to please both. Bob had reached saturation point long ago and blinked and simpered at the world. Brenda was the onlyest one sober, and I demanded to know why, and tried to top her glass.

"All this drinking and it isn't Carnival yet, Moses," she say, "My God, I haven't had a chance to recover from jet fatigue."

"How are things in Londontown, Brenda?" I ask.

"Grim, boy, grim. They have introduced even more restrictions on black immigration in the short time you have been away. You may not be able to return."

"Don't classify me among the undesirables like you and Galahad," I jeer. "I don't go around creating racial strifes and the demise of the whites. Did they deport you, fortuitously in time for Carnival?"

"Actually I am here on business, to check out the Black Power elements and do a piece for our newspaper, and to raise funds for the Party."

"What about your sidekick?"

"Ask him yourself. What's this freaky thing I hear about you playing Britannia?"

"It is one of my greatest ideas, Brenda."

"I know all about you and your great ideas. For heaven's sake, if you've got to do an impersonation, what's wrong with Amin, may I ask?"

"You can be sure that the African countries will be well represented by others," I say.

"You whitey-lover," she sneer, "you anglomaniac, after they kick you out and send you scurrying back to Trinidad, what do you do?"

"I turn the other cheek," I say, a little confusedly, and didn't know how to continue.

"An eye for an eye, Moses, and a tooth for a tooth. You've bloody got me being corny now, but that's what you should remember the good lord said. I wish I had been here to sabotage the project."

"And I wish you had kept your tail in London. You are an evil influence, Brenda. A bad egg."

"We shall see who is what when the Freedom Battle is fought. I will not forget to hang your head on the highest pole as an example of a good man wasted. You'll find you can't guile Trinidadians as easily as the English. If I see you lurking about the gateways of Brit'n, it will doubtlessly be because they excommunicated you and chased you out of the island."

"You're not addressing no Black Power meeting, girl," I sneer. "I think you need another drink."

"What I need is sleep." She got up. "I'm in no mood for a party. I am going to bed."

The moment she stand up Bob come to life and blink. "Leaving us so soon, Brenda?"

"Yeah. I'm tired, and you are all drunk."

"I'll see you to your room." His chair fall down as he get up and stagger after her.

I took a sip to wash that woman out of my hair, and turn to the others. The three of them were now in a huddle, and Jeannie was giggling as if they was telling her blue jokes. I wanted a chance to talk with Galahad, so I suggested that she should dance with Lennard. Of course Galahad jump up, but I told him his name was not Lennard, to cool it and sit down as I wanted to talk to him.

He look admiringly at Jeannie's backside as Lennard led her off.

"Man," he say, "I sure missed that piece of arse. You must of been having a ball, Moses."

"Let's discuss a few things before I pass out," I say. "First off, who is looking after my property while you are away?"

"It's in good hands."

I let that pass for the moment. "What did you find out about selling?"

"The worst. To put it like you would, you have the chance of a snowball in hell."

"Somebody will buy it."

"No, sir."

"Some desperate black?"

"None that desperate."

"Come now, Galahad, you don't mean to tell me that a man of your talents?" I left it at that, merely raising my eyebrows as if peering over spectacles.

"As a matter of fact, I have not been idle." He twirl the ice in his glass. "I have inveigled the Party into considering taking over the place, as it's impossible to set up offices in Whitehall, which is crowded. If Brenda can raise the funds in Trinidad, we'll make you an offer."

I introduced him to the Dominica laugh. At that moment I had an interesting if not original thought. I thought: How much can a man stand before he falls to pieces? Are we endowed, albeit unknowing, with an elastic capacity for adversity, which contracts or expands according to the size of the adversities, sort of like that Parkinson's law thing about work?

I began to expand. I pretended to mull over it, then said: "That won't work, Galahad. It's too risky. I'm after a quick sale, but no shady deal."

"You mean you're going to settle down in Trinidad?" His tone incredibly conveyed surprise, hope, gladness, doubt all in one.

Now, for all his failings, it is to be remembered that Galahad and I had been through a lot together, good times and bads, even to sharing one toothbrush. Also, I had reached that stage of glowing intoxication when I felt I could stretch my capacity as much as I liked and the elastic wouldn't burst. And last, but not least, as any love story would tell you, there must always be a friend to whom the lover turns for comfort and advice. So though Galahad was an ill-choice, I had no choice, and I was vastly relieved when at last my secret came out as I said gently: "Galahad, I am smitten."

He thought I said "bitten" and asked if there were mosquitoes in the hotel.

"I mean, I have fallen in love and I am actually contemplating marriage, which shows you it is no laughing matter."

They had coloured lights hang up around the pool and they was reflecting in the waters. Overhead, I actually see a star pitch, and I make a wish. The steel band was taking an interlude from Carnival music and was playing Song of Songs while the dancers rested. My confession was appropriately cocooned.

Galahad look at me. I look at Galahad.

And I must say, that though it was in his nature to laugh kiff-kiff at the disclosure he didn't, as if he too, for the first time, come upon a situation that nonplus him. It is also a measure of the intense emotion with which I spoke.

But for all that, a leopard cannot change his spots, and kiff-kiff laughter—even a Dominica laugh—would of been less distasteful than his next words, which were:

"Just because she miss her menses is no reason to be talking of wedding bells, man. I have some tablets that I always carry about for such an exigency."

"You cur!" I cried. "You despicable cur! Is there nobody left in the world who does not think evil? I pour my heart out to you, and you drag my true love to the depths of degradation!" And I reach across the table and actually collar him, like Delivery did collar Boysie in the taxi.

He was taken aback by my passionate outburst, as it was meant to be. He should of gone down on his knees, the bastard.

"It's a natural assumption, as you'll see when you cool off," he say. "In England the birthrate goes up when the electricity is on strike. In Trinidad it happens during the Carnival madness." Then he ask, with a show of concern which *I* had to pretend was genuine, "You really serious, Moses?"

"Yeah." I had to swallow his weak excuse with my pride. "Her name is Doris. I met her at my Tanty's place up John-John. You ever been in love, Galahad?"

He gave himself time to think—I could see his wits functioning as he turned over this state of affairs in his mind, to see what there was in it for him.

"No. Well," he bit his lip, ruing the denial in case it might of give him an edge to have said "yes"; played it safe by saying now, "Well, not really, I don't think."

"You'd have known the moment it happened," I say like an aged Casanova. "This is the real thing, I feel it in my bones. I don't know what to do, boy."

"Is that why you want to sell up in Brit'n? To married and settle down?"

"What you think I should do? This sort of thing never happen to me before."

"Leave it with me, Moses." He went so far as to stretch his hand across the table and pat mines. "Don't do anything, and don't tell anybody—unless you talk already?"

"It's not a subject for public discussion. You are the onlyest one who knows."

"Good. Doris have money?" Before I could retort he went on quickly, "You got to keep your head screwed on right, Moses, I am only thinking of your interests."

"She's living up John-John, man," I say, and that answer him.

"Yeah. Well, what's money anyway, it always cause trouble.

Anyway, I'm glad now that I came. You need someone you can trust at a time like this, Moses, and you can depend on me as always."

Some fresh drinks came, ordered by Lennard as he brought Jeannie back to the table. But I had just about had as much as I could of everything, drink and company, and there was a lot for me to mull over in lucubration, if I didn't drop off like a log through exhaustion and brain fatigue. Watching Jeannie hemmed in by the two boys I knew she would have a problem deciding which of them was going to be the lucky paramour to enjoy her charms when the time came to select a sleeping partner.

I took out her penny and returned it to her. "Let them toss for it, Jeannie," I told her, and to Galahad, "If I were you I would bet on Britannia."

It was a crying shame I couldn't solve *my* problems that easy.

Carnival begins, officially, foreday morning on the Monday before Ash Wednesday. That is not to say that Trinidadians say their prayers and go to bed early the Sunday night, in order to have the strength and endurance to face the rigors of the two-day mas. In truth, they have scarcely opened their eyes from dreaming of a White Christmas before the Carnival nightmare starts, and in the next two months or so, week by week the tempo and excitement, the preparations and the tuning-up work up steam for the big explosion on Monday morning when the cocks begin to crow. Some people preserve their sanity by fleeing the Mainland (as it were) and spending the two days on one of the tiny islands that dot the entrance to the harbour in Port of Spain. The city is the mecca for the majority, but this minority makes an annual pilgrimage "down the islands," to escape the bedlam, and rather than get boos for chickening out, there is some snob value in being fresh and rested on Ash Wednesday while those who masqueraded stagger and limp and totter and rub aching bones and stiff muscles, and moan about what a great time they had. Left to me, such was the stress and strain I was under, that had I not committed myself to the cause of Brit'n by impersonating Britannia (no mean task) I would of been sorely tempted to hang up a gone-fishing sign like Louis Armstrong and join the small band of deserters.

What happens the Sunday night, more than less, is drunken parties and dances all night long until foreday morning, when the revellers move out to the streets to play Jouvert, the real beginning of the Carnival. Now there are last year's costumes, and ludicrous disguises, like fixing a potty to your backside, or stuffing a pillow round your waist to simulate pregnancy, or, getting to the nitty-gritty by wearing a third leg which has to be strapped down every so often as it breaks loose like a roused penis.

Needless to say, de-Hilton was chock-a-block not only with its entire clientele and staff but hundreds of locals who consider it the best launching-pad on the eve of Carnival. The tourists let their hair down and prance and jump up in gay, wild abandon which is what they come for.

With the coming of Galahad and Brenda our party was now swollen to five, I, strangely enough, being the odd man out. And not only numerically but decoratively, being as all of them was wearing some form of disguise, whilst I was in ordinary casual clothes, making me odder still.

Galahad ask, trying to be funny, "What you disguise as, Moses?"

"I represent sanity in madness," I reparteed.

"I know you would rather be you-know-where with you-know-who," he say, "but everybody crazy tonight, man."

"You know Moses—always trying to be different from others, but not quite making it," Brenda say in her sneering voice.

And Jeannie ask: "Could you not at least have painted your face black"—and as everybody went into fits—"I mean, white?"

"Yes, you should try to be different," Bob say, sort of paraphrasing Brenda as if he was already incapable of originality.

"I don't want to be a spoilsport," I say, "but I really have nothing I can dress-up in."

"You can turn all your clothes inside out, and wear your right sandal on your left foot," Galahad suggest.

"Better yet," Brenda say, "how about wearing your clothes

back to front, as you never seem to know if you're coming or going."

"Have one of my golden earrings, Moses," Jeannie was dress as a Romany gypsy and she take off one and put it on one of my ears.

"Have some of my lipstick and powder, Moses," Brenda say, and open her handbag and take out a big set of cosmetics and applying them slapdash to my face.

Galahad· had another bash trying to be funny by saying, "Lend him some white skin, Bob."

"What are *you* donating?" Bob counter.

"Okay." Galahad had on a purple tam o' shanter and he snatch it off his head and clamp it on mines.

"I won't be left out, old boy," Bob say, and take off his false beard—he was playing Bluebeard the buccaneer, a rather incongruous role for him, anyway—and put it on me.

I suffer all these decorations in silence, it was no skin off my teeth if they wanted to amuse themselves, even at my expense.

"What do I look like?" I ask the leading question like a fool.

"A right twat!" Galahad had the answer waiting. And as they all split their sides laughing, though Jeannie had the grace to blush at his language, Brenda gasp: "Reality at last—a composite man among mimic men!"

"But I still have my own brains," I say coolly. "Small things amuse small minds, but I will prove I am no killjoy," and I take Jeannie off for a dance, to try and get into their mood of jollification: my first venture on the dance floor, incidentally.

As usual, this turn out the exact opposite: I keep thinking about Doris and grew maudlin and morose. When Lennard tap my shoulder to cut-in, Jeannie was glad to change partners, and I went and sit back down, nursing my drink. The merrier the others get, the more miserable I feel. All I could do was drink, but Brenda and Lennard was quite chummy—no doubt, as one journalist to another she was pumping out the Black Power situation from him; Jeannie and Galahad, when they wasn't jumping up, invent some kind of wrapping game with arms and legs, and Bob, well, hard to tell, as he was wearing a domino what hide his face, but I was sure it was haggard and drawn with sensuous debauchery, and his eyes red and bleary. So you will gather I was not the life of the party.

Some time during the festivities Dominica appear, playing it safe by bringing along some wanton tourist blonde as he did not know how Jeannie would be disposed, which was just as well with hustlers like Galahad and Lennard to contend with. She was from Canada which made a change: Galahad gave her a thoughtful appraisal.

As the time tick merrily by, I started to argue with myself. I was mad to go up to John-John and plead with Doris to come and join us. Then I got to thinking why the arse I should have to plead, surely I deserved some sort of reciprocation for giving my heart away? I was using the wrong methods with her. I should be manly and forceful instead of hanging on her every whim and fancy. All I was doing was spinning top in mud, getting no place with all this romantic shit like a starry-eyed idiot, when I should give her the old one-two-three and use some Trinidad tactics.

One thing I am sure you notice is that I take a long time to make up my mind, but once I decide I move into action like a bat out of hell.

I didn't even tell the others I was going, I just get a flask of rum and push it in my back pocket, and went out to look for a taxi. I thought of Boysie but I was in a hurry and I didn't owe him one bloody favour, so I hop in the nearest one and give the driver directions.

As I went up the hill the pearly light of dawn was stealing over the sky in the east, and I knew it would not be long before the morning was shattered by a thousand thousand voices.

I pound on the door of Tanty's house until a light come on inside and Doris open the door slightly, wearing babydoll pyjamas.

"That you, Francis?" She rub her eyes.

I crouch a little away from the light, and say in a squeaky voice, "Yes, Doris, is me."

"You early, man. I got to brush my teeth." She notice my composite costume now and giggle. "What you playing, the ass?"

"Do quick, Doris," I squeak again.

"Come inside and wait," she say.

"No. Just do quick." I didn't want to risk her recognising me and refusing to go: once I get she outside I would manhandle she if I had to.

She went back and come out in a few minutes wearing one of Tanty's old long frocks and her face daub up with charcoal and flour. She had a long piece of red ribbon in her hand.

"You don't have on what you said you was going to put on," she say.

"No," I say. "It's me, Moses."

"I know all the time," she sneer. "You think you fool me? You make a trip to John-John for nothing."

"Doris," I say, "you going to play Jouvert with me, else we blow off right here." And I put my thumb on my cheek, spread out the other fingers and wiggle them, and blew out, which signified that I would have nothing more to do with her.

She laugh. "You really bold-face, you know Moses, coming up here with your drunken self and waking me up!"

I knew then she was coming. I grab her hand. "Let's go."

"I should leave a message with Tanty for Francis when he come," she say.

"Don't bother with Francis, don't bother with anybody or anything, Doris. You and me going to make ruction in town today!"

I didn't need no Yank to tell me, "Have a nice day!" It was in the cards: the law of averages had to work for me some time. I put my arm around Doris waist and she make things snugger by putting hers around mines. As we went down John-John she tug off two broad banana leaves from a tree near somebody fencing and give me one to hold over my head.

It wasn't much use as a weapon, though, and in those frenzied crowds, some ragamuffin or over-eager Hercules might try to rub up and squeeze up Doris and cause botheration, and I wanted something stouter to defend my love. It had a clump of bushes by the roadside, and I tell Doris I wanted a branch to shake and wave about that wouldn't break-up quick like a banana leaf.

It was still a little dark in the bush, as the foliage was heavy, but I make out a calabash tree, and I was just going to break a branch when I notice something or somebody crouch up at the foot of the tree. I didn't know what it was, it was sort of bundle up and shapeless. It was making sounds, whimpering like a little puppy for milk, and crying in a high-pitch voice, "Daybreak or no daybreak, daybreak or no daybreak?" over and over again, sending shivers up my spine.

"Oh God Moses, come away from there!" Doris pull me back. "It's a soucouyant!"

"A who?" I ask, though the word ring a distant bell in my past.

"You don't know what a soucouyant is? Tanty say they shed their skin at midnight, and go about sucking people blood!"

"Like—like a vampire?" I quaver.

"That's it! But it got to get back in the skin before daybreak to return to normal!"

"What the hell it doing under the calabash tree?" I try to sound brave.

"Somebody must of thrown salt on the skin, and she can't put it back on! Forget about the branch, man, let's go!"

To tell you the truth I was shit-scared; I am one of those people who can't sleep when they sit up to look at a late horror film on the television, but I couldn't appear a coward in front of Doris.

"Listen," I say.

"Daybreak or no daybreak, daybreak or no daybreak?" The piteous whimper was going on and on.

"You think we should tell her it's time for Jouvert?" I whisper.

"Come and go, Moses!" Doris was tugging me, not that I needed tugging. It's all right for you to smile indulgently and pooh-pooh superstition and legend, but I was there on the spot and seen and hear it with my own eyes and ears. And they have it to say that that's how the word "Jouvert" start up: in the old days the soucouyant would of talk French and say *"Jouvay, jou paka ouvay?"* but even soucouyants got to keep abreast of the times. I for one wouldn't of been surprise in the least to hear one of them eldritch cackles like the wicked witch in *Wizard of Oz,* if we did stick around for it.

Bands was beginning to form, from all over the city we

could hear them. We join one that was just shuffling about and warming up for action, because it couldn't move off the crowds was so thick, but eventually we get on the move and head downtown.

"Jouvert!" I scream.

"Jouvert! Jouvert, Moses!" Doris leap in the air and wave the banana leaf.

So we went chanting and prancing, the whole mob moving like one, but each individual doing his own thing. Some of them running ahead when the *vap* take them to lead the band, and the true leaders don't mind, because every now and then somebody get the vap, and me and Doris do it too, shrieking and screaming like we gone mad.

And in truth, I don't know what come over me that morning, if memories of bygone Jouvert return after all my years in stuffy old Brit'n, or if it was that I was in the midst of my countrymen now, the pulse and the sweat and the smell and the hysterical excitement, but my head was giddy with a kind of irresistible exultation like I just get emancipated from slavery. *All of we chanting and slaving to out the fire in Massa sugarcane plantations; foreday morning come; Jouvert, Canboulay, Massa come to play mas too, mas in your arse; slave ancestors jump out their graves and come to play too, oh God Massa, play mas, play mas, the vap take me, the vap take the vap take all of and Last Lap go make misery!*

"Doris!" I scream, "Doris—! Let we get married."

"What you say? What you saying, Moses? I can't hear you, man!"

"Let we get married, Doris!"

"Mas, mas, play mas!"

"Doris! Oh, God, Doris, is Jouvert morning!"

"It sweet, eh?"

"It too sweet! Let we married, Doris, let we married! I don't going back!"

"I can't hear you, Moses, the music too loud!"

"I say I don't going back, Doris, I don't going back!"

"It sweet, eh?"

"It too sweet! It sweet-sweet!"

We justle up in Independence Square what used to be

Marine; we tumble and fall down and get up and *we dingalay and we dingala and we poopsing poopsing and what-it-is-at-all, Carnival is we bacchanal.*

"Oh God, Doris, we really have to get married. I don't going back!"

"I can't hear you, Moses, I can't hear you at all at all at all!"

"I say Jouvert! I say Canboulay! I say *something iron lick up gearbox!*"

"Oh God, what-it-is-at-all? Mas mas, play mas!"

We mix up and confuse up and scream up and jam up and explode up by Frederick Street, and *old lady walk a mile and a half.*

"Moses! Oh God, Moses! You not going back to England?"

"What, Doris, what?"

"Stay in Trinidad, Moses! Carnival too sweet!"

"*I went to Donkey City, to circumcise my donkey.*"

"Let we get married, Moses! You want to married?"

"Oh God! *Don't lick up my junior commando!*"

Hours, days, maybe weeks later, who keep count of time, we fall exhausted by the wayside, near the Savannah, itching to follow the band, but bone and muscle refusing to move.

"This is the best Jouvert I ever had, Moses."

"You feeling hungry?"

"More tired than hungry."

"Come back to de-Hilton with me."

"All right."

"Have a last drink before we go." I take out the flask, it still had some in it, and we finish it and I fling the bottle in the Savannah.

We catch a taxi and went to the hotel, and straight down to the room.

Doris lay down on the bed and shut her eyes.

"We going to do it, Doris, you know that?"

"No."

"Yes, we got to do it."

"I ain't ever done it before, Moses, I swear to God."

"We going to do it, though."

"You don't love me, Moses. You only want me."

"I love you, Doris."

"True?"

"True."

"What going to happen after, Moses?"

"Don't think about after now, Doris."

"But suppose we make a baby? I don't want to do it, Moses, I really don't."

I deflowered Doris that Jouvert morning in my room at de-Hilton.

"It sweet, Doris?"

"It too sweet, Moses."

When I look back on my life, I see many times when there was a climax to a certain chain of circumstances and events, when one would have gladly given up life. If one had the choice, would one opt for a demise in the past, or take pot-luck in the future? Imagine being asked by St Peter at the pearly gates, after he show you a flashback, "That was your life, my son. When would you have preferred to die?" I would say, "You remember that Jouvert morning when I was with Doris in the hotel, St Peter?"

"Yes, my boy," he might well reply. "You have chosen well, for your life before that, and after that, was full of sin and transgression. It was your finest hour."

Of course, in real life one goes on from climax to climax—one thing leads to another, as it were, and you have to apply yourself to the continuation of your existence. The onlyest thing I know that have one definite climax is fairy tales, because all of them finish by saying that they live happily ever after.

Even Doris had to go with the tide, for it appear she slip away while I was in a pleasant doze, as I discover when I stretch to touch her: in my dream-like state I merely sigh, thinking she had move a little to find a cool spot on the bed, and I went back into a deeper sleep.

Somebody was pounding on the door and shouting.

"Moses! Wake up, man. You dead or something?"

Even if you don't continue your existence for yourself somebody else bound to do it for you. I fling open the door resentfully and went back to lay down.

Lennard came in.

"Jesus man, it's twelve o'clock. Where's everybody?"

He did not look any the worse for wear: these locals are hardened customers, left to them every morning would be foreday; they even have a calypso saying don't, don't, stop the Carnival, and they were sullen and morose during World War Number Two when the English governor really stop it because it wasn't nice to debauch when we was at war and thousands was falling on the fronts.

"Get out of bed, man, we got to be in the Savannah by three o'clock!" He actually laid hands on me.

"What!"

"The Carnival Committee has so many entrants for the competitions that there has been some reshuffling and they have to start today."

"You said it would be tomorrow, when the best bands and costumes come out!"

"Don't argue, Moses. I barely managed to squeeze you in because a band dropped out. Get Jeannie and Bob. I will pick you up in an hour." He was already on the way out. "And Moses, keep an eye on Bob, don't let him drink anything or everything will really turn old mas."

It was typical of me that I made a little Dominica laugh to myself and rose to the emergency calmly. I got on the phone and ask the switchboard girl to give me Bob's room.

Galahad answer.

"Where's Bob?"

"In the bar. What you mean by this disturbance, Moses?"

"Where's Jeannie?"

"Right here. You want to talk to her?"

"Yes, pleease."

Jeannie come on. "Oh Moses—"

"Listen carefully, Jeannie. We got to for the Carnival judges in about two hours. Get rid of Galahad immediately and take a cold shower."

"Before or after, Moses?"

I bit my lip. "Get upstairs and drag Bob from the bar. Keep him sober. You too. I will meet you in a few minutes."

"But—"

"Get moving immediately, Jeannie, don't let me down."

I put down the phone and got up to shower, but it ring. It was the operator.

"Sir, the Manager would like to have a word with you in his office."

"Tell the Manager I won't have any time until Ash Wednesday."

I showered and dressed and went up to the bar. Bob was protesting to Jeannie that he only had one rum-punch and she could ask the bartender to prove it.

"Okay, okay," I say. "Just calm down. We'll all have fresh orange juice with a little Angostura bitters, and a dash of Worcester sauce."

"I understand Lennard wants me to be blackened for this farce, Moses," Bob say. "I refuse. Point-blank and categorically."

"You stay white," I say. "That's my decision."

"That's okay, then."

"Lennard has a big, boarded-up van with everything in it, parked in the Savannah," I explain to them. "We will get ready from there and set off."

"I hope I do not have to pull the contraption through the streets of the city," Bob say.

"The Grandstand is quite near," I tell him.

"I'm getting butterflies in the stomach, Moses," Jeannie said.

"Maybe we should all have one stiff drink," Bob suggest hopefully.

"Cut it out," I snarl, "can't you stay sober a few hours for the sake of your country?"

"I will perform better if I'm not thirsty," he say.

I had practically to sit on him to restrain him from going to the bar until Lennard arrived, then he suddenly decided he was hungry, so we all had a bite to eat.

Lennard had done his part, as I saw when we got to the van. All we had to do was get ready ourselves, and I was the most trouble, but Jeannie help me a lot, though I get copper paint in my eyes when she was spraying me and thought I was going blind for a minute.

Lennard had a photographer from the paper and we took some snaps outside the van, just before we set off.

Thank God he had the foresight to be close to the venue, else I do not know how we would of made it in the hot sun and the tumultuous crowds around the Savannah. Like millions of revellers was about the place, and bands, and loud steel band music. We had to queue up between a band of Zulu Warriors and an Eskimo tribe near the entrance to the competition platform, and I was sweating so much I feared for my make-up, and opened my mouth for the sweat to run into.

"I want to pee badly, Moses," Jeannie whisper urgently behind me.

I had struck my Britannia pose from the moment we left the van, and if it killed me, I was going to do my bit for Brit'n this day. Without twitching, and my head rigidly to the front, I say between my teeth, "Jeannie. Listen to me. Think of something else, how wonderful you will feel when you do get the chance to pass your water."

"I'm trying, Moses," she whisper.

The officials on the platform get the performing band of Queen Venus and her Followers off the scene at last, and the Zulu Warriors in front of us went up to do their things. We was close enough to get a view, and they really look warlike and savage, and all of them shaking spears and shields and fluttering their plumages as they do a war-dance. They must of scared the shit out of the white tourists, they were so realistic: I was sure Brenda would be tickled pink sitting in the audience.

I was very nervous about representing Great Britain now that my Big Moment was at hand. It took all I had to concentrate on maintaining my equilibrium: that bloody Jeannie make me think of peeing too. I could not see her, but I could hear a few succinct comments from standers-by: whether for Britannia or Jeannie herself I do not know. Directly in front of me Bob look as if he had fallen asleep. He was leaning forward with the rope clasped in both hands over his shoulder, resting his weight on it, his head bent, aptly reminiscent of them slaves you see hauling the stones to build the pyramids in Egypt. In fact, when the last of the Zulu Warriors left the stage, an official had to shout at him to get moving.

We trundle up a little ramp and almost had an early catastrophe when Bob stall half-way up, but two competition workers get behind and give us a push. I find myself looking down the platform which was so long and broad it look like a jumbo could of landed on it.

I take a deep breath. I was conscious of ohs and ahs from one side of the audience—there was seats on both sides of the platform, and it come from the side that could see me now. Out of the corner of my eye I notice a little section that Lennard had bribed was on their feet and applauding.

Bob was suppose to haul us to the centre of the stage and pause for a minute or so for the VIPs to have a good look, but the fool just went on and make a circle, bringing us in view now of the other side, turning the blank side of copper foil to the VIPs. Praise God, as if he realise his mistake he pull quickly now and brought us around again. The crowd roar and cheer. I hold my head proudly, looking straight in front of me, the trident balance in one hand, the other resting with casual grace on the ornamented shield. And Jesus Christ, I forget all about the tape recorder near my foot, I fumble with my big toe (I had actually have Jeannie rub it with some vaseline to make sure it didn't catch cramp or something) and switch it on, but the ovations was so loud you could hardly hear "Rule, Britannia," until I manage to turn the volume knob on full. God knows, I enough to contend with doing my part: I could only pray my assistants were getting on well, and that their white skins were showing to advantage.

I was now realising that if the tumultuous applause continue, I would be unable to make my speech. Another thing (and that bastard Lennard must of known all the time) was that in order to do so I would have to get up and leave the penny, as it were, as I was displaying Britannia's profile, and even if I get Bob to turn me the circumference of the coin would be in my way, obstructing me from the audience. Indeed, the profile pose handicap my proper look at the audience: I could only judge from the cries of "bravo!" and "mas, mas!" Disappointed as I was about my address, it was still very gratifying to hear the uproar. Perhaps some of my loyal spirit must of infected the cheerers, for after all, Brit'n was once the head of a great Empire, Mother of the Commonwealth, and it was nothing short of a stroke of genius on my part to think of depicting Britannia, the symbol of every man, woman and child who ever shelter under the Union Jack.

I see two important-looking officials whispering to one another, and was sure they was debating if it wasn't time for us to vacate the stage, in spite of the public response, and the next competitors, a big band, was already coming on at the bottom end of the platform. Good old Bob take his cue, and begin to haul us off, I was just thanking God nothing went amiss when he stop for no reason at all, causing an official to hurry up to him. It seem as if the tiniest splinter of wood from one of the platform planks give him a *chook,* and that make him stop. As it turn out it make the onlookers cheer even more, as he pull the sliver out and continue.

As we left the platform I thank God from the bottom of my heart for my short-lived glory, and for giving me this opportunity to qualify for some distinction of recognition from the British Government. The least they could do, was to inform the Immigration Authorities at Heathrow Airport that I should be welcomed back, without let or hindrance, should I decide to return.

I had the utmost difficulty trying to fall asleep on the night of Ash Wednesday. One theory that suggests itself is that after two solid days and nights of hammering at the eardrums, the comparative silence is earsplitting; I can now hear the sounds of little insects of the night, so often used to typify or illustrate the tropics, like the garrulous, cigar-smoking tourist in dark glasses, with camera, is used to typify the American. Another slight, almost negligible sound, a thin whine rather than a buzz, answered Tanty's uncertainty as to whether there was any mosquitoes in de-Hilton; whatever the precautions and safeguards, these noxious insects manage to survive and make their presence felt. One in the room now sounded like a Concorde as it circled my head looking for a place to land; what with soucouyants and mosquitoes, the blood-toll on the white visitors from the North must of been colossal: no wonder they tan to hide their bloodless pallor, and fool the folks back home with wish-you-were-here postcards.

I thought if I wrote down a description of my day and the things that happened to me, I might be able to relieve my mind of the oppressiveness that kept me awake. So I got up and got down to it, as follows:

It is ashes and sackcloth now after the tintinnabulation and the jubilation, and I for one do not regret it, I have had enough mas to last me the rest of my life, though there are regular diehards and enthusiasts who are already planning next year's do.

I won the first prize for the Most Original Individual Costume. It is a silver cup, appropriately inscribed, and one hundred dollars in cash. The former I have, the latter I gave to Lennard and Bob and Jeannie to enjoy themselves with. As results of my impersonation of Britannia, (a) I am due shortly to make a television appearance on TTT; (b) to be interviewed by Trinidad and a tape made and distributed throughout the Caribbean; (c) to have an audience with the British High Commissioner for Trinidad and Tobago; (d) Lennard has been promised a rise by *The Guardian* for his part in the whole affair.

But I do not know if I shall follow up all these requests for my time and presence; I am a mixture of emotions, precipitated early this morning by the manager of the hotel who summoned me to his office and demanded settlement of my bill.

"Sir," he told me, clearing his throat, "I do not know if you appreciate how high your bill is running. I have the following items to date," and he read off a set of fantastic and incredulous expenses and amounts.

I raise my eyebrow. "It is more than I thought," I admit, "in the excitement of Carnival one is apt to forget mundane matters."

"It is not mundane to me, sir," he say, "your account has gone up by leaps and bounds, particularly since Mr and Mrs Galahad arrived. I have them under "Sundries and Incidentals" and it is your biggest item."

"I gave you my bona fides when I took up residence," I say. "The Bank of England—"

"Your bank has withdrawn your credit." He did not say "sir" this time.

"Nonsense!" I cried. "There must be some mistake."

"On my part, yes," he say. "However. This is de—the Hilton, we do not harass our clients. I shall give you a little time before taking steps."

The second emotion that happen was Galahad come to see me.

"Moses," he say, "this is what you should do. You should remain in Trinidad and get married. You are getting on in years now, it is harder for you to withstand the rigours of the English clime, not to mention the social conditions which worsen daily for black people, and the appalling state of the economy. Remain among your own kind, and make Dorothy happy."

"I thought you might of forgotten her name," I say with irony, "but like a true friend you remember. However, I shall make my own decisions. Right now I want to know what you and Brenda are going to do about the sundries and incidentals you have incurred on my bill. You place me in an embarrassing position with the manager."

"You can hock your Carnival prize," he say, and make a laugh. "But don't worry, I left some money to be deposited in London. In due course I'll give you a full statement." He yawn. "I wish I could stay for your wedding, but I got pressing business in London. Brenda will be here, though, if you need a bridesmaid."

The third emotion that happen was Bob come soon after Galahad left. One would of thought they would have the compassion to leave me alone to recover as I did them after the celebrations, but no.

He look a mess. Dissipation, debauchery, and overindulgence had his shoulders sagged and there were lines of woe and misery on his face, and his whole body was shaking as if he had caught some tropical malady: I do not understand why white people do not keep their arses quiet with their Bank holidays in their own countries and let black people get on with their Carnival instead of coming to lacerate themselves in order to observe the Lent.

I ordered a rum-punch for him but when it came he took one look at it and began to heave as if he wanted to vomit, so I poured it down the sink.

"I'm in bad shape, Moses," he say.

"We all are," I say.

"You don't know the half of it. I wish I had never come to Trinidad."

"It's only the aftermath of Carnival. Didn't you get enough sleep?"

"It's not the Carnival, Moses." He walk about the room, rubbing his face, shaking his head, pushing his hands in his pockets, exhibiting all the signs of unrest and worry.

"You ought to of taken a couple of aspirins, Bob," I say, touched by his misery.

He did not seem to hear. He stood by the window, looking out at the Northern Range, the very picture of a man with monumental burdens. At last he turn and say in a low voice, "Moses. What I am about to tell you is between us and the four walls. You won't tell Jeannie, or anyone else."

"Cut out the drama, Bob. If anybody got cause to be histrionic it's me."

"You should have dissuaded me from researching my ancestors, Moses."

"I tried to, Bob, but you were stubborn and would have your own way. What's up, then?"

"Somewhere in the past one of my forebears committed an unforgiveable act."

"Is that all? Oh Christ, Bob, come off it! It's common history that the original whites in this part of the world were rogues and criminals deported from England. What did you expect?"

"Certainly not what I unearthed."

"Was he a buccaneer? Did he transport slaves from Africa for the sugar-cane plantations?"

Some sort of expression cross his face—it might of been a sickly smile. "Worse than that. He actually associated with one."

"So what? You're not averse to a little black pussy yourself," I chuckle. "Maybe you inherit that from him!"

The expression this time was a flush. "I told you that you would not understand! Can't you see what it means?"

"A skeleton in the cupboard?" It wasn't quite relevant, but I like the phrase.

"There were children by that association, Moses, and their children begat more children, and a chain was formed, and today I am a living link in that chain! *Now* do you understand?"

"No," I say, for honestly I didn't see he was getting at.

"Moses," he take a deep breath. "I have been touched by the tar-brush. I am tainted!" And he turn his back as if he couldn't face me any more.

Poor man. But a fool too. "Listen, Bob," I say, "perhaps I go back far enough I'd find I've got a white streak. Do you hear me 'Out damned spot'?"

"Ah," he say, looking out the window, "that would uplift you. But mine is a pox."

"I see," I say quietly, "I see." I was not hurt by his words. After all, he had been my friend for a long time, and I suppose that there are some things I would never understand about white people, no matter how hard I try. "It is all in the past, Bob," I say kindly. "In those days the planter was not worth his salt unless he knocked the pick of the crop." A picture of sweet Doris flashed in my mind. "Some of the finest specimens resulted because of those bygone unions."

"What should I tell my Dad and Mum, Moses?" He turn away from the window and face me now, depths of despair and wretchedness reflected in his eyes—he might of been shedding a tear, for all I know, that's why he had his back turn—"How will they take this terrible revelation? My poor Mother has a weak heart."

"I would forget all about it if I were you, Bob," I say. "It is nobody's business but your own. And you can rest assured your secret is safe with me."

"Will I be able to live with it?" he mutter. "And how do I know, that in a moment of rashness, your tongue will not slip?"

I make the Sign of the Cross with my forefingers and kiss it. "This satisfy you?"

"I suppose so." I see him glance at the sink where I pour the rum-punch, as he spoke, and knew that the worst was over.

I phoned up for a couple, as I, too, felt like one, and I had made no vows like other Trinidadians to do penance for Lent.

"I shall miss you, Moses," he say when the drinks come, refreshing himself with a sip. "London won't be the same without you."

"Miss me?"

"Yes. Galahad told Jeannie you were getting married. What a sly one you are, hiding it from us all this time! Who is she?"

"The miserable rotter!" I exclaim. "It never ceases to amaze me how he slips out of my strangling clutches. I'll do him yet, Bob, you wait and see."

"When is the wedding?"

"You know better than to listen to anything he says, Bob," I tell him. "You would be the first to know if I decided on anything like that."

The fourth emotion that happen was I meet Brenda and Lennard at the bar when I went up in the evening. The moment I appear—and had a glass in my hand—the both of them begin to congratulate me on my forthcoming marriage.

"This is too much," I say angrily. "I cannot think of a thought, or make an observation, before it becomes public property. Am I some sort of ridiculous buffoon that everyone makes a *pappyshow* of me?"

"It's just idle rumour, then?" Lennard ask.

"No comment."

"I'd be sorry for the woman who ever married you, Moses," Brenda say.

"You amaze me."

"I thought you might be interested in buying the return half of my ticket," Brenda say.

"Are you touting for the airlines now?" I sneer.

"There's a lot of hassling at Piarco, Moses," Lennard say. "Hundreds of people are held up at the airport, and flights are being delayed and cancelled. Brenda's ticket has premium value as it's a charter flight and they'll have less trouble getting away."

The fifth emotion happen when I trudge up John-John that evening in a miserable, pitiful state, my feet like lead, my heart heavy. Even the evening itself was sombre, there was no gay calypso steel band music on the hill, and the sun, setting over the highlands of Venezuela, painted the sky in mournful shades of grey and deep purple, like funeral drapes.

Doris and Tanty was out in the gallery talking as I approach, and something in my slouching figure must of told them that I came like a Jonah, for I saw Tanty whisper something in Doris ears and go inside.

I keep my head down as I mount the steps, and hear Doris say: "So you come, Moses. The Carnival over."

"Yes." I stay on the last step, looking up to her as she lean over the banister. I was glad she begin the talking; I wouldn't of known what to say or where to begin.

"You had a good time?"

"Yes."

"Tanty don't wish to say goodbye. That's why you come, ain't it? She say she would pretend it was somebody who masquerade for the Carnival as you."

"I better go inside."

"No, Moses, she don't want to see you, she say Carnival time everybody dress up as somebody else, that it's not real. I think so too."

"You only saying that, Doris, but you don't believe."

"Yes, I believe. I don't wish to say goodbye either. I not coming to the airport to see you off."

"Why not, Doris?"

"We better say goodbye now."

She bend down suddenly and give me a hard slap on my face. It make me happy. "I deserve that," I say.

"I would never give you what you deserve, Moses," she say, and open her hand to show me the mosquito on her palm, that she slap dead to stop it stinging me.

And the sixth emotion that happen this Ash Wednesday, when I left John-John and going down the hill, was I feel like Peter must of felt when he deny Christ.

We touch down at Heathrow about six o'clock in the morning, and there was a cold breeze blowing, and a flake of snow brush my cheek lightly on the exact spot where Doris slap me.

I clutch my passport tightly as I shuffle up in the queue to Immigration, and hand it to the officer.

He open it and peer inside. "Just one moment, sir," he say, and get up to go to the office.

"Hold on," I say, and open my plastic carrier bag and take out the silver cup first prize what I get in Trinidad for my loyal impersonation of Britannia. "I have this to declare," and I hold it up, like Arthur Ashe hold up the Wimbledon Cup when he win the tennis, for all the peoples in the airport to see. Only to me it was like holding up the Holy Grail.

"That's quite all right, sir," the officer say smoothly, "I won't keep you a minute," and he go off to the office with my passport, leaving me holding the cup up in the air like I was still playing charades.

About the Book

It has been more than twenty-five years since Moses Aloetta became one of the "Lonely Londoners" in the novel of that name. Now—though an avowed Anglophile—he hankers for Trinidad, for sunshine, Carnival, and rum punch. With characteristic irony and delicacy of touch, Sam Selvon tells the story of Moses's reencounter with his native land.

This edition of the novel includes a new introduction to Selvon's life and work by Susheila Nasta, as well as a preface by "Moses" that was written in 1991 for the first US edition of the work.

Sam Selvon (1923–1994) was one of the most popular, prolific, and internationally distinguished of Caribbean writers. A native of Trinidad, he is best known for his vivid evocation of East Indians living in the Caribbean and Europe. **Susheila Nasta** is professor of modern literature at the Open University (UK) and editor of the journal *Wasafiri*.